The Shaman Within

A Hidden Shaman Novel

Gary Wedlund

Loconeal Publishing
Amherst, OH

The Shaman Within

A Hidden Shaman Novel

This book is a work of fiction. The names, characters, places, and events in this novel are either fictitious or are used fictitiously. Any resemblance to actual events or persons is entirely coincidental.

Loconeal books may be ordered through booksellers or by contacting:
www.loconeal.com
216-772-8380

Loconeal Publishing can bring authors to your live event. Contact Loconeal Publishing at 216-772-8380.

Published by Loconeal Publishing, LLC
Printed in the United States of America

First Loconeal Publishing edition: July, 2011

Visit our website: www.loconeal.com

ISBN 978-0-9825653-7-7 (Paperback)

Table of Contents

I became terrible and unkind
As the lie of my life
Grew increasingly pressed
Beneath the weights of knowledge
Some few steps beyond my door.

Abi, to the Council.

Chapter One

The horse had been bred wide and tall for war. I held her loose reins with an arm that was little more than a stick. A uniform of sackcloth marked me as common and beyond my station. The iron-tipped lance stood straight out, though it should have been too heavy for my arm, and I carried a razor-sharp sword across my back. It was illegal for peasants to bear them. Deadly knives adorned my hips. A small archer's shield bobbed, ready at the pommel. My hand felt naked until I briefly switched the rein into the hand bearing the lance and pulled the shield up by my ten year old forearm. Holding all of that, four hands would have suited better.

We rode so swiftly toward the sea of pikes that I felt sure I'd fall.

Never had I seen the world slip by so swiftly, nor had I ever imagined the wails, stench and startled eyes of the hundreds of dying men. Flocks of arrows fell among them, swaying the masses. Their arrows missed my charge by inches. Surely, any moment I'd perish.

I heard words, seemingly from within my head, "This is nothing."

Behind came the thunder of my company. A thousand warriors included two glorious gods, one a man, the other a woman. These two nipped at my heels and laughed joyfully.

Once again, the voice, "That is nothing."

I took inventory of my young body, and, to my horror, another stranger's spirit rejoiced from within me. She helped hold my lean steady and seemed thrilled to be a part of the carnage.

And, just before my bounding horse trembled into the sea of pikes, I heard the Goddess whisper, "Compared to what shall come, these few are nothing."

* * * * *

"Wake up, girl!" The old crone swatted my shoulder. "You are not here to dream."

I rubbed my eyes and raised them to the book.

"You had that vision again, didn't you child?"

I nodded.

She finished crushing some roasted barley seeds and put them into a bowl of egg before getting up from the seat beside me. The old woman bent over and reached into her crawlspace. She extracted a wrapped bundle and opened it on the table.

I knew a bit about hazel wood. The staff was stranded with laced grays and one long thread of deep brown. It wasn't a straight staff; it rippled and spun from knot to knot as hazel will do. The wood had endured many diversions, and it meant to tell the story by the madness of its grain and wanderlust. The body had been oiled smooth, and the head carved to resemble the howling snout of a wolf.

"This is yours. Better for fighting than a stick." A finger of knuckle and skin wandered over the snout, passing downward over every knot.

"Look at it. See how it twists and turns. See that thin thread of grain that the Goddess let grow hidden from the world. There it splits, and there it comes together, but then, for a while, not entirely whole. This is your life, Abi. This is you. Mark it well. It tells a story, the same as any of our other books of kingdoms, conquests and princes."

She stared with unexpected steadiness, as if she wanted to say more, and yet something held her tongue.

I went back to my studies. The staff waited by the door where the crone put it. After a while I could hardly stand reading when sport waited so seductively. "I hate these dead kings that we study."

"You'll learn and be ready, girl. Imagine it your kingdom while working."

"My little kingdom? That's two sleeping boards in my father's rafters. I'm nobody."

"You're somebody. The Goddess knows you." Upon the last word, the crone bit her tongue, seemingly on purpose. "Just read your book, girl."

"Books give people crazy ideas. Get you put in the bad place. That's why it's illegal. That's why we have to hide what we're doing."

"Their god is a bastard. We hold no council with Sho, and instead honor the Goddess. Ask your mother."

I asked, "My mother... were you little girls together?" My hands made fists on my hips. I should have shown more respect, but I was a mighty mite back when I knew so little.

"Mind your learning. Just do as I say: When you face Sho, spit in his face for both me and your mother."

"Sho even counts our hairs, they say. The Dark One comes for us when we're bad."

"Ah yes, spit at Sho, and out come all the dark myths. Let me tell you something, girl." she leaned toward me as if she meant to keep her thought secret, "Sho's hidden name is Janus, the God of two faces. Ah! He is full of light and wonder, and all of that, they say. I say, he is both the Dark One and a firefly in a sky of flaming stars. Fireflies have no fire, child, other than what you let them take from you! You'll need to step through some trifling little fireflies before you see any light worth knowing. Understand?" She tapped on one of her books of war and history.

"No."

She struggled to her feet, eventually upended her chair, and waved me through the cottage door beside which my new and twisted staff waited.

My troubles seemed instantly over. I loved all the fighting she and my mother taught me, enduring the rest for it.

Leaping to my feet, I raced to beat her out.

I made it just to the edge of the landing before she struck me from behind with her staff. It seemed a dirty thing that she did; I recall having thought as I landed awkwardly in the yard.

"There. Go home with your new toy and think about that. Don't question my tactics, for today I am like Sho. Tomorrow, come back, and we'll read and brew cures and fight over better questions. Perhaps in the end you'll become someone other than the one he expects."

She slammed the door on my startled expression.

I now know that upon reaching the old and unmarried age of sixteen, I'd be pushed out of my father's cottage, and, without a dowry, a sure sign of a willful and worthless girl. Little did I know at that moment the actions of my teacher forewarned this fate six years earlier.

No, at the age of ten, sitting in the dirt before my teacher's step, I felt only the aching of my backside and confusion regarding the lesson I'd been taught. It was a momentary insult, and I knew I'd be back the next day, for the fierce old woman was clearly right about one thing. I knew the person Sho expected, and for the moment I was nobody.

* * * * *

I recall six years later, two months prior to my sixteenth birthday.

Having been tripped off the crossing log and into the creek, rivulets fell from my hair. Up above, the four Ranglson brothers leered like they'd come upon the goods wagon for the first time.

I waved them clear with my staff and shoved my skirt down, hiding the pink flesh of my thighs and knees. I was known-strange and heron-tall for a girl, but the lankiness filled in daily with flesh.

I recall wondering why the fancier girls in our village went on about boys. I could imagine no pleasure mingling with the likes of a Ranglson.

All of the boys were wet—I'd not been the first into the creek. They laughed and jeered anyway.

My arm covered the front of my thin blouse as I worked my way up the mud bank, beating them to the path.

Devlon and Kitchor shoved my sides, tempting me to fight them more. Young Bullor hawed like an ass.

"Soon your father will cut you loose. You'll be wantin' company then." Devlon showed a sour smile. He leaned toward my shoulder. His gait reminded me of my own father's mannerisms, further reminding me of their shared wretchedness.

I picked up the pace. My eyebrows hardened. I swore, "By the Goddess …"

"The Goddess? Do as we say, and we might not tell the priests of your witch words," threatened Devlon, though with a smile, as if he were completely unaware of the desperate danger in his threat.

The second oldest Kitchor tended a four inch gash I'd put on his head during the fight. He said, "She shows signs of a witch, sure. One look at her fire-red hair and its unnatural lightness… What might a witch do to our customers in the new brothel we intend of that old crone's shack? Particularly at night when the customers can't see what she's doing. We'll have to see to her taming."

I kicked at him but missed because I didn't want to shorten my stride.

Devlon added, "We can help you repent for fornication. And then more quietly add a whispering mention of witchcraft for Sho's ears, though too low for the priests to hear it."

He dropped to a whisper. "Might only be a few days in the pillory. Then your soul will be clean for a while."

Kitchor agreed. "Yes, we'll come by and give some pats of encouragement while you're repenting in the pillory." He'd come closer, nearly trampling my ankles.

Dangerous talk. My mother and the crone had taught me every herb trick imaginable, mostly just useful potions. Some of the spells required dances and communion with the Goddess, but that was fun, not evil. I'd even felt the Goddess's breath while dancing and had learned that Sho was not alone in the heavens. The Ranglson threats had goose bumps rising on my arms because I knew the priests and their White Shirt inquisitors took such talk seriously.

"Witch, witch," chanted three of the four brothers.

I said, "You know better than to bother a priest. They'll want to know where the Ranglsons were last summer?"

Kitchor made a little space for my elbow, deciding to walk in the weeds beside the trail. The others fell behind.

They oft went up in the mountain trails to rob priests and other vulnerable travelers with my father and brothers.

Devlon nodded to his wary brothers. "Her kin has no dowry. Let her fuss. Soon, all she'll be is a pretty turn of leg. Come her sixteenth, she'll be a calf wandering the road, looking for a bull."

Kitchor added, "Hunger turns 'em fast. By the back edge of winter, she'll take us all, that for the same copper and a black tater."

Devlon said, "We can set Abi up in the old biddy's cabin, once the crow's gone."

What an ugly little world. My look back toward Devlon

caused him to stop walking entirely. He raised his staff a little, but I moved on without threatening with mine.

If they'd rustled the leaves in my wake, I'd have murdered them all. I'd decided it was better to hang for that than to burn for witchcraft, or a worse fate.

They were right. For some reason, my father detested me and intended to turn me out. When I went, half the family labor was going to go with me. Then who would take care of my crippled mother? The farm sustained them, but we women sustained the farm. Such was just another example of my father's hate and poor judgment.

I seemed sure to spend the rest of my days crawling in the dirt with babies strapped to my back. When the stores dwindled to the last root, I'd eagerly take to the fields or the mines or onto my back as a Ranglson business. I couldn't see myself slipping to that, but I knew how things slowly shifted from unthinkable to pragmatic.

My own awareness startled me. I looked up through the leaves, seeing the bright-blue sky. Joy seemed way up there, as untouchable as the many worlds in the crone's books.

* * * * *

I emerged from the forest and into muddy furrows. Out in the fields, my mother toiled under the sun. A ragged scar ran across her ankle. I'd always known her crippled. Seeing her toiling in the fields shamed me.

My mother startled upon sensing my approach. One of the many new piles of rocks toppled. It seemed a sign. Perhaps the gods were plotting.

I ran to her. When I knelt, I coated my arms and clothing with mud in case my brothers and father were home.

I asked, "Have you taken no rest?"

"I'm fine. How went your studies? And fighting! Tell me, my trouble." My mother was on the sing-song edge of insanity.

"I've learned a little."

I walked a big rock to the edge of the plot. There I fit it into the new stone fence.

"Tell me all you can remember," she asked when I again neared.

"I've learned to love my mother. Guilt is murdering me. Out here all day by yourself."

"Then you are wasted trouble, learned nothing; you break an old woman's heart. Can't you feel my soul in you? When you are ready, I'll be happy in my mud. Happy, I say! Can you hear me? It grows close. You'll feel it, too, soon then."

My mother's eyes looked up to the heavens. "She whispers to me. Again. After so long."

My mother waxed delusional—or so I felt certain. I said, "I've a broken heart, seeing you like this. Full of crazy talk, hot from the sun."

"I want to know if this day, in this mud, is for nothing! What's crazy about that?"

I had to get rid of my frustration. I tossed a boulder the size of my head, nearly making it to the edge of the plot. I should have expected my mother's complaint, for it was the same every day.

"I've read of more dead kings and their wars. Different people in different places. Those before our time, whom I'll never meet. To make an ointment for warts. Arguing over the heavens. Still, she didn't hit me in the back and tell me, 'Come back when you have better questions,' like she oft did when I was younger."

My mother smiled and said, "She has never been patient. Now, she smells the trial. It is close."

I added, "Talk like that. You are a pair. I can't tell you why I listen to her. She teaches me of fat lives made thin and sprinkled in ink onto paper. I marvel at the battles the most, for they are bigger than us all. The worlds in her books are nothing like our little one. I told the crone that when I read today. I said, 'It seems too noble. I think the writer must be lying to us at least a little.' Then she patted my head like I was a puppy, which is how she tells me I have said something special. I never know why."

My mother nodded knowingly and even smiled a crack, though it was probably a wince caused by painful shifting.

Of course, I knew what my mother mostly wanted to hear: "Do you remember when I was ten, and she taught me to watch my backside?"

She nodded.

"Well, there is another backside; this one is on the other end of my staff. The thrust, meant only as a fake. We spent most of the day on just that, often leaving me befuddled."

"Ah, she hasn't changed entirely! In a fight, she danced. You know what surprises me; that she has stayed so long, just to teach you these things."

"What is the history between the two of you? You never visit, just sending me back and forth to learn things I can never use, and that might even get me burnt at some stake. Have you both always lived here, pretending as you do? Seems you both know a mite more than this wee place. Seems there is a story about the two of you. Not a book, but a story that ought to be told."

"An old friend, sent... Oh, I am bound to say no more than—"

"Yes, but what about when you were young? I swear she knew you in some other life. Tell me about it, just this once."

But, my mother's mind wandered just then. She mumbled on about raids, wild horses and golden necklaces sparkling in the sun. Her mind wasn't able to stick to the real world for more than a minute or two before mentally falling off a cliff. Her voice faded all the way to nothing. It was maybe even a good thing that her words rested, for she calmed.

I forced her to drink some water. She returned to crawling among the furrows. We worked the field together as the sun crept half-again closer to the horizon. Soon our work found the end of the new row of workable land. We looked back, still seeing ample rocks.

I ached a little from the crone's blows, and also felt the pains of a girl still growing, though I already stretched to the clouds.

Neither my brothers nor my father returned from wherever they'd wasted the last couple days. More than likely they were off robbing. What would we do if they never returned at all? I found the thought less than troubling, save for the thought of who might come to pitch us out. Women were not meant to keep land, though, from my experience, we were the only ones who did.

We fed mostly on hunt and forage. There was the new harvest, but the men kept a tight count on the height of the silo and larder.

Before we left the field, I smelled the deer in the wind. Upwind, a mule deer broke across our holding. I raced to head it off, grabbing my staff.

A hoof caught in a mud hole causing the deer to tumble, but it was quickly up, standing.

Farther on, I saw a friend. The wolf, Yellow Eyes, often toyed with me in the woods, but he wasn't very generous with anyone when it came to food.

Yellow Eyes stood tensely just behind the deer. He was the first of the pack to step into the dying light. With a shake of his head, the rest of the pack held back.

There was the matter of the deer between us, and friend or not, food was personal.

It was small, but one of its flanks promised to feed me and my mother a fat meal, two days of stew and a good deal of jerky. Three more wolves broke cover to my left, while a fourth stood her ground on my right, just into the field. That one had teats that hung. A favored female, she'd left her new babes for the sake of her own hunger, so I took her for both desperate and unpredictable.

Yellow Eyes walked forward another step. The others took up his example. This didn't sit well with the deer. He looked at me, thinking me the lesser risk, and he leapt.

I had to throw no farther than two feet, though quite quickly. The staff wasn't sharp, but I'd been tossing boulders. It hammered the deer's chest, stunned its heart and caused it to stumble. I fell on the kicking deer before it could recover from the blow and cracked its skull with my staff.

Straddling the kill, I watched the eyes of the great grey. Our fields were plagued by endless stones. I quartered the meat with the first one within reach that had an edge, bruising my hand as I cleaved and beat the joint to sinew. My father had taken the family knife on his business. I tossed the first thigh to the great grey. The next went to the dominant mother. She took it and raced away to feed her young. Yellow Eyes didn't touch the leg I'd tossed him, and, by not doing so, the others did no more than snarl their displeasure at having to wait for the command of their leader. With the third leg in hand, I rose slowly and kicked the rest of the deer.

Soon by her side, I gave my mother my arm, and we backed ourselves away toward the house.

That was all the waiting he had in him. The great grey jumped over the leg and landed on the bigger portion. His eyes met mine, teeth bare. Saliva dripped onto the deer's body. He leaned down and flipped the body open, feasting on the warm entrails. No sooner had he wetted his nose than the rest of them came nipping in. Some shot backwards with tidbits when the great grey growled. A rangy young female snatched up the leg behind them all and raced off toward the woods. In minutes, the body lost its head. The bony antlers left the field between the teeth of a large female.

Full for the moment, the grey regarded me where I stood by our house door. He snarled, almost politely.

Yellow Eyes spoke to me in my head. He told me all the meat was his, but he sensed that I was stronger than I looked, and he didn't feel like fighting me over just a little. Then the great wolf disappeared into the woods.

The last female carted off the remaining carcass, cleaning our field of the evidence. With luck we'd have half our leg eaten, and the extra made into jerky, or hidden under a rock in the bottom of the gruel pot before the men remembered they had a place to live and two women to keep it for them.

We used the best drinking water to clean our hands. I broke the haunch in two with our sharpest stone while kneeling in the doorway. Jerky strips were butchered on the porch foot-slate. That way I kept a lookout against the return of our men.

My mother had the kitchen stone to work with as she carved out two thin steaks and hung them with a stick over the fire. Then she worked the oldest bones out of the wide family grueling pot and ladled in the new ones.

With luck, the men wouldn't notice the better flavor, given the flavor had been better two days back, and they thought the world stopped for them when they left anyway. The anxious part was laying the strips up on strings near enough to the hearth to let them slowly smoke. Even quick jerky took time and space, the first being uncertain, and the second making it hard to hide our treason should we let down our diligence and not watch the road for their earliest sign.

I ate my steak while sitting on a log in front of the house.

My eyes were fixed on the end of the moonlit cart path. It would have tasted far better if we'd bled it and soaked it a day in brine, but my stomach didn't care that it was tough and gamy going down; to me it was the best tasting meat I'd ever eaten. It always tasted like the best meat ever when my mother and I did our little felonies against my father.

Skipping the well, I got a couple buckets from the creek, and mud washed the floor and table when I was done, allowing my mother to eat her share of the poaching while on guard. It took until the moon died for us to finish quick-drying the jerky. I dropped the bucket into the well for some drinking water. We laughed like children as we used the bucket to better wash away the blood and drippings, while filling our gullets to the brim. It was great fun knowing we'd beaten them again and that we did it so often that my brothers were skin and bones while they thought they were the pride of the litter.

I looked over at my mother when we both came to appreciate our success. My mother was the most worn and battered woman on earth. Still, she hid a secret soul and a secret history. The biggest secret of all, perhaps, was a pact she'd made with the Goddess to never show me more than a few tidbits of her past.

Her quick glance and conspiratorial smile sent me a shiver. I knew for sure that she lived for me though. She lived through me, too. And, in me, she somehow saw revenge upon the world within which we suffered.

Chapter Two

Two months later, upon the eve of my sixteenth, I had a rich knowledge of languages, cultures, wars and kingdoms, all remote and totally unrelated to my life. These distant but deeply implanted kingdoms felt like gates bursting to open and expose me for a literate. It was a good thing that we lived so removed from others. In fact, I knew nearly nothing about the tiny barony one mile from my home. I was utterly naïve regarding all that mattered and waited to touch my soul.

* * * * *

On the last day that I spoke to the crone, I said, "The men have been gone for seven nights. It has been a joyful time because of their absence, but we don't dare raid the stores much, lest we get beat when they return. We've mostly eaten rabbits and roots, whatever fills the gruel pot. Normally that's no problem, but I had to walk the creek to the Harpers just to find wild onions. It's not my fault I've been late to lessons. My mother is expert at putting her food on my plate. I can never find enough to dissuade her from starving herself for me."

My muscles bulged as we washed in the creek, proving I didn't suffer from starvation. The crone had gotten stronger the more years she'd put into training me as well. That day she'd been in good enough shape to beat me mercilessly with her staff after tying my best fighting hand behind my back.

Once I joked about my bound arm: "The off hand is made for brushing my hair back?" She'd finished my stupid thought by bashing me on the head for having a smart mouth in the midst of a fight.

"You expect your enemies to fight fairly? It's the job of generals to find you when you're squatting in the woods with your sword a field away."

Lessons done now, the creek felt cool and the sun warm for late fall. The crone's mood had softened after my explanation for being late. She poured a bucket over her sagging body, and then she tossed the bottom wash my way.

"The Goddess calls us home soon. Make your mother's life easy while you can. I'm sure she taught you how to hunt and gather herbs?"

It seemed to me the crone ate little but herbs, though I personally doubted one could live off them. Herbs heal and herbs add taste, but one can only eat so many dandelions before the stomach feels as empty as the white, wind-blown seeds on their stalks.

"The meat animals have left. I think they got tired of smelling me. I used to smell more of them as well, so my eyes are not deceiving me. I've over-hunted. What of the mating season? The wolves remain though, so we share the misery of our success."

"There are wolves. There is meat," said the crone. Her expression remained curious.

I skipped a rock across the water. "Maybe they're still here for a different reason?"

"Oh, so you think they remain just to keep you company? Maybe they intend to scare you away, as they have the meat? This, of course, suggests the Goddess has a thought on her mind."

"Where do you come up with these ideas?" I asked.

"When the Goddess tells you to go, I advise you do as told and leave the fancy thinking for later." She snapped a shirt. Flicks of water fanned my face.

"Don't be silly, woman; this is my home." The word *home* left me feeling so Goddess-awful empty.

We grabbed the rest of our clothing from the rocks. They'd half dried. After binding my leggings and slipping into my worn rabbit boots, I finished dressing while walking back to the cottage.

The day felt perfect for a moment.

The morning hadn't started with an easy feeling though. I'd had a premonition like I often did just before the men-folk returned. My senses were always good at sensing bad omens.

Sure enough, as we neared the cottage, I smelled horses and heard forest limbs breaking along the northern path. The crone shoved me in, barring the rickety door with a stout board. Without comment, she lifted a couple planks, taking out three coarsely-wrapped bundles. She tossed two of them across the room without unwrapping. Kicking the wooden planks closed, she unbound one of the treasures. I stepped back when I saw the iron sword. It was a soldier's weapon, illegal in the hands of a peasant.

The old woman smiled at the crudely-made thing. She tested the air with it. The weapon seemed to suit her in spite of its ill-forged weight and crooked blade.

I looked from the door to the woman, struck mute.

"Oh, girl, you have so much still to learn," the crone said. She showed incredible energy.

I heard men descending from their horses just beyond her porch. A leader shouted for the men to disperse.

The crone grabbed my arm, turning me, forcing me to look at her instead of the door. "Listen! This is my fight. Yours will come soon enough—soon as the Goddess decides you are ready."

A knight's armor clanked.

"Please!" I pulled at her arm. "We needed to escape."

"Ah, there is no time! All my waiting, and now so much to do and say!"

I rushed to close her only pair of curtains over the foggy window. It sounded as if an entire army of boots marched closer.

"Damn them; they're quick to have us, are they not. Goddess, there is so much the girl still needs to know," the crone lamented. She tested her sword some more, as if unwinding old muscles.

"White Shirts are outside the walls, beating on the rain barrel and porch fixtures." I shouted, "They're here to kill us! We have to run to the back woods." There wasn't even a back door, but I knew the walls were more brittle than the door.

The crone mumbled as she paced around the house: "I may be old, but I still bleed a shaman's blood."

"A shaman? What fool talk is that? Do you know some witch's trick that will help us escape?"

She frantically paced around a moment, and looked at me steadily as she moved. "Ah, that I do. I know the most magical of ways, child. No path is quicker to her side than the grave."

I startled gulping air so fast, I thought I'd choke.

She saw it and said, "Now don't you worry, Abi. I've already told you; it's not your time. My gift, as well, shall accompany your mother's on your journey. Let the Goddess see what comes of these three spirits within one so innocent!" She cackled with laughter so hearty that the battering at the door paused a second. I imagined the men outside listening and growing even angrier.

I backed a step from the crazy woman. She'd gone as mad as my mother. My staff was still in my hand, though I felt completely defenseless, and there seemed no way to escape certain death.

I watched the woman before me as if seeing her for the first time. Did I even know her? For years she'd spoken of witchery. She'd spoken of me and of my mother, some queen, a baby and even the Goddess, and also of herself, but all of it together in a jumble and with the meaningful portions omitted, like they'd been parts of a confused spell. Now this nonsense about death and gifts; I could make no sense out of any of it. The White Shirt, witch-hunters were here! The sound of their horses filled the yard beyond the door. Their boots pounded outside, seeking entry, hoping to burn us and hang us and fulfill all the rest of my worst nightmares.

I glanced through the curtains, out through the tiny, hazy-waxed window, seeing vague shapes both many and tall. A shoulder banged on the door. The crone turned to see the door straining in its frame. Upon seeing it still held, she twirled back toward me. Her dress flared. Her eyes landed on mine. They were the size of saucers, reflecting my tension. The crone laughed again.

"Oh, my Goddess," I breathed. She's been looking forward to this moment for her entire life, I realized. Her raving had not been fear, but elation!

For a moment, I felt as if I was all alone among a forest of beasts, fighting over me like I was a scrap of meat.

"Don't be afraid, my dear. You're to finally be set upon them! They should be the ones quaking in their boots." She laughed. "Command like the wind, my dear. The Goddess herself will join you on the field of battle! You'll see! I do. And, I shall be watching from the clouds."

"You're insane!" I said.

"Am I? I suppose I am. Isn't that lovely! Now, are you ready? Yes, I suppose you'll find your way. Here, let me show you the first step. Then, beyond, you will have to listen for her whispers. Such is wise for one entering her trial before the Goddess. The time is now. Look, Abi! We have already succeeded beyond measure! Don't you understand?" The back of her hand struck me on the chest.

I staggered back, limp with a sense of helplessness.

More shadows shifted beyond the waxed paper window and its curtain. Even as she spoke more of her nonsense, she grabbed me about the upper arm. I remained too much her friend and in her debt to fight her as she led me across the room to where she'd tossed the two bundles. There she dropped her sword long enough to struggle with four floorboards that I'd never before seen dismantled. Was there no end to the treasures she kept under the house?

A man outside the door yelled, "Open up! In the name of the high priests, witch! We know you're in there. There's no escape for you. We have holy water and signets. Your curses will not help!"

The man's shoulder met the door again, joined the third time by another man's weight. Obviously, the door was the stoutest portion of the cottage, though it only bought us seconds.

"Idiots," the crone mocked, as if expressing pity. Her head twisted back and forth from me to them, to me.

I bent down to help her with the escape hole. I gladdened. She'd finally come to her senses and understood that we needed to escape. Work helped unfreeze my fear. At the same time, I regretted that we were too late. Maybe fighting to the end was the better plan? At least there was honor in it. Surely we were counting our last breaths after so much delay. They'd probably sent men around. I heard them scraping at the back walls. How did it feel to get jabbed to death by pointy weapons?

The floor gave way. She tossed the two bundles in on top of yet another cloth wrapped bundle resting in the dirt a foot below.

"In you go with your treasures, dear. Now be still once

you're in there. I don't want to hear a sound. I've one last chore before my freedom. I'll not have it interrupted."

"No," I shouted from where I sat near the hole in the floor.

"Shed no tears for me, my sister. In minutes I'll be a newborn in the land of the Goddess. You've no idea how wonderful that sounds in the ears of an old woman! I'm as good as home. You, I'm afraid, must take a much longer path to glory."

In that moment I realized I loved her. It was both suicide and endearment that compelled her to confront a whole company of White Shirt witch hunters. While fixated on her, I imagined seeing her soul well enough to know that. It wasn't the soul of an old woman I sensed either. No, she'd said the word sister. The mere word felt full of power. Her spirit felt quickly filled with young energy, rather than age.

I said, "We can surrender—"

But, as I said this, she'd been speaking a chant. Her words struck me mute.

She spun a spiral into the air with a crooked finger.

Two final words slowed the world and filled my head with whispers.

So, she is a true witch after all, I thought, as my head grew light, and I toppled into the hole. The light in my green eyes faded toward the abyss of sleep.

* * * * *

The sound of the front door breaking cut through the fog of her spell. The boards had been placed above me seconds prior, though one didn't seat well, and that allowed me a thin view of the horror above.

I heard her feet race to the fireplace.

Many boots struck the flooring above. A brazier of cooking coals splashed across the room. The coals were like shooting stars as they streaked by my view.

I wished to fight, not burn to death under the house!

My body wouldn't respond to my will to rise, held there by her magic, so I could only watch, seeing tiny little flashes of the battle above. It was, I thought, just a dream, for the crone fought as well as I'd ever imagined the strongest knight. Her sword parried iron upon steel, then flashed red thrice, streaking the parts of the wall I could see with the blood of the first of the priests' troops. A body toppled right over the boards above me, cutting the slim view in half.

I heard the floor above bounce with the weight of at least three more before the room filled with even more boots, and the sound of iron on steel disappeared. Blood oozed between the floorboards as far as I could see around, dripping into the darkness. Someone turned the body of the dead man above, and, with that motion, the badly seated floorboard sealed, leaving me no view at all.

She didn't die all at once. I know this now because there lingered a pause before her magic oozed into my body. I became filled with the notion that the strange, seeping spirit didn't quite fit inside of me. The transaction lasted only seconds, but the feeling sank so deeply into my gut that I felt sure I couldn't give the extra spirit back to the world without something short of death.

I'd fallen into another trance under the totally consuming experience of her magic's invasion, but I was only gone from the conscious world a few seconds. Curling grey wisps of smoke billowed in and out of the cracks between the floorboards just over my head.

The sound of bodies being dragged out the front door told of a battle won and a quick retreat from the growing flames.

My reflexes returned. I shifted to a side before crawling toward the rear of the cabin and away from the worst of the smoke. Remembering my staff and the three bundles, I had to brave the rising heat to go back for them. It seemed a stupid thing to do, but I thought about the crone's life. She'd seemed so determined that I have the gifts, almost as if giving the things to me had been worth dying for.

The cabin was constructed of dry and thin wood. It went up over top of me as if straw. By the time I crawled the short distance to the back edge, pieces of it fell around the exterior. I shrunk back from the heat, searching along the edge of the cabin for a way out. Only the air nearest the ground remained breathable, and the heat at my back burned to differing degrees as I crawled toward the rockwork of the chimney.

There I saw an outlet where no timbers had fallen, and the skirt of the building's walls allowed a passage out. I tested it by sticking my head into the light, looking around for the dangers I figured would be everywhere.

It was with huge relief that I found the guards gone, maybe having fled to the front in the battle's confusion. Thick streams of black blew toward the back, obscuring the view as I picked my bundles up and cat-walked my way into the fringe of the forest. There I fell, crawling farther upwards into the wooded hill by use of a groundhog ditch.

Once up the overgrown slope a few yards, I put my back to a shielding pine. There I caught my breath while looking up into the forest. Nothing stirred in any direction. Even the birds were struck dumb by the horror of fire. I glanced over a shoulder and around the trunk. Over by the house, the fire weakened the last of the walls, though the flames and smoke kept me from seeing through to the front of the dwelling and to any of the soldiers I felt sure were still there. They, no doubt, amused themselves over the corpse of my teacher and only friend.

There was nothing I could do about it, I knew, though I'd have fought to my death defending the burnt ruin a few minutes earlier. I can't say I felt as if I'd have preferred dying. The forest air smelled fresh, and, as my head cleared, I enjoyed my breath more than ever before.

All of the pain from her spell on me eased out of my stomach and into my veins where whatever she'd put into me quivered. The woman had gone out in a fit of glory. I also understood that her fight remained unfinished, even though the light in her eyes had dimmed.

This was how she'd wanted to die, I seemingly heard somewhere between my brain and my ears. The thought laid me back onto my elbows.

Would they come for me now? No, they probably had no idea I'd been there, lest they'd be in the woods already. Maybe she'd known? Maybe she'd planned even that.

Only a witch could foresee something that exactly. Never suffer a witch to live, the priest had told us, and there burnt my example. I felt the chill of danger and the haunt of fear; however, that, too, subsided as I thought back on our lessons.

"Bah, what is a witch, compared to us?" I recall her having said? "No more than what the White Shirts say they are. The White Shirts serve Sho, and any god who favors women is Sho's enemy, they preach." The crone's words rang true. There'd been no evil in the crone that I'd ever witnessed, and who knew her better?

My mother did.

My mother's ramblings came back to me as well, some of them the same as the crone's. They both spoke of warriors and sisters and strange lands. Of course, they only spoke of these things in riddles. Each also shared the claim that the Goddess didn't want me to know too much.

The house turned quickly to piles of burning sticks above the flooring. I stared through and saw the enemy. Half were mounted, scanning the paths in front of the house. The soldiers of Sho wore mostly white and lighter gray tunics, though some of the newer ones wore what they had. The mounted sat on a variety of horses, nags to steeds. The eight to ten who were unmounted fussed over five bodies, one headless and separate from the others.

They'd cut her clothing from her body, tossing the rags into the still raging flames. A pair of troops dug a hole in the dirt with the crone's charred staff. They stuck her head on that.

They knew less than they thought, I realized, seeing that they'd left without her hair. Didn't every young girl know a witch's power was supposedly in her hair? These were the pious men of Sho, though, and, being men, there was much they didn't know that even the most ignorant woman in our valley did. They were even too lazy to properly bury her upside down and on her way to hell, as was custom by the more common folk.

The last of them climbed their horses. Their knight was the shortest one, a round man in heavy white armor whose face I didn't know. One of his men went to his knees, giving the knight a boost up to the saddle. From there, the leader slipped a hand into his saddlebag extracting some silver coins. He tossed four of them onto the wide part of the path. Three young peasants raced out of the shrubs, groped in the dirt and shared the coins among them. Devlon took two.

"Ranglsons!

"Devlon!

"Kitchor!" I spit out their names as loudly as I dared.

There, coming around a horse, as I expected, was the dumpy one Bullor. Four silvers to the likes of the Ranglsons was the price paid for one of the two lives that made mine worth living. They'd only lament that the shack meant for my whorehouse had burned down.

The horses galloped off, leaving four of their own dead in a neat row. They'd expected an easy time of it, failing to bring a wagon and apparently unwilling to drape the bodies across good saddle blankets. They'd commission a wagon later, I guessed, as I picked up my staff and made my way down the slope.

The Ranglsons had dispersed as soon as they'd pocketed the coins, allowing me to stand alone by the woman who'd taught me most of what I knew about the world that had killed her. There were cuts all over her body.

The crone's head came free of the stick with a sickly sucking noise. I ripped a shirt and pair of britches off one of the soldiers, dressing her.

That proved enough for a minute. I leaned over and fought my stomach still.

Once the queasy feeling passed, I stole the best pair of boots for myself.

The part of the house farthest from the hearth still burned, so that's where I laid her, placing her head as close to the neck as I could before backing away from the heat. She caught and burned as I sang her to the Goddess. I don't know why I sent her on that way. It was our custom to bury our dead in the earth. By the time I finished watching her body leave this world, ash flake by ash flake, the sun had taken me alone into the afternoon.

The fire in most of the shack extinguished itself, leaving only a stone chimney. There, under a half- charred chair, I found the crone's sword. It was a pitiful weapon, bent, chipped, and of poorly forged iron, fit for little more than a blacksmith's scrap heap. I used it to cut off the heads of the four men who'd tried to kill her. I mixed up the heads so they'd have to guess their own names in the next life, putting the first three between their neighbor's legs. They looked up at the sun with dull eyes.

Glaring away into the trees, I took some breaths of air to again settle my impulse to vomit, determined not to do it for them.

The last head went on the staff that had held the head of the only true warrior I'd ever seen in battle.

The battered sword belonged to the bones of my teacher, so I put it into the burning bones of her hand. Let them see this work and wonder about the power of the witch whom they'd thought they'd left for dead.

The magic wasn't so far from true. Something of her still lived, I knew. I smelled her on my breath, felt her buzzing under my skin and even tasted her on my tongue.

And, though she was now a ghost, long gone, she was done with waiting and very fierce with anger.

Chapter Three

I stole a shirt off one of the dead men. The means of whitening shirts could only be found in the king's city of Farstand. I'd need to stain it earth-shade if I meant to keep it.

I took the quickest path to my house, tying together my bundles and thievings, using the shirt as a sling. A fighting hand remained free for my staff. I was ready to bash my way home if the White Shirts showed.

Bullor sat on the log bridge. He polished his silver coin with the hem of his shirt. I wondered if he imagined himself a hero for his part in the murder.

The fallen trunk shook as I kicked it with my foot.

"Ha! It's Abi." He pocketed his coin and stood, barring my way across the creek.

From the look on his face, he saw I knew about the crone. He backed up a step. "I don't have a staff. I yield."

I had the height, but he had the weight and was a man nearly seventeen. It felt uneven to us both, I suppose: him thinking me a girl and me thinking him not enough. But, then again, so had it been with the crone, whose last lesson had been about uneven odds on the battlefield.

I tossed him my staff, leaving myself with my shirt-sling burden. He caught my wood with only a slight fumble. Then he held it aloft, admiring the workmanship for a moment. I imagined that he contemplated keeping it.

I guessed his thoughts and laughed.

He angered. On his first swing, I didn't duck. Instead, I

caught the staff–let it sting–raced my palm down until I held it near the center. Using every ounce of my strength, I planted my foot in his fat belly. He stumbled, fell backwards and landed atop the enormous log bridge.

The crone's rage felt like a tornado inside of me. I staved his throat with the small end of my staff. He fought for breath by grabbing his throat with his pudgy hands. While he did so, I reached down and plucked the blood coin from his shirt pocket.

"Is this the payment for a life? Now I have justice and reward." I stood over him and watched him twist and struggle on the great log. His lips turned the oddest shade of blue I'd ever seen.

No more were we children. My teacher was dead, and I was a day short of sixteen.

He watched me put his coin into my pocket. It was the last thing he saw as his eyes slowly lost the life in them. I could tell he couldn't believe he was dying, right up to the last. I felt nothing for young Bullor as I watched. It isn't right to feel empty after such an act, and yet I was numb to his suffering. The ability to feel such pain had been burnt out of me back at the cabin, replaced by a fresh and trembling desire deep within my soul for destruction.

Regret visited me a moment as I stepped over the dead boy; despite this, I immediately felt the spirit of the crone stir within me and lost that brief moment of compassion. In the end, I kicked him over into the creek. It was up a foot or two from recent rains in the higher mountain slopes, so his body rode the water past a bend and into the swampy weeds. They'll find him when the vultures come to feast, I imagined, not even caring, though I should have.

* * * * *

It wasn't until I stumbled into my father's house and saw my mother that I returned to the land of rationality. She stood from her stool without the aid of her stick when she saw me, as if startled by a stranger. For the first time in my life, I realized how tall she'd been before the awful wound on her severed ankle muscles had left her bent. The look on her face said she didn't know me. Perhaps it was the light at my back in the open doorway that hid my face. Then the look of surprise turned to recognition, though my intuition was that she still saw someone very different from the person who'd left that morning.

"They've murdered the crone in the name of Sho." My words set her off-balance. She fell back onto the stool.

When she didn't say anything, I added, "I murdered Bullor for the pleasure of it."

"They will come for you."

I sat my bundles on the table.

"Strange. I'm not afraid," I told her as I bent and hugged her.

She shoved me away and slapped me, leaving my cheek burning. Tears welled up from the unexpected pain. Once started, they refused to quit. She stood and took me back into her arms, and we cried for our friend like women should.

When our emotions settled, she said from near my ear, "Learn to be afraid, Abi. They'll come to take you away if you don't know when to run and hide. When they do, it'll be as if they've killed all three of us. You understand me?"

I understood her reasoning, but I still felt nothing for the dead boy or even my own safety. Ever since the crone's death, I'd felt a fire within my soul that wouldn't afford me the fear my mother spoke about. Worse than that, there was no guilt for what I'd done to defenseless Bullor, and his little part in my teacher's murder seemed too small of an excuse for my actions. I felt so hollow.

She was right, though, to say that I brought her danger and that the death of the crone should be for something. That stirred my emotions back to life.

I explained, "There's no place for me here anyway, Mother. Soon, Father will put me out. His heart holds only hatred for me, so I'll soon become the property of the first man who finds a use for me on my back or bent as his field slave."

"Abi!"

"No, listen, Mother. At least the crone died in a battle! She killed four of them with a blunt blade so heavy that two of them would have outweighed her. You should have seen how she died. It was the most beautiful thing I've ever witnessed! I wanted to feel that beautiful with Bullor, but it came out empty when I'd finished killing the toad. So, let them come in all of their pure white shirts so I might feel alive before I am dead!"

I expected another slap; instead, she held me closer than ever, and, after a very long pause, whispered as if one of the men stood near and might overhear: "This is not the duty the Goddess calls you for. My friend has burdened you with her untamed gift. Think now. Listen quietly, my trouble. What does the Goddess whisper to you when you stop this spinning in your head?"

I took a breath and said the first thing that came to mind. It was so ridiculous that I felt sure she'd slap me again. "The Goddess whispers that I need to dye that shirt with butternut so I might keep it."

My mother's mood brightened. "Yes. Now you're listening. Busy work. That's what we do to fresh, young warriors, too eager for battle."

Had I been so full of myself? My face flushed.

She added, "And when you do, take your treasures away to the woods, lest the men come back and take them. That'd be a loss greater than the life paid to give them to you. Pack them tight. They've been yours since you were born."

I was hearing so much mystery. My mother seemed

unusually sharp, though I felt the strain she struggled under as she tried to keep her senses alert.

I paced before her. "What is this all about? All of my life I've heard this kind of talk from you and the crone. She spoke of adventures and gifts. She said you'd once been a great woman. Today, the excitement made her say so many new things. Are you sisters? Is there some kind of scheme you've designed to confound me?"

"That is between us. The Goddess expects a great, but naked trial. She wants to forge something special out of you by beating on you some. Those were the Goddess's exact words last we talked, so long ago. I tried to argue with her. Even these things I say will be lost within you because of her promise to meddle with your memories, should we slip and say too much."

"Oh, hush!"

"Yes, it is magic. She plays upon your memories."

"My memories are fine, and I don't intend to go anywhere." I'd heard enough of packing and leaving on some unfathomable quest. Part of me couldn't imagine leaving her. The rest of me didn't know how.

"You're a criminal now. On the run," my mother said, reminding me of what I'd said before.

I was conflicted. "I can't leave you to the men!"

Again she heard nothing. Her mind resided in two places as she rambled, "I can make a coin for you. You've earned it." Hearing that, I suspected the great craziness had returned.

She stood, with her cane's help this time. I saw how old she'd become, and before her time. Without my help, even as hard as she worked to take up my slack, the men would maltreat her for not doing enough.

My mother took a pinch of red clay in her cracked hands. I'd fetched it from a creek only a day ago, and my mother had already made three unfired bowls, keeping the last bits of earth wet under a soaked rag.

"I'll make your first coin of clay, and fire it with a pyrite glaze. Then when you've earned your first gold coin, melt it and use this to make your mold."

"Yes, mother." I was sure my mother had fallen into another of her insane fantasies then. Yet, as I watched my mother fashion the coin, it took on the beauty of jewelry. I'd never owned jewelry. I'd only seen a few items on women of better station, mostly worn on visitors during my rare trips to our tiny village.

I got some gruel and biscuits my mother had made earlier. As I ate and tended the jerky by the fire, she worked details into the coin's face. My mother put the coin near the hearth to dry before firing, and then she turned to gather butternuts from the box.

As if an afterthought, she said, "Listen to the Goddess when she whispers to you. She has given you some protection! The coin will call to that."

"Yes, Mother," I repeated. I considered: Did the Goddess really trouble over me? The whole thing about a coin didn't make any sense either. Wouldn't a gold coin be what I needed for a dowry instead of jewelry about my neck? Did my mother think I'd waste gold on fancies?

I was moments from my coming of age and one night before the road, should my father so determine. I was sure he would. I had to go, but I couldn't go; all of that turned in my head. In the end, it was she who pushed me toward the door. She put my bundles behind a bush, just into the forest. She helped me dye my shirt in a yard hole, too, our conspiracy easy enough to see on our darkly stained hands. It was quite a contrast, my skin being by far the fairest I'd ever known, as was my hair, though it was also aflame.

I returned to the house when we were done, but she shoved

me away with a blanket and all the jerky we had in store. I stood dumbfounded when the door slammed in my face!

It was very dark by then, and the house had not been lit, but I have good eyes in the dark, and I'd seen the first wetness in my mother's eye before she'd vanished beyond the wood and brace.

I'd never before felt so alone, not even under the crone's house and surrounded by fire.

I dared not knock.

I dared not listen to her weeping, for it came back to me that the villagers might find Bullor, or that the priest's White Shirts might also suspect me for a witch. I was a danger to her. Had I not confessed that already?

Heartsick, I took my things into the woods. There I camped without a fire under my best new shirt where it dried in the breeze. I had but three, one more than I had in skirts.

I lay back and tried to sleep, having convinced myself that sleeping under the stars was prudent. After a warm day, fall was coming back with the night, brisk and windy. I wrapped myself in my second shirt and rustled up a few more leaves for under my blanket. When I'd gotten comfortable, I heard feet on the earth. Through a parted bush, I witnessed my father and at least one of my brothers breaking the shadows of the distant valley path. Their shadows merged and then passed into the house.

The door closed, and soon the chimney smoked heavily from a new log. After a while my father came out with his lantern, looked briefly around the cabin, and then went back in, probably looking to find me after the excuse my mother had made to cover my absence. I could imagine his turmoil. My mother had kicked me out, denying him the pleasure.

The moon came up, and I was finally nine months and sixteen years from the terrible planting that had predestined my birth. Such thoughts lulled me to sleep.

* * * * *

The day was not yet lit, but the stars told me it was time to get up and think. I had no plan, nor did I have prospects. If the Goddess wanted me to go on an adventure, she'd forgotten a direction. I heard no whispers from her either.

All I had were my things, including the dark shirt snapping in the brisk morning breeze, the same breeze that numbed me on one side. Beside it, dangling on the same limb, the clay coin sparkled as if it were gold, hanging on a leather string. She must have worked all night to secretly dry, glaze and fire it so quickly. I snatched it down, somewhat concerned that my mother had been able to sneak right up to me while I slept. Nobody could do that. I knew my woodsman senses to be decent, though I had nobody to compare them to because of our isolation. Maybe she'd done it by witch magic. That idea was the most believable, knowing the dances and cures we'd practiced together.

I sniffed. It was easy to smell her in the air, in spite of the cleaning wind. Though it was still half dark, I looked around, seeing all of our meager holdings—but not her. She was the last of the people I loved, and I had no choice but to leave her behind.

After the sadness wore its edges, I came to study and admire the artistry in the coin. She'd made a nice likeness of a wolf on the face. She'd poked a hole in the coin so it could be hung. I liked it more than I thought I would.

The coin fell between my breasts, nearly all the way to my navel when I sat stooped over. I stuffed it under the two shirts I wore. It would be best to keep it hidden there, given the way the visiting priest spoke so unkindly of vanity among the peasant class. Oddly, it took a few moments for me to realize that the circuit priest served the same men who'd murdered my best friend less than a day ago. What did I care what he thought, as

long as it didn't bring me attention.

I had neglected to open my gifts for fear of what I'd find. I unwrapped the thin one first. The knife was a good steel blade, leather for a grip and a slight finger guard in between. It wasn't ornate, for all the craftsmanship had gone into its steel and utility. It had been wrapped in enough fabric to make five sets of leggings. I cut some of the precious fabric off the roll and made a new hand grip of cloth so I could wear my knife without too much suspicion being drawn to its quality. Even a bad knife was worth a silver piece. It was best to make mine look as if the grip was of peasant quality if I hoped to put it in my pocket or fashion a scabbard in order to wear it hidden just under the hem of my shirt.

The next bundle was wrapped in enough cloth to make a pair of new skirts. When I first saw the sword, my stomach turned. How would I hide such an illegal instrument? Unlike the crone's ugly piece of iron, this was folded steel. The grip had the same leather as the knife. The finger guard was two fingers tall at the top and three at the bottom. I took my time looking over the steel. One try scraped the hairs right off the side of my leg. A soldier might cut a man in half with this thing, I imagined. I swirled it around as if to fight forest ghosts.

It was instant infatuation. The grip fit my hand like it'd been made for me. If the crone, with all of her skill, had chosen this one, perhaps she'd still be alive. Why had she given this to me instead?

I gripped the blade in two hands, slicing down with power. There was much about swords that I didn't know. I tried it each way. First, one handed, I worked on the footwork and balance I'd learned with the staff. I imagined how it might go if the crone's staff were my opponent. She'd fought with seeming ease, well schooled motions that made her tough to beat. I danced about as if she were still teaching me, longing to feel her blows.

Two handed cuts were for slow brutes. I'd have to work on my grip, I decided. I chipped an inch out of the log in front of me. After having seen what little I had of the crone's sword work, I figured I knew enough to get killed on maybe the second swipe, and that would probably only be the result of my good footwork, which I'd learned from my extensive staff training.

Very exciting.

When I calmed down, I sat and read the inscription across the base of the blade: *Anabi_didaokaAia*. It was in something close to ancient Vennian. I recognized it from my years of toil over the crone's books. I had no problem with the word, sword, but it took me some time and worry over the word, teacher. *The sword of a teacher*, I concluded.

Of course, I thought; that made perfect sense, given she'd

had so many books and had dedicated so much of her time to the task of my education. I'd been silly to think myself the only student in her lifetime. It was well known that peasants weren't smart enough for real study, so I'd surely been her most daunting student. Perhaps her father had been a teacher, too, and from a better class, such as a wealthy merchant's household in Farstand. There, blades were supposedly allowed for protection against bandits like my father, possibly explaining how she'd come by it.

I put the sword back into its highly crafted leather sheath before opening my last gift.

The unwrapped book was no bigger than the size of my outstretched fingers. There were only two score pages, and a few words on each page. In poet's verse, the language was a newer variation of Vennian, and thus much easier to read than the sword's inscription. The first page translated to something like:

The... truth... is burden as
(something)... boulder left by oxen.
Lift not as you fly falsely.
Hide in earth's eye.
Come one as you say deception.
I pray you spell... (something).
Goddess praise, pass fair.

I'd found only a few poems in those larger books of histories. They all wandered around the point, but not as badly as this one did, and, of course, the translation didn't quite rhyme. Maybe it did in Vennian?

I tried the trick the crone taught me of fidgeting over it as if it were a riddle. So, it means the truth is sometimes hard and heavy like a rock, and the poet wishes for some sort of ability to lie and get away with it. The Goddess was giving him a pass and would make sure he went unaccountable. That fairly explained half the community I knew. Most of the people around my home lived like squirrels. Each stole the same nut back and forth from the other and lied about it to the point where nobody could figure out who'd owned the stupid thing first.

Right under the poem were the words, *Tpunwvw Own*, followed by a big and wandering circle. Well, that was something to mull over as I traveled, I decided.

The sword wasn't an overly long one. It disguised pretty easily as the core of a roll of cloth. It went into the bottom of my long bag. I found two thumb-sized branches, cutting the bark off to make them look like whittle sticks. A little bit of wood explained the shape in the bag. An interest in cutting wood was a good excuse for owning a knife, too.

I had my staff for walking, neatly whittled already, proof that I had some skill for those inclined to look at me closely. Such work was even marketable if I learned it. A woman couldn't keep a job without a man's consent, nor could she own land, but nothing kept a woman from making a copper or two from the spot sale of something as common and useful as a walking stick. I'd honed no such skill, but then again, the Goddess maybe hinted.

The rest of my stuff went over the illegal book of poems. I had jerky, a skin full of wheat, apples, carrots, a sewing kit, an extra pair of soldier's boots, rags and a few other things that I stuffed in tightly with the fabric and old clothing. My new shirt and blanket were last before I tied the long bag with two ropes and slung the whole thing over my back. My knife had seamstress utility to go along with my sewing kit, so I'd not go naked for a while. I wrapped the blade in cloth to keep it from poking a hole in my one deep tunic pocket. A hole might cause me to lose my silver coin before I got a chance to make my first drawstring purse.

I turned away from our farm, ready for adult life, or at least the first few hours of it. My stomach was tied into knots. I tried to walk off the homesick feeling. Fretting about my mother was painful and desperately hard work. To help divert those thoughts, I watched for any animal poking his head up in the woods. I saw the wolf, Yellow Eyes, once, but only in passing.

Skirting the holding, I gained the path when I was sure I was out of view of my father, should he be about.

The trip to town was twice interrupted by hiding from messengers on horseback. They raced toward the holdings that included my father's. There weren't all that many people living down our way, and no horses at all, so seeing horses was special. Early on, old man Scoodle wheeled by on one of Sir Lastion's wagons like he was in the races. Three from the village in just one day! I'd never heard of so much hopping about in my life and grew tired of hiding from all the travelers. Finding a witch, of course, was a significant event. I had expected some activity, but not nearly as much as all that.

Our town consisted of a few houses, two barns and, most importantly, the front parlor of Sir Lastion's two story house, nearly our only commerce. He was said to be related to royalty, but I think he was seven or eight cousins past forgetting. Maybe he'd even made up having weak royal blood. Nobody asked because he owned the large house. The men drank and gambled in his front parlor, so I figured this was the hole that held all the money my father and brothers stole before they wandered home. We didn't even have a store, though Lastion made money by running dry goods and tools from Lettoir Manor or even from as far away as the baron's city of Helfax.

I'd heard there had twice been a traveling store in a grand and colorfully painted goods wagon, but my father had never let me near town when it was in, nor did I ever have any money with which to pay for anything I'd have liked to buy. I didn't know what they had on the wagon, but I wanted to know. The priest hadn't spoken kindly of the traveling wagon, claiming it temptation. If there was one here now, I'd buy something, I thought. I didn't need anything, but I just wanted to know once what it felt like to buy something.

The town was still half asleep, and that suited my purpose, given I needed to see the posting board. It was said that every day Sir Lastion came out to read what was on it, assuming someone was out wanting the news. On the few times I'd been able to come and hear the traveling priest call us sinners, he'd read off the posting board as an added service. I'd never been to town so early, when nobody was about, tempting me to go read it. I risked the sin and looked at the only thing posted:

Witch!
Lone ole' biddy out Nor lane.
Go on three miles
Cabin by White Creek Nor o' path.
Acteun pendin
Stay way till dune.'
Under that, new and watered down ink had scrawled:
'Kilt the biddy n tuuk her head.
Witch magac kilt 2 soldures.
Spiruts afoot.
Pray 2 Sho.

It was signed by Sir Lastion himself, probably because the remaining White Shirts couldn't write. Of course, it didn't look much like Sir Lastion could write all that well either, I noticed, scrutinizing the first post I'd ever read from a scholar's perspective.

Certainly they lied about only two soldiers dead and about my crone's skill, but I'd expected some lying, even on expensive paper. The good part was no mention of me. Nor was there anything about a dead Ranglson.

I heard the wheels of a wagon and scooted into a barn door where I hid. From there I watched old man Scoodle bring in the four bodies. It seemed everybody else eventually heard it, too. Some of them waited to come out after he circled the posting board and stopped his wagon in the midst of the housing. Five soldiers of Sho came out of Sir Lastion's house, their white shirts unbuttoned and boots all floppy and untied. They buckled on their swords as they walked up to the wagon as if they owned it. I hid in the even darker shadows of the barn, hoping they couldn't smell out a witch as easily as I could smell the dirt weighing down their souls.

There, plain as day were four half-stripped dead men, not just the two the board had mentioned. Their heads rolled around in the space between their necks and the front of the wagon. They put some of the town men to digging up on dead man's hill. While all the inspecting was being done, others came into town from down the road and from various paths. I'd never seen so many people in one place. There were over a hundred country people shuffling by the posting board in no time at all, adding to the fifty who lived in the village.

Then the Ranglsons were there, all except for Bullor. They didn't seem all that troubled by his not being in the brood either. Their look was, maybe, the same as my father's was when he came in with only my brother Kevin. Keith and my mother were probably left home to work the farm, I figured, given I wasn't there to work it for the brother who was only one year older than I. Just to see Keith working, I was half tempted to walk back to our holding; I'd not seen him do any work since I'd turned ten and took over his part.

Dicket Ranglson came right up to my father and started a conversation. I couldn't make out the words with everybody gossiping at one time and my being so far away, but they seemed serious. Maybe Dicket was worried about Bullor, and maybe my father was worried about where I'd gone off to before he could kick me out. And, perhaps they both decided we were with each other because after a while they both laughed as if coming to a conclusion that satisfied.

"Congratulations. Fat Bullor and the useless wench have run off together," I whispered irreverently.

The barn had a hay loft, and it was a good thing because I had to race up the ladder when people came in on horses, wanting to stable their beasts. Soon, the whole place was filled with whinnying and fresh new piles of manure. I picked just the right pile of hay to hide behind, too, because Lastion sent Scoodle up to pitch down some hay, and he missed me all around with his pitchfork. There grew a huge crowd, maybe two hundred, down out the loft window. I didn't think so many as that lived within twenty miles of our village. Almost half of them I'd never met.

A rumble of horse hooves came down the road, hushing the crowd. The people, twice as many as my last count, backed against the sides of the road. Soldiers stopped at the meeting ground by the post. These were darkly-clad soldiers, a score of them I noticed, not the priest's sort. All five of the remaining priests' guards, in their ugly whites, mingled now in two groups among the peasants. I had a quarrel with them, but not with the darkly-clad soldiers, though I didn't feel that any of the soldiers were safe. There were too many twists and turns in what was happening for me to trust any man.

Sir Lastion met a lady and a gentleman, both of whom seemed leading the troops. The three appeared to decide upon waiting for even more folks, maybe the whole world, before doing whatever it was everybody had come to do. Someone set up a tarp because our village had no good inn, and Sir Lastion brought food out for the two lords and soldiers. It was a grand thing to see, and had I not been so guilty of so much and so uncertain about where I stood in the middle of it all, I'd have gone down to watch them eat. Their clothing was strangely pretty and their manners inspirational.

Meanwhile, the lady's soldiers stood around. Most of them were well turned out, but a couple of them were in peasant clothing. These were new recruits I guessed, given they'd arrived doubled up on one of the lumbering pack animals. These new fellows were nervously following orders from the rest and were quickly put to guarding around a single horse, employing nothing more than wood spears. They rubbed their butts as they were likely unused to riding and seemingly thankful for the stop, even if it did mean more work.

Only the guarded horse still had a rider. On its back was a peasant with his hands bound to the front and a cloth sack over his head.

* * * * *

I got bored as the next hour passed, so I pulled my book out and read the first lines again. I think I sorted it out a little better on my second translation, this time working out the literal from the metaphoric tendencies in the older language; a skill the crone had abused me into learning:

When the truth brings evil
And is as heavy as a big boulder.
And you cannot avoid your duty.
You may hide in plain sight.
None will see your deception.
Pray that the Goddess grants your prayer.

When I'd sorted it all out in the literal, it made more sense, but it still left me with a mystery. It was witchcraft to cast spells, or even to try magic. As I read more, I grew certain that I held a spell book! They could murder me legally for even reading the text. Of course, they could murder me for about ten things I'd done over the past day, so what was the difference? If

I were a sinner, I was a sinner; it was done and to be sure, if tossed in the river, I'd float as proof of my witch born evil, witch or not.

I was very excited, and eager to think this through.

I'd never seen anyone actually do a big spell. Then I had a second reflection and realized the crone had spelled me twice in a row less than a day ago. She'd said some words and just spun her finger in something like a circle. The next thing I knew, I'd fallen into the hole in the floor and gone stone mute.

I put the book down, but picked it back up quickly, turning back to the first page: Under the poem were the words, *Tpunwvw Own*, followed by a swirl of ink that reminded me of someone's finger tracing a whimsical circle in the air.

I could do that. All I needed was some good lie to cast on myself. It wouldn't do to engage in witchery without a decent lie that made sinning worth its while, on the off chance I actually succeeded. I thought about how I'd get past all the people down there, now having gotten myself soundly stuck in a rabbit's hole and surrounded by foxes. If I weren't cursed by being born a woman and, in particular, Abi, I could just walk around like everybody else, I figured.

After a little thinking, I came up with a plan. If I had some britches and waited until it got really dark, nobody would stop me from walking off because men went everywhere they wanted. This, of course, assumes they wouldn't see me too closely.

I got to work cutting my spare skirt down the middle. I doubled the legs up inside so I'd not have to cut the material all the way off and lose my skirt. Then I loosely stitched upwards in a V shape to make legs. By the time lunch was over for the nobles under the canopy, I had britches. They looked just like the ones I'd made for my brothers. When done, my skirt went back on over the britches so I could quickly change when the time came to shift into my disguise. It seemed to me at the time that the book had already proven itself useful.

The hair was going to be a bigger problem. I had no brush, so I combed it with my fingers, and then three-braided it back into one long warrior's tail. I noticed that down on the street, some of the older soldiers had theirs long and braided back like that, though none were nearly as long as mine, which hung down all the way to my butt. If I put my bundle up behind me like I usually carried it, the length might not be all that unusual looking, particularly in the dark.

All I had to do was wait half a day, I thought, sitting back in the straw. Good thing such excellent entertainment was milling below. I watched it from the cloak of a shadowed loft window.

Chapter Four

"Taxes are due. Irvan Lastion, man of the Baron of Helfax, has assured the Lady Mayran Lettoir, keeper of the lands under Lettoir Manor and protector of the peace, that any not represented here, those unable to pay this day, and any tenant rights forfeit for failure to comply, will be granted one reprieve by visit from him or any man he contracts for the purpose of the collection of taxation, though this legal day be the day of final appeal and proper payment. Each and every household is subject to a taxation of one part in ten, to be determined by record and testimony, as the first is held in Lettoir Manor, and the latter is heard this day. Two years have passed, so twenty parts are due. Thus shall be posted at the end of this accounting."

I'd never thought such an eloquent speaker existed, his sentences long and woven like fine cloth. He didn't resemble the knight who'd led the killers, so I determined to judge him separately and put value to his demeanor. Though the man was elderly, he stood tall and spoke with such clear language that I doubted I'd forget a word. I tried it on my tongue, "The Lady Mayran Lettoir, Keeper of the land under Lettoir Manor, and—" I had to hush, for the pause was not long, and I dared not miss the rest.

He spoke some more about the laws of taxation and allowances. Then there was a delay when a guardsman leaned in and whispered into the noble's ear. It was the soldier with a black slash across the arm of his uniform, so I took him for someone of good rank.

The noble nodded, and then he loudly said to all, "Before we can start, we have been inconvenienced by the detainment of a prisoner. Several merchants did disarm and deter an attacker in one of the eastern passes. Hear ye all that this man was caught red-handed in the art of thieving with both knife and bludgeon, though his fellow highwaymen escaped. He has been handed off to us to dispose of as the law dictates, and at the earliest convenience. Given that he was caught without defense, there is no need for trial beyond this summary and the nod of the local lord of rank. Do you concur, Lady Lettoir?"

The fine lady stepped up and gave a short nod. She showed some hesitation before the approval, obviously giving the thief thought of fair judgment, though she resigned to the need, as all could see that he was guilty from the telling of the story.

The crowd had given a gasp of shock upon hearing the charge and another one upon the Lady's well considered trial, as if such a charge was odious and new to them. Half of the town made their tax payments thanks to the same profession as the accused, and the other half owed their businesses to the coin that floated around because of the trade of the highwaymen who got away. Still, it was great pleasure to gasp and to see punishment dealt out to the unfortunate who had proven too slow to get away.

"Given the rise in crime through these mountains, I condemn the prisoner to the example of hanging. This is to be carried out this moment and in the honor of your presence. Rebind the prisoner's hands behind his back, and set him under the village oak," declared the noble.

Three of the older guards pulled the man from his mount and refastened his hands behind him. Several others worked a rope over the yard's biggest tree. People fought for a view closer to the dangling rope. Soldiers had to clasp hands to hold them back.

I felt a little pity, but not much; this was, after all, the stakes in the gamble of thievery, and our Lady probably had little use for slaves who needed watching. They pushed him back onto his mount, but facing the horse's rump, and then led the mare under the noose. The head guard with the black stripe mounted his own horse and was thus high enough to affix the rope tight about the man's neck.

I heard the first of the condemned man's muffled wailings while he still had his hood on. People chided him, drowning out most of his pleas. I was like them some, I suppose, transfixed by the excitement. Our emotions hid the fact that it could have been any of us.

Would it be like this if they caught a witch in this public place and put her to the test?

"Who knows or speaks for this man?" asked the noble when he waved for the soldier on the horse to pull the hood off.

I could have. He was my brother Keith.

His frantic glances passed by the faces of the soldiers, both brown and white shirted, and then the other faces, those he knew well. There might not have been one peasant in our village who didn't know his name. Not one said a word to give away their recognition, obviously for fear of suspicion. Some jeered, and then others joined in, and then the whole crowd became so loud that even if someone had spoken, they'd not have been heard.

It was almost genius, seeing them work up the defensives. The soldiers in white screamed just as loudly, though only a few of the darker clad ones broke professional rank. We were wretched.

Lady Lettoir and the older noble with the clear and beautiful speaking skills learned nothing new, for Keith's pleas were drowned on his lips.

Then I saw Kevin and my father. They, too, screamed to drown out any tattle, though their faces showed no joy in it. I imagined it all very painful for them, and though it heartened me much to see my father so tortured, and forced to pretend otherwise, the whole show was an exceedingly sad display.

It was one thing to wish misery on a brother who'd shown me no love, but it was another thing to linger in glee over his death. My heart surprised me at first. After all of the abuse, I cared. My tears fell, and then they stopped halfway down my cheeks. I was quickly hardened by the spirit of the crone that infested me, for she ate upon my compassion until, within seconds, my sorrow vanished. It made what remained of my old self feel empty, not glad, not sorrowful, not anything at all. Curiosity alone lingered way up in a loft portion of my mind, old me as invisible to the new me as I'd been to my father's love.

The noble nodded. My brother was going to die nameless.

The guardsman casually led the horse forward, literally leading it to a water trough. Keith ran out of horse and fell off the animal's rump as it walked out from under him.

The hood hadn't been replaced. It is said that they do this so the evil among us can see the price of our sins.

My brother screamed while falling. The scream was cut in half. My own heart jumped, in spite of the hostile spirit that haunted me.

There he dangled. He looked like he wanted to gag but couldn't. His feet kicked at the air, running as if into the sky. They slowed only seconds after they'd started. Much more slowly, Keith's head reddened, his lips blued and his tongue fattened too much for his mouth, while his eyes pushed and pleaded, trying to drop out of his face entirely. Still, his heart beat within his chest. My wolf-talented ears seemed tuned to such rhythms, sensing it even above the applause. Then his toes flicked for long enough to make me think he'd not die at all until we all stopped looking at him. His water dripped off one of his feet, making a small puddle and causing some of the smaller children to laugh while pointing.

When he quit, we were still unsure because the rope kept swinging just enough to make us wonder if we'd see another twitch. I had to crawl back into the darkness of my window for I'd leaned too far out in awe. I breathed heavily, clutching near my heart.

The noble returned to his seat under the canopy. The reminder of his law swung under its own dead weight.

"Silence!" As if not having been interrupted, he said, "Now, the first to be called is Alandrew, surnamed Abakeson. His hold is assessed the equal to a gold, four silvers, eight coppers and three slivers."

A peasant I'd seen only once in my life came forward. He spilled the contents of a bag on the table, and then he sorted back into the bag a few coins and slivers. The elderly tax collector counted out the taxes left there and nodded. Sir Lastion put the coins in an iron-strapped box and marked the taxes paid.

It went that way until the fifth man came forward. He appealed only that he'd done Sir Lastion several communal favors and was due a half copper for each on his list. The noble found the man thankful when he was granting half of his request without quibble, though I knew Sarsion Cadwiller to be a rogue and never truthful in much he ever said. One glance between Sarsion and Sir Lastion produced a nod that told me one of the two coppers he'd saved was due Sir Lastion when all was done.

The sixth man wasn't as fortunate, making many excuses before admitting he was five coppers short what was owed. The noble asked if any would honor his debt and pay the remainder for the man who was short his taxes. None came forward for the pittance. Sir Lastion offered to send his man in a week's time, giving the debtor time to come up with the coppers.

I thought it chancy that a week was enough time to find a buyer for anything the man had to spare when the harvest was in, seemingly ample and either sold or settled in for winter. Who would buy his wheat? He had little else. They moved on.

Deficiency didn't happen again until they called the name of Garette Tokenhold. My father had been hiding well in the crowd, along with his firstborn and only remaining son Kevin. After he pushed to the fore, I read his face, expecting anger and pain behind the mask. Instead, I sensed fear and shame. So, I thought, the week of stalking the mountain roads had earned him too little to even make our taxes.

I heard his rough voice stammer a lie that his holding wasn't nearly as wealthy as the records of Lettoir suggested.

Lady Lettoir sat up and listened more intently. It was the first word of any error in the records held by her late husband and now herself. She asked, "Have you two sons and two score acres? The survey claims half are cleared, but only half a score are basis for taxes due upon them under prior claim that the clearing has been recent. That error is in your favor."

"Is true, but I've got a crip for wife. The girl she dotes on is lazy. She spends her time at play. They both eat more than ten men and work not a minute. My duties take me abroad, and there was a recent setback in trade."

"If there is no profit in trade, there certainly should be plenty in tending a farm. How much can you afford to pay, Garette?" asked the lady.

"Six coppers and two slivers, and for that I'd have aught for the winter," said my father.

I was appalled at the insulting sum, for it was nearly two golds short. My mother would be cast out into the forest and left to die under the ice of winter. As for my last brother and father, they'd probably turn to full-time thieving, as was their greater talent. The land had been a purely secondary vocation for them, after all.

"I rule you are forfeit all lands, given such a difference in sum cannot be mediated, nor lawfully accumulated in any less than several seasons. The details of your eviction will be sorted out between us and Sir Lastion upon completion of the ledger of names. Till that time you shall hold yourself at our pleasure." Lady Lettoir's word carried much threat and weight, for I noticed nods from the tall noble, as well as from Sir Lastion and even from some of the lady's troops, as if they had been called to alert. I caught my own head nodding, though my opinion hardly mattered, particularly from so deep within the shadows.

Two of the lady's soldiers eased themselves closer to my father, hands on their hilts, as if expecting him to dart. I was impressed. This was the very first time I'd ever seen a woman take such command of a man. It felt doubly good to see my own father fall to her whim, though of course, it remained problematic.

Would that I could serve such a woman.

There was such a thing as too much good excitement and too many problems all at once. I had to sit back from the window and think over what I already had mounting on my mind. Could I go back to my mother? If so, what could I do to save her when it seemed I couldn't even save myself from the coming winter cold? It would be a lot simpler if I had two golds. With two golds I could buy her at least what she had, though no more, regardless of what I did thereafter. I felt in my pocket, fingering the silver, a fortune to me a small time ago, but as good as nothing all of a sudden.

Looking back out the window, I studied to see who might loan me such a fortune. None in our village would. Five coppers had been too much for a better neighbor in dire need. The White Shirts would as soon cut my throat in the name of their God as barter with me. As fine as the nobles seemed, they couldn't give money to every peasant who came short and maintain order. Thus they were disinclined to help, regardless of their fine countenance. I imagined the lady's soldiers as the only chance of compassion, and yet I didn't imagine them wealthy servants, regardless of how well turned out they appeared. The last I saw in the yard were the recruits. They might well have less than us all, excepting new and shiny hope for a future—a future, the very stuff of my dreams. I sat back away from the window again and lamented that none would help, not for a copper, much less a gold. My thoughts on that seemed futile.

Recruits! Ah, now that was a thing to ponder! I'd love to be one, off to adventures, away from this plague of a life; fighting evil warlords on the open plains of some distant lands like in the crone's books of glory, all of which I knew by heart.

I picked up my own book and read the lines to the first riddle again. What would it hurt to see if the crone's magic had teeth?

I prayed the verse, *"When the truth brings evil, and is as heavy as a boulder, and I cannot escape my duty, I may hide in plain sight. None of those I serve will see me as a woman. Let me appear as a man to the nobles and soldier, worthy of service in the guard of the lady. May I be worth the fee of two golds for my indentured service, and may I walk among them in deception for as long as I have need of the lie. I pray the Goddess grants my spell."*

I finished my spell with the words, *"Tpunwvw Own,"* and then spun my finger into the air as I'd seen the crone do to me before she'd pushed me into the crawlspace like a bag of seeds.

There seemed a tickle around my finger, and a breeze blew up from the window, but I was looking for signs, so I knew it to be my imagination.

Then I waited. Nothing felt different.

I looked at my hands, and they were the same, as were my ankles. I felt my breasts, though they were modestly bound.

My disappointment wasn't large, given that in order to pass as a recruit I'd have to be a boy of age. I didn't particularly like boys and truly didn't want to become one. Perhaps, I thought, the Goddess knew my heart, and I had to not only ask, but also want to be one in order to have my wish granted. Thinking back, I hadn't even had the heart to directly ask to be changed into a young man, so it wasn't surprising that she'd ignored me. Might the Goddess also think men an abomination, and thus feel disinclined to grant my request? Perhaps there was a God for men and a Goddess for women, and each godly noble guarded their kingdom selfishly.

I mostly thought that I was an idiot for imagining myself a magician.

All of my thinking bought me nothing! I funneled my anger into packing my gear and readied myself to leave the barn. I would leave as quickly as I could after the proceedings and with the end of the long afternoon of tax collecting. The road would be full of travelers if I hesitated. Every group of travelers might put a lone woman to the question. Every rogue might see me as their next delight. I was doomed but eager to see night and take my chances with staffing as many as got in my way.

"You there!"

I froze at the challenge that came from the direction of the barn's floor.

"I say, you there, up in the loft. What are you up to and why've you no respect for the lords who have called the village to their attention?"

I leaned over the rail. Down below was a priest's White Shirt. I felt my hate rising, a cramping thing that crawled up my neck. I considered the chances of taking him by dropping on him with my knife, but, just as I readied the blade, my fist in my pocket, a second soldier walked into view from the open doorway.

"Fine, Ser, I've been sent to ease down straw for the many horses who never seem to cease eating. I meant no disrespect, for many of the horses bear the lady's mark, and the whole village wants them happy."

"Well, be at it quickly, boy. Then be you back quickly. You are near of age and need to be familiar with the law when it visits." He nodded at his companion, and they moved after I tossed some hay over the side.

The Goddess says to be bold. I decided to test the Goddess's gift after hearing the white demon call me boy. He'd looked me fully in the face, as had his fellow.

I got my gear and made my way to the big barn door. I took my skirt off, folded it, and draped it under my arm, thus leaving on the britches I'd fashioned. After stuffing my pocket with my knife and feeling my silver, I left the shade. Two White Shirts nodded approval as I passed at a shuffle.

The nobles were finishing with the last man. My own father had just been called forward to hear the details of his eviction and any added punishments. His steps were slow, but mine were swift as I parted the crowd and made my way through. I crossed my father's path and stood before the fair Lady Lettoir and the tax man with the silver tongue.

"Abi—" my father's stern voice said. I felt my name hit my back. I'd made the mistake of not including the peasants in my chant, I realized. My confidence sank. Maybe they all saw me as a woman, and it was just my luck the priest's guards had bad eyes. I was sure I'd make an even bigger fool of myself with my next words.

I said, "Yes, Father, Abi is at home and safe with mother

where I left her! She has need of safekeeping, lest someone creep up in the wee hours and slit a throat." It saddened me that threatening my father was all I felt safe to give my mother.

To the nobles I quickly followed, "Ser and lady. I am the get of my father, Garette Tokenhold. I stand as debt in his stead so he and my family may not face eviction." I gave as polite of a bow as I knew. I'd just managed to avoid a curtsy, not that I had the least bit of practice at either.

"Boy?" the man enquired.

"All here know me as Keith of Garette!" I turned around in a swift circle so everybody in the town could plainly see I was lying. They were all in on the crime, after all. My ears were keen, allowing me to hear their knowing whispers.

I continued: "Who here wishes to speak ill of Keith Tokenhold? None, I see, for I am strong. I have trained with staff, and I am ready for the service I am offering to the lady's guard."

Clearly nobody here wanted to say a thing about Keith, good or bad, given he swung on a rope, and any word at all might implicate the lot of them. His ghost hadn't even had time to leave the village. Surely an air of haunting touched every breath. Even my father had been struck mute.

Still, one boy near the back yelled, "It's a girl!"

"Quiet! We will tolerate no disruptions!" yelled the elderly noble. I noticed the father put his hand over the boy's mouth before I returned my attention back to the noble.

"Do you make an offer of such service?" he asked.

"I do so as payment for the debt of my father, Ser. And for my mother as well, who needs a roof over her head. I offer two years of indentured service, one for each gold demanded, as I hope is sufficient for payment of his debt. For this I promise daily devotion to duty and king."

The murmurs behind me grew. I needed something else to

dissuade the next idiot's blundering mouth. I added, "I further offer five coppers for the release of the debt owed by our fine neighbor, who is only five coppers short. It is best that all of my neighbors are thought of ... without suspicion." Oh, how I enjoyed that pause. "This I pay in full so the whole valley may be free of censure and the close eye of our lords. I do this without request for repayment, but simply out of the kindness of Sho's blessings, and in gratitude for the kindness of all my neighbors who have generously helped raise me unto the age of sixteen so I may be a warrior ... and keep them safe from strange and prying eyes." I put the only silver I'd ever owned on the table, showing proof of my payment.

The two nobles looked me over, possibly seeking the source of my madness. They took a moment to confer among themselves. Behind me, the tension was sharp, but at least the murmurs had softened upon my words about censure under the close eye of the lords.

The soldier with the one stripe watched me closely. I gave him a deep and respectful bow as we awaited the nobles' decision.

He leaned in and whispered to the nobles, "Ser and Lady, we can be done with this dirty valley. Though the boy is not thick in the arms or back, I can at least get enough work from him to make close to the fee. The difference between it and two golds won't be worth another trip."

The elderly noble's head shook no to the lady, but the Goddess softened her heart, and she nodded back.

He paused, perhaps hoping she'd reconsider, then turned to me and said, "It is decided that you will join Lady Lettoir's service in exchange for the taxes due. Let the record indicate a transfer of one gold, eight silver, one copper and a sliver, in the name of commoner Garette Tokenhold. If the obligation is not met in full through service, all will be forfeit."

The lady added, "Son, that is in exchange for a four year contract of service, to be paid at the normal soldier's wages of two silvers per month. For the first two years you shall forfeit one silver per month as payment upon the debt. That is a premium to me in exchange for my trust. Do not grieve it, for I have already fulfilled my quota of two recruits on this trip and have determined to take you as extra."

"The offer is kind, even at the near six silvers in interest, my Lady. As it stands, it is far more than I have, and far more generous than I have right to expect."

The older taxman looked at me queerly. Then he said, "You speak far better than expected for these parts and seem to have a good head for numbers. You have gained the lady's trust, but not mine, for these things are suspicious. I am a tax collector. There is no lie I have not sniffed out. There is much amiss in this valley, and, if we did not lack in time, I'd have the trees shaken until all of the rotten apples fell." He took the silver and set down my change of five coppers.

I looked him in the eye when I leaned close to gather the coppers. With a wee voice I said, "Fine Ser, you are no fool, for I confess to having told my share of lies. Yet, the fair lady has seen a deeper part of my soul, for it is plain that I am the most honest person here. I owe the lady a debt larger than I can repay. Know, too, that I relish leaving this place more than your guards relish their meals and beds. Trust not this den of thieves."

Beside him, Lady Lettoir spelled out my contract. She looked up from her work, startled upon hearing me speak, as if seeing me and the potential riot behind me for the first time. Then she put the contract before me. I read it for a few breaths time, but it said only what we'd agreed, and so I signed my name, Abe son of Garette Tokenhold. The Ab part had come out of my hand so swiftly that I had no recourse but to add the e and cover my mistake.

"The wording ... of the contract seems to have met with your approval ... Keith; and a name so well written," noted the man before me.

Had my illegal reading skill been that obvious?

"Abe is the name I go by now, or so the priest told me when he taught me to make the marks. Does it say, Abe, son of Garette Tokenhold, Ser, like he told me it would? Abe is not my birth name, Ser, but I hope this is a clean start for me from this point on, and I have taken a liking to the more holy namesake, for surely the Divine is at work in my life," I said, listing off in my mind the range of errors I'd already made in front of the perceptive lords who now owned my service. I'll have to watch my mouth much more closely than I have so far, I thought. I didn't want to gain the habit of lying to those I liked.

"I think the boy is eager to enter service, Lord Irstan. Should we help this Abe, born of Garette, on his way, given that our duties seem to have come to an end?" said the lady.

"Yes, yes. Let us dine and retire," said the lord as he stood. Bones creaked.

She stood, fussed with her colorful riding skirt and then leaned into Lord Irstan's ear, though I could easily hear her say, "No. I do not much like this valley. There is no inn, and this self -proclaimed Sir Lastion has his parlor full of the priest's men. We can make a proper village not long after dark."

Lord Irstan obviously wanted to protest, but instead took a last look at me, as if to say it was my fault the lady had turned so sheepish. "Sergeant, we leave at once."

* * * * *

It was amazing to see an army at work. The men skillfully bound the packs back onto the animals and mounted quickly. I walked near the head of the column at first, out of place, and told so by a soldier, but I was that much farther from those who knew me as Abi. I took my time letting everyone pass me and slowing toward the rear.

I was light on my feet, bearing only my staff. Everything else was stashed in my tight pack, including my dull copper coins, book, sword and dagger. These were carried on the same horse that had walked out from under my brother. I could have let the baggage horse bear the staff as well, but it was something to hold onto that marked me as a fellow warrior. It also reminded me of my mother. The other two recruits laughed at me for carrying it, though I was met with reassuring disinterest from the older body of troops.

The company had taken on some oats, so with the money box heavier, the horses were loaded until their backs sagged. As we crested a tall hill, I took one look back. I saw my swinging brother and felt myself most fortunate to be gone from the place I'd once called home. At least something good had come of him.

Sergeant Hadarm had introduced himself earlier by yelling for me to give a hand up with the provisions. It was his idea that the recruits should train at once by only letting one of us ride at a time. This suited me fine, for I had two good legs, but no experience with horses. No doubt I could sit one, but getting up on it properly enough to keep from looking the fool was my greatest concern.

It was clear to all that, even among the recruits, I was spare and thus last in rank. More important to me, though, in half of an afternoon I'd walked and raced to catch up to the horses enough to get farther into the world than I'd ever been before. It reminded me of how small my life had been.

Of course, it soon became impossible to march any more without their thinking I feared the animal. I stuffed my staff between some packs and decided that the best way to mount the beast was to take a run and leap at it. The horse apparently didn't feel as sure as I did about it, so he moved away when I came at him. I wasn't too sure how far he'd go, so I leapt as hard as I could. I sailed right over his back, hitting the flank of a soldier's horse on the other side. That sent four of the beasts squealing and kicking around as if they'd been attacked by wolves. I was hard pressed to get out from under their feet in one piece. So much for not proving myself a stupid peasant.

"Get your foot in the stirrup, you idiot!" Sergeant Hadarm yelled back.

I thanked him for his instruction.

Another soldier was a little softer spoken. He yelled, "You can't run at a horse until he knows who you are."

His fellows chuckled. The idea made perfect sense to me, so I told the horse I was sorry. He seemed to hear my thoughts and let me get up on his back without a fuss.

Then I learned it was easier to get up on a horse than to sit on top too long. In no more time than it took to round a couple of bends, my thighs felt like they were going to break off, and my ass felt like all of my clothing was seeping into every crack. My seat itched, and, even in the cooling dusk, my butt sweated. I sat up and sat down, and looked around at the others who rode like it was just a regular stool, feeling even more the country bumpkin than ever as I fidgeted. When it came my time to walk again, I was happy, not even using the stirrup step to leap down because of my joy.

The first thing the other walking recruit said to me was, "Ain't fair to hog the horse. Next time, come down sooner and give us real recruits a break."

I figured that for all the meat on his body, he was bound up and lazy. He couldn't tell time without an hourglass or sunsticks either, meaning he'd make a bad scout. We had nothing in common, so I decided to talk to a pack horse instead.

A pack horse can see and think two different things out of

each eye. That's probably because they are on opposite sides of his head and haven't been introduced. I caught glimpses of his two minds. The right eye was on some purple flowers in the ravine by a cliff, while his left eye wanted to get his feet wet in a field of delicious grass that had water running all through it.

We rode down to some swamps that were full of frogs wanting to part with their hind legs. Nothing tastes better in the whole world. I saw their little eyes, like ghost bubbles on the water, from a field away. Nobody else seemed to notice, or maybe they couldn't see as far as me. I was hungry, and frogs couldn't hide from me that easily, but I wasn't free to go get any of them, and we always took our breaks in the drier heights like we intentionally avoided the free small game and soft roots.

Out farther in the trees, I saw Yellow Eyes looking down at us. He watched me licking my lips and trying to think the frogs into my mouth as we marched down into another valley marsh. I could tell he wanted us to get on by so he could race around in the marshy grasses and gobble up both his and my share.

I didn't have any time to play with the animals in the woods, I wanted him to see, for I was a soldier now, and had to be on the lookout for the enemy should they lie in wait in hopes of coming up on us like they always did in the histories.

It got dark. "What color does the enemy wear?" I asked the second recruit when he'd come down off his turn on the horse.

He proved to be another idiot and didn't know much. Instead, he made a face at me and didn't know what to answer. I took him for a grand coward, too, but he was a man, so it was to be expected. I wanted to hit him when he kept looking at me funny. He didn't outrank me, so I thought I might be allowed, but I also didn't want to draw attention or take any chances of overstepping my bounds with the wise sergeant, so I let him off. Besides, I figured that, if we were attacked, we'd need every man we had. At the least he'd be good for a spear stopper while

I fended off the others, like Claudius had demonstrated in *Antoneo's Last Bloodbath.* I just decided to keep looking instead, knowing that any man who might be sneaking out in the woods in the night was apt to be a spy or at least up to no good.

When the moon came up, they decided the next village was too far. Our horses were too tired to do much more walking, so we made a camp. After pleasing the horses, the sergeant had us pitch tents on a knoll and get fire wood to make these really large fires that anybody could see for two hundred acres off. A decent scout could probably smell the fire all the way back to our village—even if the wind was blowing the other way. The food was good jerky and only three-day-old dark bread that tasted of a dab of molasses. I was severely impressed with the provisions, leaving my own alone.

The three of us recruits were supposed to sleep in the same little tent with our feet hanging out of the end and our backs rubbing up against one another. I took my own blanket into the woods and found a place a deer had rutted out. There I stashed some leaves, my bundle and blanket. Then I went to the creek and took a bath to get rid of my smell so I'd not be so obvious that I even scared the coons away. If we were attacked, I'd be the only one left to tell the king, I thought, when I finally got to sleep.

Later, someone came to the tent to tell me it was my turn to guard. He was so noisy to my good ears that he woke me while I was still far out in the woods. I walked over, pretending I'd just gone into the woods to do my business. The guard told me to stand guard over by the fire where the blaze half blinded me to anything else. I had every disadvantage the crone had ever taught me and was glad when it got light, though the sergeant came over and scolded me for not waking up the next man on the guard list. He was a good sergeant, I'd determined, but he didn't know how bad the others were at guarding, and how inclined they were to get us all killed if even a tiny group of good soldiers were out there hunting our fires.

That was how my first day of soldiering went. The day of marching and camping was my sixteenth birthday, but it ran right into the day after when we marched into the next town to get more money for the box.

* * * * *

Confronting peasants was a new problem for me because I didn't want to get out the book and correct my error of not casting my spell wide enough to include the peasantry. The fact is that I didn't think the spell worked for fixing mistakes anyway because the gods are fickle about errors, and everybody knew they didn't like to be told they'd been part of a muddle. This I later found to not be true because the gods never remember any of their muddles.

I put on my good dark shirt, layering it over the other one I wore to fatten me, and then I darkened my face a little with some dirt. I stood in the middle of the troops while putting on my most mean and serious countenance.

I'd never seen a real village before. This one even had an inn where they rented out rooms and gave out supper over real saw-fashioned tables and split-log chairs. A girl with her breasts squeezed tightly and half out of her shirt, clearly advertising for a marriage, handed things around. She took the unit's daily ration money from the sergeant without his acting suspicious that she'd keep the change, fib about having taken it and get rich enough for a dowry off the shorting.

The town had a goods store with a glass window full of things you could mostly make all by yourself once you saw how they were put together, and a smith who mended tools for lazy people. He kept horses for everybody, too. He made a wonderful racket with a hammer and played in the fire. All of this I just looked at because I was on duty, but I wanted to see what it felt like to actually spend a copper, so I kept one in my pocket just in case I came across something I thought I needed in order to be a better soldier.

We didn't have time for any of the pleasures of the big town though, beyond looking into doors. When the taxes were settled, the nobles and sergeant went into the inn and ate. They were to sleep there, and we were to camp out on the smooth side lawn, which was ample and had no tree root lumps on it. That was good by me. Somebody had to keep watch outside for the enemy, but I was beginning to think there weren't many of the enemy left because the woman who ran the kitchen at the inn was more concerned that we were ruining her lawn than that we were keeping an eye out for her safety.

I liked the inn lady, though, because she served us. She and the girl showing her breasts came out with a wide iron pot full of gruel made from fresh meat and vegetables, sat it by our fire to keep it warm, and even loaned us some bowls so we could eat alone and not out of the same ladle. I figured the locals would know if there was something afoot, so I ate with only one eye to the distance.

The inn lady came out a second time with some tankards of ale. She passed the first four around to the oldest soldiers as the other girl brought out more trays. When they got to me, they took too much time looking at my tiny nose, fat lips and long eyelashes, and almost didn't give me any at all until one of the men poked fun at me and said, "Oh, come on, give the lad a tankard. He's been walking two days, and I've yet to see him stagger."

"Sure enough, he needs something to top the leaping at the horse trick. As young and thin as he is, I doubt he'll hold two before he's face down in the dirt!" declared another seasoned veteran. Everybody laughed at that, and I do admit it was funny enough to be worthy of the reaction.

"Thank you. I've a mind to do just that. If you could work your way to bringing out a third, I'll be most happy to oblige you by drinking it as well," I said, knowing that being boastful about how much one could eat or drink was the easiest way to prove oneself a man. I took two tankards and started in on the first as soon as I'd put my back to the inn woman's probing eyeballs.

Everybody looked at me when I chugged the first one down far too fast to enjoy the new taste. All I'd ever drunk before was tea, goat milk and mostly water, so I felt my mouth sourly pucker after a little coughing. Anyway, I'd been standing and walking and through it all, hadn't had the sense to drink as much water as I should, lest I make some movement that would displease the sergeant, so two tankards were truly what I needed to quench me and set me on my way. I drank the second, right on the first one's rump, and then turned, lighting the two empties on the inn lady's tray. She'd been so curious that she'd not even moved, which was convenient.

It wasn't the inn lady who gave me my third, but one of my fellows. He was grinning, but it was all teeth because his eyes were glossy, and he moved oddly from side to side, and he said something in funny words that I only half pieced together. He was obviously thinking kindly, giving me his own half-finished tankard. Before I lifted the huge cup to my face, some of his buddies came over, seemingly in pairs, and poured a little of theirs into it until it was full. Just about then, the other girl who had grown a twin onto her side, came out and handed me the third that I'd requested, so I had two – or four; I'm not too clear on this point. I brought the four up to my face at once, but then thought better of it and drank them a pair at a time.

When I turned to put the tankards on the tray, the inn lady was still there watching me, but with a smile on her face like she liked me. I thought she was pretty for a middling-year woman, but not my type. Besides, she had two heads, which was pretty bugaboo and telling of a fellow witch. I felt I'd help allay suspicion if I spoke only some of that out loud, so I said, "She be mighty purdy nan nuff, but an 'ol woman ain't drinking an, my, you know wha ... two heads!"

Then I fell face first into the fire.

* * * * *

I was sure I'd done just that the next day when I woke up in the tent with my head feeling like there were hornets in it trying to pry their way out with rocks. I jumped up, ending up not all that happy that I had when the world wouldn't stop racing around me, but at least I saw I wasn't all burnt up.

"Bout time you got up. The sergeant's mad at us for getting you drunk. We've your share of the packing to make up for it. We're moving out in no time at all. Get your boots on, here," complained the recruit who thought he was my boss and relished it highly because everybody else was his.

It was a long day's march, for my stomach couldn't bear the horse's slow, rolling style. The soldiers looked over at me a lot, and they chuckled every time I came back out of the woods from losing that fine crock meal and the morning's road-march breakfast. What hurt the most was noticing that Lady Lettoir looked back at me from time to time, repeatedly shaking her head when her eye returned forward, as if telling her companions I was lacking. I felt lacking. The other recruits had taken to doubling up on a horse, so I felt all the smaller for being the only soldier guarding the ground. By afternoon our horses found a faster pace to their liking, and so I had to run the rest of the day just to keep up.

Chapter Five

I raced the trotting horses to the locked gate. A guard, pretending to be awake, sat on a stool inside, but the stool wasn't so high that I couldn't scale it and remove the board that kept it fastened. I handed the board to the guard when he stood up. Having barely beaten them there, I managed to get the gate open just before Lady Lettoir and Lord Irstan pranced through at the head of the score of men. Everybody went straight to a big stable.

She had the biggest house I'd ever seen. It was built very stoutly. Flat river slates were used in place of straw for the roof. A broad porch wound all the way around the house, and expensive chairs sat out in the open for any thief to steal. The house was both a marvel and a disappointment, for I'd expected a castle.

I knew it wasn't a proper castle because good castles had keeps made of stone and tall towers with narrow holes for shooting arrows. They also had deep moats of water that you could only get over if you had a drawbridge. If you were the enemy, and you tried to get over, they poured oil on your head and lit you up with torches. If you climbed a ladder, they had places where people walked around the roof and pushed you backwards. The higher you climbed, the longer you swung back before you splattered. The manor wasn't anything like that; it was just a big, pretty house.

Later I learned that like her house castle, Lady Mayran Lettoir wasn't a very high noble, as nobles went. In fact, she was the lowest ranking noble anybody had ever heard of, made worse by the fact that she was a childless widow, meaning she was a woman they let squat, something like the crone. Her kinless dead husband had been the true inheritor. She was fairly new to the job of Manor Lord and didn't have any friends or kin around to help her. The tax collector even outranked her, although he was on loan from Helfax, so he didn't bother to do much more than advise her. This was nice of the old, wiry man, a good man mostly, even if he didn't think I belonged in the army. As soon as we got to the manor, he left for Helfax anyway, so his help didn't last. I marveled at how Lady Lettoir did her duty on her own with nobody to speak for her and with only men afoot, other than two female house servants.

She had the biggest lawn of waist-high grass I'd ever seen, too. There was a rock fence that went all around the grounds in a wide circle. The fence was only high enough to stop someone running if they were bad at jumping, but there was a slow drainage ditch on the inside of it, and several hundred scores of pikes stuck in the ground and pointed out from just inside the fence and gully ring. Most of them were rotten and had probably been planted before any of us were alive.

Any enemy with legs could scale the defenses like they were flatland and run to the house in less time than I could count to thirty. Worse still, it would take twenty score men to defend it thinly, and they'd not be good with anything but arrows until the host of the intruders got all the way through the defenses. Any kind of concentrated push with half an army would best twice the defenders.

I determined on the road that I was getting unpopular because of my tendency to give advice about things that were important to our defense, so I thought it best to wait until I got some rank, or at least a uniform, before telling them my ideas about how to make the manor safe from being swamped in the first minute of a siege.

I wished I could go back and dig under the crone's wrecked house to see if the histories were still there. Then I could show Lady Lettoir why it was important to funnel the enemy into one wee place where you could dump rocks on their heads and poke them with pikes and short swords out from behind some stout advancing shields. If I did that though, she'd know I could read and find it her duty to lock me in a storeroom. They'd wait for a priest to burn me up or hang me, or, most likely, do both at the same enjoyable moment.

Anyway, all of this wasn't terribly important to fix right away, I determined, for on the way to the manor I'd come to the conclusion that the reason they weren't diligent was because we were at peace. When I'd asked around the last fire, some of the men spoke of sheriffing rogues and tales of skirmishes with the men of Lacellor way up in the north corners of the kingdom. That place wasn't in the Helfax baronage, or even the next one over. None of them had been there recently, so other than policing crooks like my dead brother, they mostly just practiced at being soldiers.

After a few minutes, the lay of the manor grew firm in my mind. I walked to the stable to help with the horses. On the way there, I decided that when war came, I'd run right to the house and defend the good Lady Lettoir in person, given her parlor was the only place I was sure to find the main body of the enemy one minute after it all started. I could imagine myself sneaking in and out of the manor all day long, probably in the heat of battle with all of their eyes looking for me, and I didn't even have a dark grey uniform yet.

By the time I got there, the horses were in the cribs, and the men were taking their gear into the bunkhouse, back a ways more. I went in the bunkhouse just in time to see Sergeant Hadarm handing Hobar and Horatio their new uniforms. They got instructions to keep at least one of them clean at all times, and even the one they were wearing was to be clean by first thing in the morning. I thought they were going to go looking around for a woman to do that for them, but they looked at each other and admired themselves instead.

The wise sergeant noticed me, and he came over with a shirt. I had three shirts already, but this was a dark grey uniform shirt. Once I put it on, I was going to be a real soldier, I realized, but, instead of handing it to me, he took me outside and led me back to the stable. There he introduced me to an old man with a belly as rotund as a prize melon and legs as thin as ropes.

"This is Tom, son of Calligor, Abe. I'm leaving you in his care. He's to work you and teach you everything he can about horses. Soldiers need to know about horses, and soldiers need someone else to keep care of them. You're to work doubly hard for him because two silvers a month is a lot to pay for such help. I'll have other duties for you, too, to make up the difference."

"Yes, Sergeant Hadarm," I said as he handed me my new shirt. I knew they were short the other, so I decided to work on the color and cuffs of the stolen one to make it match as best I could so I could have two like the other soldiers.

While I pondered that, the sergeant thought up an even worse thing to say: "You know, when we were on the road, I had second thoughts about you. I got to thinking you'd quit, and one of us would have to go back and take your father's farm. I'm half sorry you didn't right now. I've never seen someone do so much running before, though, so you deserve at least a job until you prove to be worthless. You don't seem to know that the duty around here is all about horses. We don't have footmen unless we're called up by the Baron and take some levies under our wing. Can't have a lone soldier running around like a fool when everybody else is riding either; it would slow us all down. You do this job well, and learn about horses, or I'll take you back home myself. I might just do it even if you do your work."

He walked out and went back to his men. I wasn't to be an equal among them, apparently. My heart sank into my gut. What kind of chance had he given me?

Old Tom seemed to see me for the first time just then. It was like some part of the chair moved, and all of a sudden he was no longer furniture.

"Might as well start by feeding some oats and hay to the horses. They'll all need fresh water. Then they'll muck up the stalls and need that forked out. After that, you can take them out one at a time and brush them down."

* * * * *

I worked for Tom for nearly a year before the sergeant realized I'd been there too long to take back home. In all of that time, I never saw Tom out of his chair more than long enough to go out back and do his business or go to the kitchen and find a meal. Mostly I brought that to him, and, if he could have found a way to have me piss for him, he'd have had me do that for him as well. Sometimes the smell around him had me thinking he'd decided it wasn't worth the trip. This proved convenient, for, as long as my work was tended, none were underfoot to snoop on me in my free time.

Other than feeding, brushing, cleaning, watering, fetching, saddling, thatching the roof, mending the walls, and everything else, I had loads of time on my hands most evenings. I'd never had it so good, to be honest. The food was fresh and plentiful. There were pickings all over the place to spice up my food. I grew new muscles and learned a lot about horses. I had my own little stall that I'd fixed up to look like a house.

Then again, I never had it so bad either. The fresh recruits, Hobar and Horatio, were real soldiers already, riding sheriff rounds somewhere in the Lettoir region every few weeks. I watched them practicing with staves and then lances. They moved on to knives, and then finally shields with wooden swords, all practiced in the extra corral near the barracks every time the sergeant scheduled it. Winter came and went, and, after the summer, I was sent into the fields to help the women cut the last of the hay. Could the sergeant have sensed something about me that led to that decision? I didn't know, but I did all I could to hide my femininity behind my britches. Being away from the troops helped that at least, but I wasn't happy with the safety.

All through this year, I practiced just like the soldiers but only at night after sneaking out. I made it a game to come as close to the guards at the gate as I could, testing my skill and their lack of it. I was a woman, I had to remind myself, and thus I had the advantage of being inherently sneaky, lest we all starve. I wasn't truly a part of any of the soldiering beyond what I made of it, so I determined to make my own soldier out of me and make the best of the fact that I'd at least escaped certain death by being where I was.

Thinking back to the earlier days, only a month into my stable hand duties, I'd discovered how to conjure the image of my dead crone by employing a spell out of my book. During my time with her, I got out my new sword, working oil and dirt into a rag grip until it suited me. At least the hilt looked properly worn and ill suited for hanging above mantels on castle walls.

We bowed one to the other. She had nothing to say because she was just a magical ghost, but I felt comforted by her face. That is, I felt that way right up to when we she took the first swing. This practice had a giant advantage over the pretend male soldiers. I could cut her any way I wanted without killing her, assuming I could get at her.

When I cut her, she misted up before disappearing, and then she came back together. She smiled at me like when I'd first conjured her. We started back up without even a decent breather, just like when she was real. She almost always smiled, regardless of the tide of our battle, which was soon annoying. I was heartened that I could slice her up without hurting her one bit, but it takes a lot out of a victory when your ghost smiles like you've just given her a petunia instead of dropping her arm onto her foot.

When she sliced or poked me, however, I felt the blade ripping right through my gut, though only like a tingly little knife. There wasn't much pain, but I learned what it was like to be done in. I'd see the mistake even as the sword came at me. My ghost crone was twice as strong as the real woman, so, when she cleaved me in two, it was pretty hard to forget. I'd look down and see my guts spilling out as my bottom got numb and my legs turned into sticks, and then the ghost always poked me a second time somewhere else to make sure of me. Finally, it all went away like I'd gone through two winks of a really bad dream.

The worst part of it was that she reminded me of the real crone's company. She never said squat, and was too cooperative about dying to be a real person, but just the idea of her being there, like a painting, had me longing for her real company. I even craved her scorn. I never got a correction for making the same mistake over and over again. One time I even screamed at her to tell me off when I'd died ten times in one night, my head lopped off twice. Through it all, my ghost crone didn't do much of anything except fight like a demon. There wasn't even the same old limp. The only real personal contact I had with her was when our swords met or our bodies butted in combat, and that kind of touching was no fun because she was amazingly agile in combat. It was metal on metal, legs into guts, heads knocking heads, all of it not unlike the sound of the blacksmith visiting to make shoes for the horses. We had to go way out into the woods for this, lest someone came running in response to the noises.

It was strange, fighting a ghost, but some small voice kept telling me I'd been fighting ghosts all my life, and nothing was going to be different about it if they started bleeding real blood.

My sword helped me learn with its own steely voice, too. It had a voice that sang to me when it moved through the air just right. I wanted to hear it. My staff did that, too, but not like the sword because the sword stopped singing if I made a blunder, while my staff didn't care if I did anything wrong. When the sword stopped talking altogether, I'd feel the punctuation on the next swing when the crone split me or poked me in all sorts of odd places. I knew it was coming every time my sword stopped speaking to me, so I worked to please my sword, given the crone no longer cared and spent her whole night smiling at me like a ninny.

I put my sword away when the moon came down and hid it back in the little home I'd made for myself in a stall in the stable, so nobody would know I had it.

During that year I also learned that the soldiers were in love with their horses, but I got to know the animals better than they ever did. For example, a horse can't even love his mate for longer than it takes to do the business of making a baby horse. All a horse loves is apples and the hand that rubs him down. The apples are for eating, and the rubbing is for pleasure. When a soldier gets the notion that his horse loves him, what he's really seeing is that the horse knows who gives him apples and pats him where his tail and nose can't reach. Regarding all others, a horse is suspicious. Knowing that made it easier for all of us stable dwellers to come to an early understanding after I mentally communicated with the horses that I wasn't going to put up with any foolishness from anyone bearing a nose as long as my arm.

The hardest part to understanding a horse, other than riding one all day long, is the fixings they wear. I noted how the saddles and harnesses were put together by mending them instead of wasting the lady's money by sending them into town or having her buy new. I ran out of cinches and leather, but Tom thought to put a word into the ears of anybody who'd listen that he was in the mending business, and I soon had all the cow leather and cinches anybody could ever need. Tom was awfully proud of himself when the soldiers came by to compliment him on his suddenly industrious nature. I was happy, too, because the happier Tom was, the more he slept, and the more he slept, the more I got things done without his getting underfoot.

Coming to respect the value of leather, I'd started curing a batch of elk in a tanning pit I'd dug on month three of that first year. I fired the pit hard enough to hold the hen dung and soap I used to soak leather in before I pulled the hair off my elk hide. I had to sneak the soap out of the kitchen, but the hen dung was free and all over the yard behind the barn. When the hair fell off, I had six months of waiting while the hemlock and oak bark soaked the leather ready for me to stretch, smoke and beat the softness into it.

I'd caught the elk between myself and my wolf friend, Yellow Eyes, as he'd driven it to me. After we'd downed it together, I with my knife and Yellow Eyes with what the Goddess gave him, we shared it out. I took a shank and the hide, while my friend got to take the rest home a piece at a time and brag about making a solo kill on a buck twice bigger than the size of the sergeant.

I carved the saddle out of a log, using the stable's saw and awl to poke a bunch of holes in it to make it lighter than any of the other saddles. I had no interest in crippling my horse by being too much of a burden on her back. The elk was fashioned over a layer of cowhide, for I wanted to be kind to my butt as well. The elk ended up looking just like the other saddles, only it was less bulky, lighter, softer and a little more handsome than I wanted it to be.

I didn't have any butternuts to make the elk a dangerous looking color. The only dyes handy were too joyful, and I was short on time in the cure anyway, that taking half a year alone, so I determined to live with the auburn color that matched my hair almost too perfectly.

There was one last thing to do before the year ended, and I could go to the sergeant and tell him I was ready to stop pretending and be one of our lady's guards. I had eleven silvers in pay to go along with my five coppers. It was illegal to talk to our Lady, but only in the sergeant's eyes, and he was busy. I bowed to her and asked her if I could trade ten of my silvers for a good gold piece.

She seemed startled. Then she said, "Abe is it?"

"Yes, my Lady." I remained on one knee like they said servants and soldiers always did when in the presence of nobility.

"Where did you get ten silvers?"

"It's my pay, ma'am. I have one more and five coppers as well."

"My Lord, you are on only half wages. Haven't you spent anything we've paid you?"

"No ma'am. I have everything I need right here, and, besides, I'm too busy to go looking for ways to waste my money."

"Don't you know that good soldiers have to find a way to waste all their money on unchaste women and ale?"

I looked at her funny but then thought about my other problem of not fitting in very well. Maybe it was that I only looked like a man to them and didn't know how to act like one.

I answered, "I'm doing better at my other duties, Lady Lettoir. I can fix these deficiencies you've noted, too, soon as I get rid of these silvers and find me a gold one."

She gave me another startled look and then laughed. "It's a joke, Abe. I didn't mean to imply that it was a duty to abandon the virtue of thriftiness, nor is it your duty to despoil the maidens and go to drink. I, for one, will never forget what happened at the inn when they got you drunk. My only mistake was in assuming it was your habit."

"No, ma'am, I have no such habit. It was a surprise to me more than anyone, I can assure you that. I've had only the ration of ale since."

"Well, in a way, your temperance explains your reaction even better." She seemed more content with my being there, pausing to enjoy the breeze. "You can get up and sit if you want. I'll not tell the sergeant, and, if he comes checking, I'll say you were summoned."

I remained nervous, though. "I can't take the chance on that, ma'am. I'll have to be off to do my duty of soldiering. Are the ten silvers enough, or do they charge for trading it in for a gold one?"

"Oh, of course, Abe. I'll not want you in trouble with the sergeant. Just leave the coins on the porch, and I'll have maid Minari bring your gold out for you as soon as I go in and unfasten the safe-box."

"Thank you, my Lady, if you think she can do it without biting a piece off it. I need it all because I promised my mother I'd earn or steal a gold coin to melt into a medallion to wear for her. At first I didn't see the point in it, but her words haunt me, so, now that it has been earned, I'm relieved to have the metal."

She gave me yet another odd look, though I hadn't thought I'd said anything confusing. "I'll make sure to tell her, and make sure that the one I send you is of good weight."

"That's excellent of you, my Lady. And I'll have you know that I've been contemplating doing you a favor as well. At the first sign of the enemy, I have resolved to come straightway to your parlor and defend you personally. That is, if you'll have me as your personal guard in times of trouble?"

"Well, Abe, that's nice, but I don't think it's quite necessary for you to come all the way up here. I'm sure the sergeant will find a place to put you that will defend the grounds more generally. It's just a good thing that we have no armies marching on the kingdom at this time, don't you think?"

"Oh, yes, I suppose, though it's mighty boring that way. I'd rather someone like King Ansion of Vennia were riding on us with his chest all swelled up on pride and legions of stiff shirted pikers, just so I could give them a poke or two and get the want of some action out. Sooner or later they'll come, too, because peace isn't what they write about in the histories and the books are mighty thick … I hear. Best I prepare. Around here that's simple enough; they'll be up your steps in a minute the way the walls are so wide, short and worthless. Well, good day to you, My Ladyship. I'll be back to my duties, small though they may be at this time in my life, and again thank you for changing my silver."

"That's fine, Abe. Good day to you as well," she said, though she looked troubled.

I left her, thinking that it was strange how every time I'd said something to her she'd either looked at me oddly or laughed. As far as I knew, I'd never cracked a joke, nor had I been rude enough to make her overly concerned. I guessed that nobles' ways of thinking were strange to the rest of us. Odd though she was, I loved her as a lord and would protect her with my life. After all, she had nobody else to protect her, other than the men, of course.

After the hot work of duplicating my mother's clay

medallion into gold, I was all set for my confrontation with the sergeant. I'd done as he asked: Learned my horses and tended to them much more than twice as hard as ole' Tom. I'd even made a point of riding them every chance I got to take them around in their tending, though most of the trips were mighty short, and most of my practice was just getting on and off in a flash between two or three steps inside the stable, saddled or not. They grew to know and like me pretty well, as much as horses do when they figure out who has the apples and brush. Honestly, most of them were pretty boring to talk to.

I'd even picked one out for my mount. It was a nag named Ella. I'd set my eyes on her as long back as the month after I'd found out I was stuck in the stable while the idiot recruits got to move on to soldiering.

Ella was old and lame, just like my mother. She had a bad right foot. I asked the soldier who fancied himself a horse midwife, and he said she was born with a short leg. I looked at the leg and then measured it with a stick. It was the same as all the others, so I decided that the horse-expert was pretending to know about horses about as much as he pretended to be at war while only practicing.

The soldier never bothered to just ask her what ailed her. Apparently this was a skill unique to me. It was interesting, what she said back in my head. She was just a baby when she noticed that they fussed over her when she limped. She liked that so much that she just kept on limping every day thereafter. Every time the pretend horse expert came, he gave her an apple and rubbed her flanks.

I told her she was a fool, even for a horse. She didn't like that and turned around in her crib, but I went around with her, daring her to pin me.

I said, "Not only are you a fool, even for a horse, but don't you know you get a lot more apples and rubbing when you are out racing on the rounds? Don't you know you have a mighty chest and could have knocked a hundred footmen off their feet with it, building yourself some pride by this late in your life? That's the reason they've bred you and not turned you to slaughter. What are you doing wasting here in your crib when you could have been a warrior and known what it was like to have your rider look at you with a twinkle in his eye? You've sat here in this big barn and wasted your whole stupid life sulking for an apple and a rub! There are more apples and rubs out there than you can dream of in the barn, some you could have had by now, right off the tree, but you're too lazy to go out and find them. Now you've missed out! Now you're nothing but a horse!"

Some of the other horses were listening in. They whinnied and snorted, agreeing with me, but also informing me that they thought the horse part was the other way around, and I was nothing but a human.

Ella didn't like any of that and wouldn't talk to me.

When she finished sulking, she wanted me to help her, so I looked in the book and found a spell to give her back some of her youthful vigor. I guess the Goddess forgave her a few spunky years, probably because the nag hadn't used up any of them when she should have. I thought, maybe Ella will last until my four years are done, and I've gained enough standing to find another one who hasn't wasted so many of her years limping for apples and brushes.

So, around month three of that year, I started riding her around at night, employing the aid of a fixed-up saddle that everybody had taken for useless because back then my elk one had just started tanning in the pit. When she'd gotten her nerve up, we sneaked out by the back pikes and fences. When our men guarded, they only guarded the front gate, so it was nothing to pull out some pikes and get up some steam and then turn her from racing along beside the heaped up rock fence for a long race without anybody even close. The pair of us flew over the fence, and there was nothing lame about that at all. After once or twice doing that, I actually started to like riding horses.

Nobody knew about my relationship with Ella except for Yellow Eyes. He wanted to eat her the first time they met. Ella got so nervous that she started limping around in front of him. I swatted her ear and told her to knock it off because it only attracted Yellow Eye's attention.

It was like that for a while until I told Yellow Eyes that, if he did manage to kill my friend without getting trampled to death in the process, he'd have no way to get her home and brag about it. All of his friends would laugh at him when he told them about it and say he was exaggerating. And, if he broke something in the process, someone else would take his place, and his days with any lady he wanted would be over. I think what really convinced him to join up with Ella, though, was when I told him that Ella didn't eat anything but grass, apples and the new purple flowers I'd just introduced her to. He smiled at that and then laughed with his tongue almost all the way out of the side of his lips. He'd never been too happy about my eating my quarter; it was a major disagreement we always had to deal with.

Thus, Yellow Eyes and Ella practiced with me for most of that first year. It was good that Ella carried me. We were able to get well away from the manor, so far into the woods that the ruckus my ghost and I made was never discovered. All of the riding built up my thighs and butt, and, when I finally got done with my new saddle and fixed my britches to look like the rest of the soldier uniform, we cut an impressive image. I knew this because, when the moon was full and we crossed the creek, I could see us in the water's reflection. The three of us looked as tall as the sky.

* * * * *

Finally, only one more night stood between me and the old-maid age of seventeen. The moon was full, the Goddess's favorite light. Shadows shifted under every tree and hedge. A late-fall chill swept across, raking the leaves. I stopped my horse at a familiar clearing, and then called with the chant that brought forth the ghost. It was always the crone—I expected no different – and, to be sure, I'd never imagined any better. *"Tpunwvw Own."* I yanked off the blanket that I'd wrapped myself in to ease the chill. My finger twirled into the air a second before I pulled my sword out of the scabbard which I'd strapped to my side before racing off to the practice.

Nothing happened.

Maybe the crone was busy in the afterworld? Maybe the Goddess was being fickle? She always felt that way to me, the way she only whispered, and in so small of voice that I thought it was my own imagination all of the time.

Just when I thought the spell wasn't going to work, the loose leaves rustled in a spiral from a tiny twister, and the leaves beyond that, in the forest itself, blew back and forth while still on the limbs. Feet crushed the undergrowth in the gloom even deeper within. Yellow Eyes snarled. Ella went hoofing around where I'd tied her, and then she loudly whinnied her fright.

I smelled the wind that raced around in all directions, but there was no new scent in the mix. Lances of moonlight didn't help, nor did my good eyes that could see so well into the dark, for as the sound of feet came closer I still saw nothing until the full moon touched the guest when he emerged out of the canopy and into my meadow.

There before me stood the priest's fat knight, the same man who'd murdered my mentor.

His broad chest was sheeted in white steel, and his blade

was already in his mail plated hand. Chilling cold rushed off him, so much so that I could have shut my eyes and told which direction he stood. He shimmered a little, such that the trees appeared behind him when I looked through his body and armor, and then he snapped into a solid mass. No longer short, he stood a head taller than my sergeant. In two more steps, he'd come near enough to fight.

I hated him too much to even remember my lessons, and more than even that when he shouted, "What is this? Is it you who took me from my bed and the first whore worth plowing in a week? Another witch? Ah, yes, another witch I can see, and pretending to be a soldier! Yet a new blasphemy! There is no end to the depths of some in the chore of inventing sins. Well then, I'm made to get up and find myself in the night for a good cause. Come, wench, and, if you show remorse for the sin of turning your face from Sho, I shall dispatch you swiftly by lopping your head off your shoulders in one neat swing. Then your body will be free to come with me as a fondling prize, and your head can stay and serve a while as minces for the crows!"

Those didn't sound like easy terms. I had to try to beat his boast if I was ever to call myself a warrior. I shrugged at him. "I will cut you in three good places and watch you spend the night trying to hold back the flow of blood with only your two filthy hands."

I must have had that part of the fighting down pretty well, for it unnerved him, and he made the first mistake, crashing down at me so that his sword slashed into the place I vacated with a simple roll through the leaves. When his sword cleaved a root the size of my arm and the root didn't heal like it had with the crone's carnage, I knew something special was afoot.

I ran to the edge of the clearing, giving myself some time to think. All around crept a growing fog. To one side stood a shadowy figure of a woman with a wreath of flowers in her hair. To the other towered an old man with a long white beard.

I was startled to actually see the gods. Not so much, though, that I dared not speak to Sho: "So, you've brought a champion, have you." I disliked him for his insistence upon belittling women, but he was still the God of majority in our land, and, thus, there was no doubt a host of ways in which he could plague me. Thinking about it, I tempered my words by adding, "If it's your will that I fight your champion, I shall do as pleases you, my Lord."

He seemed very happy upon hearing this. He nodded to me, and then to his champion, and thus his knight advanced.

The words of my mother came back to me. I should learn the value of fear, but it was one lesson I never excelled at until I was knee deep in trouble.

He was more careful with his next move, holding his sword out in front with two mighty hands, and testing how it felt when I tapped it. I circled and backed to the center of the meadow, swinging my sword around in a tiny circle before him in order to keep him from guessing my tendencies. As I did, my sword sang its lullaby. I refused his sword's request for another tap.

The broadsword reached into the sky, and I was too far back from him to counter with a quick jab and live after it, so I stepped as close as I could while holding my sword up as a shield. My sword wasn't happy with that move, and it stopped its singing, causing my heart to ripple. The power of the chop on my blade bent my wrists back, so I ducked under and let my sword tip slant toward the ground. The mighty sword of the oversized knight screeched down my metal. Sparks showered over me. His weapon finished with its tip in the dirt to my side, near an ankle.

I scooted under the man, right between his legs, where I doubted he'd strike with such a brutal blow coming down. When I came out behind him, my sword dragged. I cut him nicely in the thigh as I slid and scrambled clear.

He turned my way, screaming. "Look what you've done to me! I'm bleeding. That was illegal and cowardly!"

He was right. The law said that peasants were obliged to let nobles kill them if it suited their fancy. I realized that I'd decided a year ago to take the laws that pleased me and leave the rest to those who were so afraid of dying that they sat still and let themselves be murdered.

The most important thing to me was that my sword started singing again, as if it hadn't expected me to sneak between the man's legs. It was a new sword trick that had gone unanticipated by the sword's many experiences, I guessed, so my sword forgave.

The slow knight turned around and swiped at me broadside. By the time I got up from clawing in the dirt, I didn't have time to get my sword up and block him, so I flinched back. The tip of his long sword tugged at my sleeve. I looked over and saw the tatter and blood. I felt better of my wound when I noticed I could still bring my sword up with both arms working fine enough to whack him on the barrel breastplate, producing a fierce bang.

He was slow as Tom, but he weighed as much as Ella because of some enhancement Sho had blessed him with in order to cheat. Banging his armor was a mistake. He butted me to the ground, and he came down with the point of his weapon. I had no protection other than my shirt and courage.

While waiting for the blade to kill me, I slashed the knight's leg again, though the response was pitifully little.

Yellow Eyes was a blur as he hit the man from behind, sending them both toppling over me in a rush that caused the blade's tip to miss my gut by the width of a hair. Swipes of the knight's armored fingers smashed at my head on the way across.

Yellow Eyes didn't stay.

The knight's chain mail undershirt seemed no match for my sharp blade. I stabbed him right under the breastplate. There, I held fast with both hands and ducked under the inevitable blow of his weapon. His claymore fell on my steel even as I sank under my hilt and blade. I held on for my life. The power of his own blow caused my stuck sword to slice down so hard that it cut him from belly to groin, finishing by wedging into his pelvis bone. Foul smelling intestines splashed across my body like an emptying night bucket.

The knight was dying then. He dropped his weapon from the shock of knowing he'd killed himself with it. My weapon also proved cantankerous, stuck in the bone and temporarily useless to me. I plucked my knife out of the sheath and jabbed at his soft parts while his armored fingers clawed and beat about my head. When he finally keeled over, it took both of my feet and some wiggling to free my weapons from the pelvis of the enormous corpse.

He breathed a moment more, but then sighed. His slipping away felt almost peaceful and unfinished. My heart raced rapidly, however, and my sense of justice remained far from satisfied. Something unsettled lingered within me, something maybe even bigger than the murder of the crone—I knew not what.

I sat back and looked at him as he shrank, thinking he'd just disappear like the crone did when she lost. I worried that he'd recover and come back like she had. I was breathing too hard to have a go at him again, so I looked back and forth from him to my horse. Ella looked more than ready to help me run. Nonetheless, when he shrank to normal size, he remained dead. I soon realized I'd killed him for real. The rush of blood seemed endless before it stopped.

The waiting grew long enough for me to clean my blade,

wash off in the creek, bandage my arm with a rag off his leggings and look around the whole clearing. From the tramplings, we'd fought everywhere, and yet I saw it in my memory as a short struggle of only a few blows and all of it in only one or two places.

The fog had gone, too, along with the audience of gods. That's when I was sure the killing was over.

It was a fine thing to rid the world of such a man, I determined. So, I dropped some rocks on the body to bury it in the weeds and hide the evidence. Somebody might complain and start looking around if they found a dead noble too close to Lettoir.

Chapter Six

I couldn't expose my good sword on my seventeenth birthday, but I did show off my hand-woven blanket and saddle. I wore a uniform shirt and britches that looked better than those worn by the other soldiers. In my hip belt was my knife, and in the lance holder I set my staff. I'd gotten up early to hide my curls by doing my warrior tail up as tightly as possible.

I had bruises all over my face and neck, and those that weren't purple were black. My left eye had swelled shut from all the head butts. I'd worked much of my stock of mustard and coneflower root into the cut on my arm, sewn it two stitches, and wrapped it with some tea leaves and rags. Some of that had brought tears, but I tucked my emotions in and bore up.

Yellow Eyes was home and sleeping off the excitement, but Ella stood under me, and held her head almost too high for me to see over as she pranced up to the corral where the soldiers mustered for practice with their swords. They pretended that I was invisible, so I raced Ella around the outside of the corral, raising dust. I think the fight in the forest had done Ella some good. I had to shush her, though, because she ceaselessly bragged about not yanking her reins free and running off.

The sergeant had to stop pretending he didn't see me proving that I could ride better than little hops around the stable. "What in Sho's name are you doing out there, Abe? Get that horse back in the barn and get back to work. You're raising a dust storm, and we can't get on with it!"

I'd been waiting for his undivided attention, so I turned my galloping Ella toward the four foot fence, and we jumped right in between them all. I halted her in an orderly fashion, and then flipped over her head, landing on both feet with my staff still in my hand.

Some of the older soldiers laughed, but Hobar and Horatio acted unimpressed. They'd gotten all of the breaks of being real recruits and undoubtedly saw my exclusion as proof that they deserved it.

"I've done as you've said, and I've learned all there is to know about horses. Also, Ella has decided that she wants to be my horse, given she is spare, old and in need of a firm hand. Also, you can see that she is refreshed and randy. She has been convinced to lose her limp and is provisioned. There is not a happier horse in the stable. In there, I've worked doubly hard as you instructed. I have made my own saddle for her and dyed my own uniform, so you need not worry for a spare. I don't have two pair of decent britches, but I will clean mine every night. If you are short on swords, I'll fight with my stick until I capture one from the enemy."

Certainly the sergeant could see that I was a very good deal, and yet his face showed the same old reluctance to include me. I tried to square up my shoulders and not stand on one hip so much.

"I'm sorry, Abe. You seem tall enough and light enough on your feet, but I can't take you on. Though you've proven yourself valuable as a hand in the stable, where we'll be wanting to keep you permanently and at the pay we promised. You've proven handy and brought new skills. Still, there is not enough thickness to your meat to warrant putting your life in danger on the road. Guards have to be intimidating," declared the sergeant.

"I'm a warrior and will prove it." I stomped my foot.

"Yes, and I've been meaning to speak to you about that as

well. You do know that it is improper for a man to wear the warrior's tail unless he has slain a foe in battle. I'll have to see to it that your hair is shorn, if you persist on wearing it in such fashion."

"I've earned it properly, for I've slain the same as a thief in the night."

Some of the men looked at me with smiles, the rest with ridiculing laughter, perhaps thinking my boast ill-timed humor. They never believed me, so I walked to the center of their circle and said, "I challenge any man here. If you lose, you can take up my chores in the stable, and I'll take up your risks with the enemy, wherever they may be hiding."

Horatio spoke first, reminding me of why I found men hard to love. "That's a peasant's weapon. Get back to watering and brushing my horse."

"I'll deal with you later, Horatio. I prefer starting on a real man, and not some boys in need of lessons. As for weapons, I'll make my challenge with swords if you like, should any here lend me one."

The sergeant said, "That's enough, Abe. I can see by your bruises that you've had a row with some stubborn horse, and I forgive you because of the trauma to your head, but now I insist that you get on with your work, or take a needed rest, before you over-tax my patience."

"Do you accept the challenge, Sergeant Hadarm? Swords it shall be, for I've heard you are nearly a master!" I backed up to an old soldier I trusted and swiped his sword from his scabbard before he realized my intentions. I tossed him my staff as security. With a spin of the metal, I showed the pointed end of it to the sergeant from across a small distance. It was no worthless wooden thing either. It was a mite heavy and not perfectly straight, but it was far better than the one the crone had used when she'd died a warrior. If they gave me one of these, I'd be long hours filing it down into something decent.

"Hold on, Abe. I have no intention of harming you in a poorly bartered match."

I bowed and declared, "Flat of the blade alone for blows. None to the head. Let the consensus agree on the winner of two of three." I'd heard them say the same words in many practices, though the blades were never steel.

I could see in his eyes that the sergeant thought me a mouse, and, thus, he wasn't afraid that I held steel instead of wood. That it would never come to much more than he could handle was his likely thought. And, it wouldn't be good to send me away now without some discipline. Maybe, as well, he didn't want to spoil my whole spirit by refusing me entirely. Or, in any event, all of that I hoped. That's not to say that he wasn't angry. He wasn't good at holding his anger most mornings.

He came forward, employing half a stance.

I spent the next few minutes backing away and swatting at his swipes and thrusts, as if all I had going for me was quickness and flight of foot. Then he lunged with more confidence than I could credit without making my pretend incompetence obvious. I lightly poked him in the ribs just enough to make it clear that I could have killed him. Catcalls of "False blow," rang out from the soldiers, but the sergeant would hear none of it and gave me credit for one of the three.

I suppose he thought I'd tire of my prancing, and be bested after that, and to be sure I was tired from a long night awake, part of it in mortal combat with a demon twice the size of Hadarm.

It was in my own interest to let our wise sergeant strike me next. The flat of his sword came under my shabby defense and smacked me hard enough to make me think I might have purpled yet another rib. I'd run out of pink ones.

The soldiers roared approval, and the sergeant smiled as

well, though he was good enough of a man to help me up from the dirt. He'd backed me all across the corral, and now he had smacked me a good one. His confidence was at a peak, just as I wanted.

I thanked him for his gentlemanly spirit. He offered to end it. I told him, "We have only one more to go."

The sergeant shook his head, knowing I'd spent my energy running around and playing tap for tap with him. In battle, neither of us would have prevailed. The crone had often warned me about prolonged fights on a battlefield, which gave others time to stab you in the back.

I set my hands high and faked a high cut down to his torso, but then I backed without delivering the swipe. When his sword whipped by, I poked at his heart and backed off just in time to keep from entering the skin and killing him. Some didn't even see the poke. It had been too fast and clean. Others claimed I'd come too short and couldn't have driven it farther.

Sergeant Hadarm looked at me curiously, and continued.

Three times more I caught him overreaching on just three more moves. Three times more I sent the message back in the form of a certain kill or a likely cut that would have had him bleeding to death before the battlefield cleared. The soldiers chanted:

"Unfair cut."

"No reach!"

"Not the flat!"

I quit killing him, lest someone suspect my skill. Instead I battered his blade. I was no longer backing away, for Hadarm had grown hesitant, not sure if what he was seeing was deadly or a demonstration of the limits to my reach. The next meaningful swing he mustered was a blade edged swing that I caught and held in the air, steel on steel and unyielding. Blades and hand-guards locked. I had the leverage and backed him up a half step.

No longer were we tapping, and no longer was I running away like a mouse. It was my field, and he finally knew it. The meat in me was sufficient, for, by using thighs as leverage, I pushed the large man back with two hands on my hilt, having found and kept the better stance. I heard the crone say to me in my memory that such things were done by the feet. I couldn't kill him because he was my sergeant, and I loved him for his leadership. Though he had treated me unfairly, it wasn't for lack of his own reasons. There, steel to steel, and testing our bodies, I loosened a hand and pulled my knife. The flat of it smacked across the back of his hand as I backed away. Our blades shrieked as they parted. I put my knife back and made myself ready for more.

"Unfair cut! It was to be sword to sword," yelled Horatio. The older soldiers took up the opposite view. I thought Horatio silly. Hadn't the white knight nearly killed me with his armored fingers alone?

"Enough!" My sergeant put his sword into his scabbard and looked around at the soldiers surrounding us. "Use of his knife was unfair, but so it is in battle. What is most important is that Abe has shown he has enough meat to fight, not to mention enough nerve to try such a trick on his sergeant—more than some here. He, of course, has much to learn about holding his place early on in the contest. Yet, I could see his skill growing in just this one lesson. It would be wrong to hold him back further. Now I have a problem I'd not anticipated: Who will keep our horses safe from Tom Calligor's laziness and dirty habits?"

I told the sergeant, "I can keep an eye on the horses and even bed down in the stable, Sergeant. All I want is to be a soldier like the rest of the men. I want to learn what you can teach me and do my share of ranging out and protecting the lands of Lady Lettoir. There should be some time left over to keep the horses safe, as long as Tom can keep them happy while I'm on the road."

One of the soldiers said, "That suits me. If Abe wants to be in my squad and still keep track of my mount, I say, let it happen. He can go on patrols with my patrol as well, for he can fight, and he can keep my horse happy. There's not much more to want."

"So be it," said the sergeant. "No guard duty for you, in exchange for living with the horses. You'll do half afternoons at that, and mornings until noon meal with the company. You eat with the troops though, all three meals, so you can be seen as a part of us. You train and go on tours with Ankind. He picked you; he has to live with you. Give back the sword, and Ankind will find you your own, along with the rest of your issue that you're short. You've gotten what you've wanted. Don't come to me later and say you don't like it."

I felt giddy as I bowed. I was in the army, finally. I couldn't wait to start practicing and, most of all, I couldn't wait to go out on one of those tours and maybe meet the enemy, even if he was nothing more than a bandit.

After that, the hardest part of being in the army was keeping away from teaching everybody what I knew about fighting. I had to take a lot of wasted hits that I'd rather have avoided. It was almost as if I was unlearning good instincts, pretending to be as awful as the rest of them. Ankind was good to me, though, and he kept nodding every time I pretended I'd learned something new. I saved most of my pretend spankings for when he fought me, so as to be on his good side. He was a good fighter, too, younger and better skilled than the sergeant, so I didn't mind listening hard for the occasional tricks I'd not already learned from my crone.

There were a few whole new things to learn as well. Most of

that included the horses and how to fight from them with a group of soldiers. We went out on squad drills, keeping our horses in lines and moving the lines around in circles or rotating them at angles. I liked charging in triangles formed to break up the enemy by stabbing and bashing them with a whole host of horses.

We had short lances with which to spear the straw dummies. When they stuck, we circled around and lopped off chunks of their stuffing with our swords. I could have done that all day long, and I did until everybody complained about the dummies being beaten into sticks with hay under them.

We only had a score of soldiers, so we kept it at three, seven - man squads for most practices. One squad was out on patrol at a time, but we'd sometimes bunch the other two and call it a company, though a real company is much bigger, and our whole company was really just a squad in numbers. The sergeant told us it didn't matter that we were a little group because the same idea could relate to an entire army of horsemen. Now there was something I couldn't wait to see; maybe it was the crone inside of me wanting to, but I think I also lusted after war more than a little.

Being horsemen was special, everybody thought, particularly because Lettoir Manor didn't have any nobles, and it was home-spun, passed down from commoner sergeant to commoner sergeant. Lettoir Manor didn't have many resources to waste either, so we kept our guard small and quick, as opposed to having sheriffs in every town. Footmen drew less than half of the pay of the horsemen of Lettoir, down to only a few coppers per month.

"A footman can't go much farther than the little place he has been charged to police. He can't go for help either. In a fight, he's nearly worthless if outnumbered. Best to let the towns sheriff themselves, and make a call upon us or hold their rogues until we pass," explained squad leader Ankind, the only man I knew, beside the sergeant, who had a mind for tactics.

* * * * *

One thing we learned with the horses, I already knew from Yellow Eyes. Two or three men would circle around in the woods, either to the right or left or both directions, and then the others would work forward until they came into contact with whomever the scout had sniffed out earlier.

Ankind explained, "This way the rogues will think we aren't all that many, or they might even try to sneak away in a direction that drives them right into our flanks."

I mentioned to Ankind that wolves paid attention to the direction of their smell, but he didn't think it was a problem. I told him that lots of baths might help, but it wasn't good enough if we got too close or if the wind blew toward the enemy. It was one of those times when Ankind said I should just do what I'd been told and not think. Then he got stupid and added, "Besides, nobody can smell that well."

The other new thing we learned was finger talking. I gobbled that right up, though nobody would talk to me that way when we weren't in the woods practicing it. They only used a few words, so I made new ones for mushrooms and the smell of fear and the idea that my horse was worried about snakes, and I even invented a way to do all the letters in the alphabet. I decided to keep specific letters to myself because reading was illegal for the peasantry.

They used me as the enemy on my first practice in the woods. I was supposed to find a place to hide but leave a trail they could track. I couldn't try to leave my hide until I saw somebody coming. After that, I was supposed to make it difficult for them, which was a mistake because the scout was always too noisy or easy to smell, and I knew they were going to surround me. All I had to do was hide under the leaves, or find a fold of land between their groups then disappear. I could hear them, and smell them and even see them better than they could me. Lots of days I came in late, walking all the way home because they had my horse, and the whole idea was to not let them have me.

After a couple days of this, Ankind got mad at me and said I was cheating, so he wouldn't let me hide anymore. He kept me on my horse with the rest of the troops. This was much easier, and, most of the time, I was the first to the goat with my lance out. Ankind got mad at me for that, too, saying I wasn't keeping in position on the flank, and was charging in too suddenly for the rest of the men to join.

"The idea," he said, "is to come in together and overwhelm the enemy as a group while trapping him between us." I thought that was a good idea, but the enemy was only one of us, so he was mighty small and awfully hard not to get. It was kind of like waiting for Yellow Eyes to help when it was only a groundhog.

Ankind put me at scout, and things were a lot better after that. Part of the job was to not go in and get the enemy at all, but to be slow and easy in order to not scare him away. When I found him, I was ordered to go back to the squad leader and report, after which we used our hand words, and everybody was assigned a part in the trap.

The scout always rode in with the squad leader, so I stayed out of trouble, and Ankind said, "I think we've found your calling, Abe." The only thing he faulted me for after that was for telling him where the goat was moving off to while we drove in. "You can't see him from here. He's over the hill," he'd tell me, but, when he saw that I was right, he'd add, "That's why we circle on the flanks and don't go in one at a time," as if he hadn't noticed I'd been right.

It was all to the good, I figured, given Ankind and the rest couldn't see too well, were terribly bad at smelling things, and didn't seem to feel anybody else's tension or fear at all. A good pack would have been better at the chore. Still, I grew to like my squad. Horatio and Hobar weren't in it, and most of the other soldiers were too old to buck for scout, which was more fun than any other job.

This practice lasted three weeks, after which I was sent on patrol with Ankind and the four others in our smallest squad. I didn't know what to take with me. In the end I took my issued sword and hid my staff and good sword in the stall. I had a ton of herbs and rags and things that might be useful, but I had to camp and fight and keep the rest of it light. We had lances and swords and the right to tell everybody what to do.

I tried to explain why my staff was a good weapon, saying, "The staff is helpful if you don't want to kill the enemy, or if there's a lot of them, and you don't want your weapon stuck into someone's bones. You can keep a whole lot of them away from you, too, and, when they're all on the ground, round them up and put them to justice."

Ankind corrected me by saying, "Not even a peasant will respect you if they see you with it. Respect is important because it will help you avoid fighting altogether, in some instances."

Such news didn't please the spirit of the crone within me, for she wished to do less persuading than fighting.

On the road out of Lettoir, Ankind told me, "Around here, justice is the problem. We don't beat them about the head much, nor do we have a dungeon like in Helfax. The truly evil ones who surrender, we have to hang in the first good public place. If they didn't do much wrong, then we've little to do at all but scold them, and we won't even be out looking for them if they've done something small like keeping a neighbor's wandering lamb or killing their woman for being unchaste."

That startled me, though I knew that such was how men

were taught to think in Farstand. "What if they killed their woman for something else?"

"Then we have to hang them. I've never had to do that, though, because no man would ever do more than spank his woman if she was faithful. What would be the point of it? Who would feed him and keep the children quiet?"

He made a wee point, somewhere in all that. On the other hand, I thought it possible that a man might just get too drunk and carried away with beating her, maybe for being too slow with his supper or eating up the stores while he was out robbing merchants on the highways. I forgave Ankind his naivety because he thought certain things through ignorance, and he was also easy on the eyes.

We stopped at several villages where I was tempted by several stores to buy something. Most of the time, I hid in amongst the others. I tried not to draw too much attention to myself, lest one of the peasants look too closely and see that I was a woman. It was hard, given I was lanky, my lips were like apples and my breast lacings were fighting a losing battle. It helped that the bruises on my face had gone from purple and black to yellow and purple, making me look rough-faced enough to be a man.

Way up on my horse it was hard to see me as a mite female, and I looked overly-curious people in the face, too, just to give them the frights and make myself look meaner than I felt. The magic helped, of course, for I imagined that even if my squad members chanced on me naked, they'd still be completely blinded by it. The men bantered with me as if I were a man. There are many fair skinned boys, and I learned that much of what we see in one another is social; I had only to nod their way, spit their way and laugh loudly in proportion to the crudeness of their jokes.

We slept in the fields, out in the open by the fires that we kept all night. I was no longer worried about being so lit up, hoping to keep warm and knowing that war wasn't to be our destiny right away. We slept close to the fires, under leaning tents of canvas.

One of the men fancied himself a cook, but he wasn't good at it, burning everything to a cinder, including the water for our tea, which bubbled down to nothing but black leaves, for lack of tending. I dared not touch the chore, worried that it would tattle on my gender.

My baths were frequent, even when I had to chip the ice and steal away in the dead of night because I didn't want to give away my smell and was keen to know others by it. How could anyone not know I was a woman during my time, I wondered? Clearly the Goddesses magic was sure, even having sustained me through that unpleasant annoyance. It was powerful magic affecting the men, for even Yellow Eyes could tell my state from so far enough away that I couldn't even see him before he turned back and stayed away each month during my cranky period.

At every place where we saw people, Ankind or one of the others asked if there was any trouble about. Our mission took us into every valley along a long stretch. I thought Lettoir's lands vast. There seemed endless people living along Lettoir's many tenant fields, but Ankind corrected me and told me that it was a midget land in the kingdom of Helfax baronage, and that beyond, Helfax was a mite in the order of baronages among the lands of the great King Falstaff of Farstand.

He said, "When called upon, we may need to augment the army of the baron and then maybe even the duke or king. Though we regard ourselves among the best of Falstaff's common soldiers, the great lords know us not, for we are small and stand as no more than a dash of salt among the armored cavalry if it was put together on one field."

I worried naught about that, for I knew it was the tip of the blade that did most of the cutting.

Then one night I could no longer take the bad food, and I ventured out into the lowland marshes we'd been passing, looking for those frogs I'd been aching to eat since over a year back. The frogs croaked up a storm as I waded into the water. I watched for the reflection of moonlight off their eyes.

I came upon a patch of them, one every step, and waded into the bank where they always looked out at the water as if looking at it was all they needed in order to be safe from invading foxes. I put a water lily in my hair, and pretended to be a flower. This helped me attack from the water, holding a long poking stick I'd whittled to spit them with. Only one in ten thought to jump into the water right in front of me where I'd let them go. I'd poked a good five score of them in no time at all, one right after the other; they were so dumb. I put them into a bag that was so squirmy and heavy I let it drag in the water as I carried it along.

It wasn't until I'd cut them all in two and was stripping off the skins that Yellow Eyes came running up to see what I'd caught. He thought it was funny how the top halves of all those frogs walked everywhere he stepped, none of them with hind legs.

I tossed him a meaty leg that stretched nearly as long as my forearm, and he chewed it up in nearly one bite, pleased with the taste.

"What you been doing all this time, Yellow Eyes?"

He said in my head that he'd been at home, making as many pups as he could before it got too cold to stick his private parts out.

He thought I'd do well to get on home and make some pups, too, reminding him of my nature. I told him I wasn't ready for babies and was unlikely to be pleasing to a man, as unsettled as I felt, though I often yearned for company. Besides, I didn't have a dowry, and, while it was fun looking at the butts and shoulders of my fellow soldier, I found it hard to trust them.

He didn't understand any of that, but all of the discussing was only his way of telling me that he was hanging around in hopes of some more of the frog legs. While I cleaned them up, he started batting the wandering top halves of the frogs around in a moonlit game of paw-paddle.

When the rest of the men got up, I was already frying the legs up in the wide squad pan, having coated them with salt, fennel and flour. I had to catch some of the legs when they tried to jump out of the pan. I only had a half dozen for each man after Yellow Eyes had spent half the night begging for so many that he succumbed to food sleep right there by the pond and didn't even have the energy to say goodbye when I walked off with the meager remains.

I told the men that it was a mess of bird wings, and they ate them without thinking too hard about it, except to tell me that it was the best bird wing batch they'd ever eaten. "How'd you catch all them birds?" one of them asked.

I decided that I couldn't explain it, so I replied, "I was just sitting here ready to fry up some flaps, and they flew into the pan among the flour, dropped off their wings, pulled out their own feathers with their beaks and breaded themselves with their feet for me. Next thing you know, I had four pans of wings to cook before the sun even came up. Last I saw, they were walking on down the road daring us to go scout them and flank them and put them to the question before hanging what's left for supper. See, there are their tracks." I pointed to some possum marks in the dirt around the campfire. Oddly enough, that worked. I think they were fooled because they thought the birds a different species than regular birds. One of the men even started looking for where the marks in the dirt went into the brush. Others saw my extra uniform drying over a string near the fire and told me I'd caught some strange, little ducks.

The subject never came up again. It was a good thing because eating lizards and toads was considered demon work. That wasn't true, though, because I'd already seen a demon, and he was a lot bigger than any frog I'd ever eaten, which was a delicacy my mother and I never passed up. Even if it was demon work, I was already tainted with it for being a woman, and it would do the men some good to catch up.

Those kinds of thoughts got me thinking about my mother. I wanted to go home and see how she managed, but I knew it was a bad idea to go anywhere near that place. Too many knew me, and they'd be looking to comment, should I ever go back, now that the shock of my leaving had passed. The Ranglsons were probably eager to see me, too, about murdering their brother. Luck kept our squad from that direction.

* * * * *

I ran up on some poachers on Lady Lettoir's best gaming lands while out front scouting. There were only three of them and none had a sword—just knives and a bow with some arrows without fletching. Instead of racing back to tell the others, I rode up on them as they were cutting a deer. They were bad at poaching, having let me get so close that the first thing they saw was my horse's legs when Ella almost walked on top of the deer they were hacking into quarters.

"What are you doing poaching deer so close to the lady's manor?"

All three of them jumped back and sized me up, one with a bloody knife in his hand, and another grabbing at one stuck in the deer thigh. "Who wants to know, woman?"

I'd not expected such a quick recognition, but my bruises were healing, and I attributed it to that. "I'm a soldier in the Lady's guard, and will have you call me Ser! Answer my question, for the penance for poaching noble lands is hanging."

"You're no soldier. Just because you have a horse and have stolen a uniform doesn't make you anything at all," declared the biggest man in the middle.

I took my lance out of the holder and aimed it at him.

I nudged Ella, and she walked sideways into the man closest to me, pushing him over with her broad breast. The man probably didn't know how to properly kill a horse, I guessed, seeing his hesitation. Doing it wrong tended to make horses angry, not to mention their riders. The other men scampered back a few steps. I threatened with the end of my lance pointed at the mouthy one's chest.

"I said I would have you listen to me and do as I say. If not, I'll have to dispatch you here for a crime I have no heart in enforcing!"

I had to inch toward the leader until he listened well enough to please me.

"Now hear this. I am a scout, and the rest of my squad is coming this way. If you leave to the south, and then turn to the left, you'll escape with a couple of quarters of Lady Lettoir's meat. Else, I'll tell them how to flank you, and you'll not fare too well with my knight." I always found it convenient to add title to my sergeant (though Ankind wasn't even a sergeant), when trying to impress the serfs.

They scrambled, picking up two portions. I took my time reporting back.

"My clumsiness has given warning, but we are in luck for the night's spit." Ankind was happy with the news, so I asked him what the penalty really was for a man taking a deer right on the lady's best hunting grounds.

He whispered, "I'd let them go with a spanking. Seems a bit much to hang a man for eating. I've seen the sergeant do it that way after keeping the meat as penalty. Don't do that if in the service of the baron. He'd see any sign of leniency as treason.

Not soft like the lady."

I nodded. It was a good thing I was in the service of Lady Lettoir instead of the baron. I wasn't happy with the idea of hanging anyone for eating what the Goddess put on their table. If so, I'd have hanged many times over.

The next day, however, all of this lazy soldiering changed, as did my service to the good Lady Lettoir, for we were not more than half a day into the manor before we heard the hoof beats of the baron's messenger. His message bore the tidings of war. Levies of footmen were to be recruited and trained. Most of those who were ready and not needed for the training would depart upon the gathering of supplies.

It made no sense for peace to linger, for I'd long suspected that the gods had plans for the course of my life, and it had something to do with bloody fields and the continually discontented spirit of an old warrior I felt beating through my veins.

Chapter Seven

I stood naked beside the icy creek. Limbs lay bare of leaves. Clouds drifted by in tiny puffs. Not a sign from the Goddess showed anywhere.

"I can't wait to fight. The art of maiming and murdering sings to me. Oh my Goddess, what kind of woman am I? Is it not my duty to bear life instead of death? No, I cannot feel it. Ever since the crone's death ..."

I'd changed the words from a spell about bravery, addressing my sense of emptiness instead. Bravery I didn't need, for it was courage that plagued me.

"It is women who bear forth spring; yet, I crave the sword. What does that make me?" I received only silence in reply. To be honest, I didn't want spring, and that stood at the core of my guilt.

"So be it." Obedience is blind, I'd once read. I raised my sword, saluting the darkening world.

"Let my sword slay these foreign invaders, and let my body hide the blessings of womanhood, so that it may kill the enemies of the Goddess. Let none who live under the king's banner see me as a woman while I fight in this war. The Goddess will know, even the king's peasants should know, of my glory as a warrior of our king. Your magic is mighty. I pray, my Goddess, grant this spell. *Tpunwvw Own.*" I twirled my finger in the air, signing the benediction.

The wind paused over the still and frozen creek. My skin felt covered with prickly chills. I had to will my body to stop shivering, for I was trying my best to look worthy of the Goddess's attention. I waited until a cloud passed beyond the falling sun. The warm breath of the Goddess kissed my skin. I'd grown to recognize when she gave her blessing.

Two days later, our squads traveled the road to Helfax. The peasants saw me as a man. They bowed and cast wary eyes. I had no taste for their deference, for I found it dishonest. All of the cold judgments were gone, reminding me that I'd become a traitor to womanhood.

Ankind had made sergeant, for our old sergeant was needed to recruit and train the foot pikers that our lady felt obliged to send behind us. We were two of the three squads, the first sixteen lent to war. Tom had been left with only a third of our horses. Other than Hadarm's squad of seven, the reinforcements would come on foot. They'd march, weeks late, and with a dyed shirt and some handmade pikes for uniforms.

Women tended the fields when their men went to war. It wasn't very polite of Sir Lacellor to turn his border raids into a war so close to early planting.

We were more fortunate than most of the soldiers we came across. We had winter tunics and solid boots that the lady's holding held in reserve for such occasions. The lady had sent us with all of her blessings and more than half of her gear. She'd watched us depart with tears falling from her eyes.

As we departed, Ankind said, "If all the nobles were the same as her, I'd have no concerns about how we'll get on under the flag of Helfax."

"I can't wait to see the great baron." We rode over another mountain foothill.

"Well, nobles are not all the same, I have come to know."

"Hum. I guess I will withhold my judgment."

"Better to stay clear and judge nothing."

I watched Ankind's face, seeing concern in a wrinkled

brow.

Early in the march, we took up a rag collection from the peasants we passed. From those we fashioned motley hats that helped hide our heads while traversing tall fields. Lettoir's dark greys and browns proved practically invisible among the forest stands, though of course, earthen colors suggested the peasantry. On the road, our blankets and tunic tails flapped as if we were rogues coming forth from a dark realm and not from some noble holding.

In nightly camps, Hobar and Horatio thought it their job to play top cocks. They were in the second, and I in the first with Sergeant Ankind, so I practiced patience by ignoring their constant pestering.

As Ankind's scout, I rode at his side and scouted, the first out during practices while on the march toward Helfax. This hurt Hobar's and Horatio's feelings. They knew I'd been hired last, and obviously thought I should ride in the dust, attending the pack horses.

I drew Ankind's attention to dust ahead on the third day out.

"Go find out who is ahead, and report back," Ankind commanded.

"My pleasure." I checked my long spear and sword, then took off, hoping it was the enemy. At the bend, I diverted to the forest.

"And be careful!" He yelled when I started off.

I came out of the forest behind a score of White Shirts destined for Helfax. Unlike others we'd passed, who were slowed by wagons, soft nobles, footmen, archers and servants, this was a lightly armored company of cavalry, much like our own. The sign of Sho shone off overly large shields. They bore them resting on pike holders, as if they continually needed something to hide behind.

I nosed my horse in between the two columns of ten. Ella

enjoyed parting them as easily as walking through a gaggle of house-fed geese. When I got to the front, I cantered over to the outside of a young man who had far more armor than the others.

I glanced left and right. "Have you seen the enemy? I've heard that he ventures close, and my noble wants me to scout carefully. They say many peasants have come running from the woodcuts, as if racing from a dragon-storm."

The boy noble made a tight fist, squeezing his reins. He lifted his head in order to fashion the image of an older man.

He said, "I've heard no such thing. Superstitions, I suspect, and you will call me Ser. I am Sir Allen Wencor, second son to High Lord Wencor, himself second cousin to Baron Eron Prescott of Olan. I've entered the service of Sho as a holy gift to our Lord and Savior."

I imagined the cold chill within his steel unbearable. I also noticed twenty places through which I'd be able to slip my sword if I ever had the chance to meet him alone in some woods.

"Well, Ser, that is a powerful name, Ser, with mighty kin … honored Ser." I really had nothing meaningful to say to him, except maybe that I'd enjoy cutting his throat for the mere pleasure of it, and that I felt that the longer his name, the better served the cut. As long as his name, I'd not be done until his head fell off entirely.

The man across from him asked, "Do you have your own troops to rejoin?"

I rode beside them for a while, and then said, "Yes, I do … Ser. Yet, I have been given the duty to determine all loyalties, so you do well to indulge me a little, regardless of my low rank."

The same man said, "Well, you've seen us now. Best begone."

"Yes, I'd best. And, I'd best keep an eye out for enemies. I hear they are huge and ferocious. They are nothing like the old women that some hunt in order to appease their gods. Should I describe for you what a real enemy looks like? To start with, they are big and ferocious, or have I already told that part ... Ser?"

"Watch your tongue, young serf!" said the older knight beside the youthful leader, the dangerous one, I determined, given mandate to watch over the nobler son. Rough experience rumbled from his voice.

"I'm sorry, Ser, and Ser, but I have been told to take care, and I have not yet determined where you stand. If you are found to be the enemy, then I am ordered to cut your heads off forthwith and leave them dangling on the ends of your pikes for the old women to look up at and admire. I would, of course, not bother my noble with the matter, it being little work and not outside my duty."

Both of them glared.

"But, now that I've seen you, I am leaning toward believing that you have entered the same quest as I." I winked at the younger man. "Should I take up humor as a profession?"

"I do not think it. Rudeness, perhaps. Now, be away with you before I have you arrested," said the young knight.

He looked directly into my eyes, challenging me to back away. His God Sho had many talents worthy of my admiration, for talents were not at the core of our disagreement, but Sho did not tell his men that I was a woman. Sho occasionally played fair in his games with the Goddess, I suspected.

"I have need, Ser. You could be in disguise. I hear the enemy even rides with their women on occasion. Can I see your private parts? They would help me tell if you are a witch. You must be sitting upon them—I have seen no evidence to the contrary. Perhaps you've noticed an unusual skill at floating upon water, for instance? I hear water is the finest test of witchery." I nodded my head and raised an eyebrow. "Has my jesting improved some? Is there a future for me at court?"

The man on the other side of the overly-armored boy nodded back to his troops. One of the men came around to my free side while another drew more closely behind. I felt surrounded. It wasn't a good spot to have me, for I felt as bound up as a spring, and my fingers itched for a grip on a rag-wrapped hilt. The landscape had greened some, the farther we travelled from the heights. Great expanses of oaks hid us from the world and, perhaps, all need of mercy.

I sighed. "Ah, I see I must beg your forgiveness. Let me ask a serious question before I go, however. I seem to recall an older man, with a round barrel breastplate. It was painted white. He led some men of Sho. What happened to him?"

The young knight replied, "The man you speak of was in a brother company. He was honored by dying peacefully in his sleep, I've heard. Speak no ill of him, else I will run you through."

I said, "I will speak well of him now. He was good in a fight, if not before." I touched a slow-healing bruise on my cheek, and found myself reflecting: "I fear that I shall not go so easily in my sleep. A path of dying men lay before my eyes."

"Bah!" said the boy in armor.

"Oh yes, God has given me this vision. God said, 'Thousands shall fall before your horse's feet.' That is certain."

I felt the protector's patience turning from hot to boiling. He'd obviously been well trained to keep most of his emotions hidden, but I was keen to smell out the limit to his wrath.

As for the boy, this seemed his first time out of the cradle. I saw him swallow hard. Still, the boy did not flinch.

"Well, good day to you, Sers, and, if you find yourself in battle, do not lie idly in front of my horse, for I come fast, with steel and bearing God's vengeance upon those who slaughter women."

"Is that a friendly piece of advice or a threat?" asked the older noble.

"I am duty bound to not make idle threats to our allies. I'll trouble you no further and report to my knight that I've found none of Lacellor's troops."

I stopped my horse, nearly causing the riders behind me to run into Ella. The banner of Sho waved by. I watched them ride away. Eyes turned, apparently seeing me grow small.

"Whose house is dark grey and brown?" The young noble asked the older man. He must have thought me deaf, for his whisper carried all the way back beyond their pack.

"The widow Lettoir allowed to rule in a man's stead. Still, there is something particularly odd in that one, my Lord."

"I had very ill feelings as well."

"He could be brought before the ...."

"... found on ... battlefield...."

I circled Ella in the road, hoping they'd turn back and have a try at me. I hated them beyond reason and had far overstepped my bounds, somehow getting away with it, or so I thought. They rounded the bend before their whispers faded from my ears, and I suppose they bent past another couple of bends before I stopped feeling their evil whiteness in my bones.

I leaned over the neck of Ella, fighting the cramps in my gut. They danced around inside like clawing crabs. It was all that I could do to hold my last meal inside because of the nagging of the crone's spirit. I wanted to kick my horse and ride the score of them down in one blazing rush.

Gods, I wanted them dead! What was wrong with me? Without cautious reason, something inside drove me to open wrath on occasions. I knew it. I couldn't help myself.

I even thought I heard the Goddess whispering for me to attack them, but then I also sensed the Goddess whispering for me to wait. I eventually realized it had been the two whispering faces of my own soul that had me so befuddled; maybe the crone and my old self were having a spat inside my stomach, and it was loud enough to reach my most hidden thoughts.

With great reluctance, I returned to report that nothing but a squad of the priests' men rode ahead.

I said, "I suppose that instead of watching for their plodding dust, we'll have a better sign of the enemy when they are slaughtered, and stop raising such a cloud of it." The men around me laughed.

"I am not overly fond of White Shirts," one man said.

Another agreed, "They undo much of the good work we do. Some mistakenly think we shared their same zealous ideas about how to handle things."

I saw that attitude as an opportunity: "They said Lady Lettoir was ill suited to lead us. They were most offensive, even to the point of suggesting that she was stained by some womanly evil, and any noble would do if put above her."

"Daft!" an older soldier said. "She'd spoil us with cakes two times daily if she could do so and still call us soldiers."

"That's true enough," another said. "It's a sacrifice that she's been burdened with because of the bad fortune of her husband's death. I'll not take kindly to ill words about her sweet ass."

"I would have run them all through, but I think we should win the war first,"

Ankind looked at me strangely, and then he seemed to have decided that I'd told him a joke, and he laughed. After he thought some more, he said, "Abe, I hope you know better than to try such a stunt. It is against the law to run people through without notice. I'll have to command you to not do it, just because I wonder if you know it can't be done. You are a fine soldier, but your manners are often odd, and it is sometimes hard to determine your knowledge of the broader world."

He squinted at me with one eye. Even while scolding me, I thought him handsome, particularly with his better tailored tunic and bright sergeant's stripe.

"I know it, Sergeant Ankind. I lived my early years on a scrape of a farm with nobody about but women teaching me about men and their ways. Men didn't seem important to us."

"Ah, it relieves me to know that your manners can be explained so easily. Now, as a soldier, you are in service to your lady, but also to the law and the people. What was once not important to you is where you are lacking. Follow my lead then, as we commune with others. In time you'll learn the ways of the world, and stay out of trouble." I could tell that Ankind's heart was right, so I determined that I would, as best I could. That, of course, didn't set the men of Sho free of an obligation to die someday.

We passed the white knights a few villages ahead, as well as several other small groups of soldiers. None, of course, were as small as our sixteen, though far fewer than one in twenty were horsemen, and all of those were nobles or their servants. These troops we passed took up residence in or around many large houses.

"Every lordly holding in Helfax has sent a contingent," Ankind told me. "And every decent peasant residence has been invaded for lodging. The king has decided, no doubt, that our strategically placed baronage is to bear the brunt of his war against Lacellor."

"It's cold, but I'm happy to leave others to the towns," I said.

"Me as well," agreed Ankind. "I have no desire to waste the resources of Lady Lettoir, nor do I relish a company of troops who need looked after. They'd have us fetching their water both up and down the stairs." Ankind seemed well aware that he was only a sergeant.

We came down out of the mountainous region, and into the flat fertile plains of Helfax proper. This part of Helfax felt warmer. It was outside of the mountains, so, even in winter, chill only numbed us at night. Vast expanses of wheat stretched near the rivers, some without a single boulder troubling the black soil. In one field, highly-pruned fruit trees lined up like soldiers.

We moved slowly, practicing caution, and camped three nights. Sergeant Ankind taught us what he could about reading the maps of lowland areas where the subtle folds of the land were not as obvious as they had been in the holding of Lettoir. Finally, we aimed directly for the keep of Helfax.

At the edge of the city, we stopped at a horse breeder's pastures. His house wasn't large, but the three stables were long and ample enough for ten times our company. I noticed few horses in the fields. The breeder came to the door. His wife appeared with three small children tugging on her skirt.

He said, "There are no more studs for breeding, Ser. The baron has claimed most of my stock for the war. I have only a few mares left and no studs."

Ankind knew him: "I've a proposal for you. Lady Lettoir also has no desire to show her horses to Lord Eron Prescott. She is loyal, but she knows the workings of court. Every noble will covet a third horse to hold his purses and stockings. Now, we need to make our presence known to the high baron, but we'd prefer to do so while dismounted to save our horses for battle."

"Ah, I see. They think my stock bare and won't think to look here further. Perhaps we can come to some solution, Ankind," said the smiling breeder.

Soon, a deal was struck that traded only a little coin and the services of our studs in exchange for shelter and a home away from Lettoir.

The breeder said, "Perhaps luck will cause one or two of my mares to be in season. Do me one more favor. Keep an eye open on the battlefield for any decent stock that might wander loose."

Ankind agreed with a smile, saying, "If extra are found, we will run them through here, so that half go to our lady, and the other to you at half normal price. In exchange, you give our men a way-station, for those sent up and those retiring from the battle."

The horse breeder took Ankind's horse out first, finding him a mate. Each of the men with studs was put to the task of sleeping near the larger breeding stalls and overseeing any chance mating.

At first nothing happened. I went over and impressed upon our studs the importance of getting down to business and not engaging in a long courtship. I spoke into their minds that I knew they didn't understand it, but some things were too important to discuss and had to be done right away if there were oats to be had. They remembered when I'd been their main source of oats and obeyed my voice. Soon, all of the studs got down to the business of helping out the mares that were willing and even a few that were not. It was hard to sleep after that, with all of the horse noises. The breeder woke those of us near the door. He was in good spirits when he came in and saw what all the whinnying was about. He said he'd never seen anything like it, and that he was mightily pleased with his deal.

At dawn, we put our best uniforms on and put ourselves into our best formation. Then we walked out toward Helfax Keep. I noticed that the long city road was too crowded with houses to be healthy. To make matters worse, we were no parade; everybody ignored us, seeing us as just more hungry mouths and filled beds.

Being the scout, I rode on Ella beside Ankind. We were the only two mounted. Ella did her best to look as old as she could.

She even limped a little for me, at my suggestion this time, bringing curious glances from Ankind. She had no desire to be plucked up by some idiot noble. Ankind had a pack animal under him. Two more in our second squad rode pack animals. No noble would want those pack horses either. Each of our men was happy to act like a foot piker saving the horses, and none of the soldiers had the heart to interrupt these animals in their pleasant new duties.

As footmen, we sported swords and steel tipped lances. Our uniforms were clean and matching darks, and our stride was much practiced, making us as orderly as the king's own pikers, or so Ankind told us. I could see for myself that most of the other footmen only had sticks and peasant rags and looked about to die from the cold.

Maybe it was for the best that we walked in, I realized, upon seeing the noble cavalry, almost all of whom rode horses as nice as the ones we'd left in the stables. Some of the animals even wore horse armor. I almost never saw a rider without at least chain on his chest. Most of the nobles had a second horse. Ankind said the knights rode into battle on the large one, and they saved their butts by riding around the countryside on the smaller one. I looked around at all the peasants who were pikers, and realized we could have twice the cavalry if the lords weren't so picky about who rode and on what.

Helfax was a city, not just a town. We passed at least two of every kind of shop, and signs suggested guilds that kept them up to standards and stopped the people from fighting with one another. It was no use, I could see, for everywhere we passed there was someone shouting at someone else, and people passing so closely to one another that they had to look where they were going. Soldiers added to the mess. Groups of them sat on all of the porches or milled around and engaged in the important duty of waiting.

A woman sat on a soldier's lap, right in front of a drinking parlor. She wore a dress the color of spring flowers. One glance at her pretty round face, and I saw the sparse color of winter. Her dress hung mostly open in front, though she had buttons. I'd never really seen a whore before. I'd heard of them all of my life, been threatened to be made into one, and the men were always bragging about having their way with them. I wondered why this one wasn't hiding in a bedroom. I gave her a look that spoke my displeasure for betraying herself. She started to smile back at me, maybe to tell me she didn't care what I thought, but then she saw something in my eye that I suspect told her I knew more about it than she wanted to hear. The whore got off the soldier and ran into the drinking parlor.

I took my hand off the hilt of my sword, not sure when I'd put it there.

The houses didn't quit. They ran within a few feet of the keep's walls. The shops and houses close to the keep were built of brick or stone. Their foundations arched right over the moat, making the defenses nearly useless against a siege. Near the gates, the shops were largest, less open to the public, and more formally adorned. All of them wore little shields by their doors, announcing that they were official shops of the baron. We passed fletchers and blacksmiths working in teams so large that I wondered how anybody moved to do their work. Their products spilled out into the streets. Arrows were so numerous that they were bound like hay, and short swords were made so quickly that some had square, unsharpened edges.

A stone block house rose beside the battlements. The keep's rampart's walls were only a little higher than those on the house, allowing the view to be swamped by the dwelling when we rode close. "That," said Ankind, "is the residence of the baron himself. The keep isn't a comfortable home and was originally built for defense alone.

I glanced up at a top window of the baron's house. It seemingly looked down upon the main gate's allure. If I were an enemy, I'd attack the house and climb the stairs. Then I'd send my men jumping down upon the main gate's walkway, or even the ramparts. Maybe it was a trap, I considered, though there were many other ideas I got just looking around at the way the city had encroached upon the utility of the moat and gate defenses.

I determined that the best way to defend the keep was to fight the enemy in the streets. The problem was there were too many streets, which meant I'd need to have my army topple some houses. The sacking of Roan, the old Vennian capital, was told about in several of the crone's histories, and nowhere in any of them was the chore of scaling keep walls thought worth mentioning, for the wealth was the city itself. I decided not to tell Ankind my discoveries. He already thought my ideas dangerous.

The closer we got, the better turned out were the troops we passed. Clearly, the baron was keeping the serf levies well away from his front door. We passed well enough, having taken the time to clean ourselves from road dust. We looked both disciplined and seasoned in our dark greys and browns.

I turned to Ankind and said, "We're by far the best turned out pikers in the baronage. I hope they don't see through our ruse by noticing the wear on our seats and asking about our horses."

He nodded that he, too, was worried, and then we dismounted and walked right up to the gate where we were asked our lord's name and were told to wait. A captain came out and looked us over, as if he were Sergeant Hadarm giving us an inspection, and then he went back in without a word. When he came back out, he said we were meant to occupy houses eight and nine down on the left side of the street where he pointed. Ankind had to pick two of his men and follow the captain under a great portcullis in front of the draw-bridge.

Ankind had come to rely upon me as his scout, so I was chosen along with second squad leader Wistriff. Glancing up, I saw the portcullis gate was rusted tightly in the upright position. I suppose the gatehouse was a formality, though the huge doors on the other side of the moat looked very stout.

Ankind assigned our few horses to our men. They went to find the houses on their own, saying how eager they were to see a bed and to spend some money on women who couldn't fasten their shirts properly.

It was an honor being invited into the keep, although peasant soldiers usually only visited the keep to do some duty. Perhaps they needed guards for the prisoners, but I expected some chore like gong farming, judging from the smell of the moat. The standing water had no means of releasing the scum. From way up high, privy holes dripped mud honey into the moat like the keep was a tree on a windy fall day, dropping seeds into the swamp.

When I looked up the great wall of the keep, I marveled at its height. I was also amazed at the size of the sandstone blocks that made it up. Here, just inside of the great gates, but outside of the inner gate, was where they'd pour the oil down on my head if I'd not been invited. It was grand just thinking about it, leaving me with the idea that it was better to be invited. Of course, I didn't need to worry, for I was not an enemy; Lady Lettoir had loaned me to the great baron, so I was sworn to not kill him and invite boiling oil on my head.

We walked into the first floor of the keep. The captain left us. He went up the stairs to the next level advising us to find the kitchen at the back of the ground-floor room.

The first floor was filled with square pillars that held up the rest of the building. In between them, scores of soldiers made places to sleep and store their gear. Only the center aisle was kept empty. There were no nobles among the soldiers, though they were the best turned-out professional troops in the land, and many of them bore the slash of sergeants. Several groups of them played stones and dice on the rock floor. There was little else to do beyond cleaning and sharpening our gear.

The kitchen was here, off to the back and separated by the only wall in the place. Clearly, nothing on the first level was suited to nobility.

We looked around the kitchen wall, only to be met by a scullery maid who'd been put there on a stool to tell us we couldn't go in. We told her that we were new and that the captain had told us to get some food, so she came back with a small amount of bread and cheese, along with a bucket of water. It wasn't much, and I worried that we'd be stuck there with the rude and stingy scullions feeding us while our own men set up more properly in the houses where they'd also taken all of our stores.

A long while later, the scullery maids came out with trays of food. The smell made my mouth water all afternoon. They carried pigs and fowl and baked tubers up the stairs, only to come down again and get the breads and butters. Once again they came down and got ale and wine and long bowls filled with raisins. Three or four more trips, and we were famished from watching. Our tongues hung out like we were Yellow Eyes after a long run. Yellow Eyes, of course, wouldn't have put up with it.

The procession of food settled down, so we waited. After a time they brought down the bones and leavings, letting us have what we could pick over, which was nearly nothing. A day of this useless waiting went by until everybody was sure we were going to starve to death. Starving would have been much more pleasant had we not been so close to the kitchen.

I told the sergeant that it was easy to fix the problem by just going into the kitchen and telling the women that we were hungry. He didn't think it was a good idea because we'd been getting up to bow all of the time. We did this every time a noble came down the stairs to leave or came in to go up the steps, and we were clearly not any kind of authority. All of the hints at the scullery maid on the stool had been for nothing, so someone in authority must have determined the method of distribution.

I didn't care about authority. I went into the kitchen, and right off I had to put my hand on the chest of the maid guarding the entrance. She bounced back down on her stool. An older woman came up, and she was good at shaking a spoon. She told me I was supposed to mind my business, or she'd tell some fool named the chamberlain. The rest of them looked at me with contempt, obviously sure that I was going to mind an old woman with a spoon. There, just inside of the doorway, were a couple of oxen hanging half butchered. Another ox turned on a spit, just enough for the baron's nobles I imagined. I pulled my knife out and sliced a tiny chunk off the nearly raw carcass. I let some blood trickle across my chin when I put the bite into my mouth. That got the cooks looking at me differently.

"You, old woman with a spoon, if you don't start cooking the soldiers some food, I'm going to have to tell the baron that you've left his troops to starve." I swallowed the raw meat, licking the blood off my lips.

That didn't move her, for she was stubborn, and so I picked up a large wooden bread turner and invited a couple of the scullery maids to participate by insisting that they stoke the fire up on the spitted beast. I patted them on the bums with the flat of my bread tool to make them understand that the old woman was no longer their minder. I made the minder sit in the corner so she wouldn't make trouble.

I found the women to be good cooks and spirited workers

who had enjoyed no voice, either, in the uneven distribution. In no time at all, I had no need for the bread turner, and we traded bread recipes for some herbal tricks that I knew to be good at improving taste and regularity.

Trays of cheese and the bread departed for the men, along with plenty of buckets of water. They only half cooked the ox, and they didn't spend any time carving it up for us, but they did bring it out hot on a cart, and the five score of us feasted with our knives as if we were all around one fancy campfire.

The captain apparently found out about our trouble, and came down to collect me, Ankind, and Wistriff. We were led up past a hall full of nobles. Their rooms were full, and each had great shining armor that took up more hall space than five fat men. Up one more was the grand throne room where the baron kept his court. There we were told to wait while the baron attended other business of court.

It took no time at all for Baron Eron Prescott of Olan to decide to see us. He was a man the age of my father. A stout but short man, most of his muscles had gone to fat. He wore a robe over a pair of britches. The robe was partly open, showing a hairy chest. His feet were in slippers. In one hand he held a tankard of ale. I had expected something more like the God Sho, white bearded with a crown on his head and looking all serious, but I guess we were just supposed to be impressed that he'd gotten out of bed for us before the late afternoon meal.

Beside him stood a bear of a man who wore chain over a purple shirt with lace trim and black leather britches that must have taken a whole cow to make. He stood at rough attention, one arm on the great throne's back. Every so often the baron whispered to the man as if he dared make no decisions without his advice. Over on the other side of the baron was the man I guessed to be the chamberlain, noted because of the many keys on a belt. He was a thin man in a blue robe. He often leaned over and gave the baron his advice without being asked. The chamberlain was the one who looked at us most unkindly. He eventually announced that it was our turn to be noticed by the baron.

"These three are the ones I've told you about, Lord Prescott. They disrupted the servants in the hall with threats." The chamberlain whispered this to the baron, but my good ears heard every bit of it.

We marched past a score of nobles who stood around a long rug leading up to the great wooden throne. We knelt and waited for the baron to spank us with his words.

"Well then, you are here for tempting the wrath of your baron? This is not a good start for you. Where do you come from, soldiers?" The baron leaned forward.

Ankind answered, "We've come as leaders of the first contingent from Lady Lettoir. As for disruption, we did no such dishonor, High Lord Prescott, for we are always in your service. My men are usually some of the most disciplined of your troops. All of your sergeants and troop leaders went two days without a meal, so I sent my soldier to assist in the kitchen, lest the men starve and have no strength left to fight in the war. We found provisions ample in the kitchen once things were set right and the situation explained to them."

I admired my sergeant mightily for taking such upon himself when it had been my fault that we were here at all.

"I see. Is this true, Chamberlain?"

The chamberlain answered with a lie that he didn't know I could hear: "They'd been fed well enough from the lord's own table, and to include all the cheeses and breads the cooks could make. It seemed they had an interest in an ox."

"Well now, my man tells me a different story."

I stood, and took one step forward. I would not have my sergeant punished for my impatience. "The chamberlain's intentions may not have been understood, my Lord. The cheese and bread were not forthcoming, and the pickings were so little that they wouldn't have fed a squad, much less the five score below. As for the ox, it was I who picked it, for it alone seemed the quickest solution to our problem. As you know, an ox alone is plenty for five score, so I put the maids to flaming the closest spitted beast at once."

"And who are you to call my chamberlain mistaken and to tell my maids their duty?" asked the baron.

"I am Abe, soldier on loan to the baron, eager to kill the enemy of the king in battle, as are all below who did feast upon the ox. Being ready for battle is a soldier's duty, for fighting appeals to us." I pulled my sword from my sheath and raised it toward the ceiling of timbers.

The giant beside the baron took a step up but then waited when he saw that I meant no harm, and that the baron had his hand out halting him.

The baron stared at me for a long while, but then he laughed, motioning with his hand for me to lower my sword before my arm wore out. I put it back into my sheath. He said to Ankind, "I suspect you have your hands full with this one, Sergeant."

"That I do, my Lord, but he is worth the trouble. He is the best scout I've ever seen. At times I suspect he can see through the hills themselves. Used properly, I suspect he will save the lives of many of the king's soldiers."

"Well then, it is not for manners that he was recruited, I suppose," observed the baron.

Ankind answered, "He is being tutored in the skill, my Lord, having come from the deep and mountainous passes where he must have learned his scouting skills from the bears. Abe is coarse in manners, but Lady Lettoir didn't see lordly manners as the skill she needed when she hired him on."

The baron looked at his chamberlain and then back at me. I could see by looking into his eyes that, in spite of his lazy and excessively fed condition, the baron took pride in his judgment.

"Lady Lettoir seems a wise noble, for a woman. All right then, I have decided. I have to punish you, you know. So, I've decided that you and your soldiers should be sent to the duke's front line forces as quickly as we can send you. Will that suit you, my chamberlain?"

The thin man looked stricken. I had to agree; waiting around in the keep was worse. Being sent on seemed quite the reward to me. None of us had the faintest idea why we were waiting in Helfax anyway.

The baron turned to the large man who'd not yet spoken. "Brother, can you arrange to send Lady Lettoir's scouts forward? Will the next group formed have good use for the contingent?"

"I will be leading the next, Eron. Did you forget that we bargained that the next group would be my own guard and that I'd hand-pick the first fifty score in my own personal corps?" I later learned that the baron's brother was named Sir Randolf.

"How many are you?" asked the baron.

"Only four short of a score, my Lord, though the lady is working toward three times our number in non-professional footmen after she has spent some time in their training," said Ankind.

Sir Randolf's mood lightened. "I see no problem with including so few."

"Then it is settled. Sergeant, take your unmannered but eager men from the keep, and go to the master of provisions, three buildings down from the main gate. Tell him that the baron has seen fit to provision your sixteen for battle. Account for your current provisions, and then see him so he may fill the remainder. Ask no more than you need for a week's march, for I have a vast army to assemble. You will have no use for any ox, which should please my chamberlain. The day after tomorrow, join the forces gathering two miles on the north road. The master shall tell you the captain under whom you are assigned. My brother marches by end week."

"Thank you, my Baron," said Sergeant Ankind. We all bowed.

I was pleased to be done with the keep. Donjons are not fit for people, as they are cold, damp, surrounded by rock, and everybody always on display. It was the last part that I disliked the most, given that I had little privacy for myself as a woman. Some things couldn't be hidden forever from plain view, for my breasts would not stop their growth, and I'd felt my first aches of the month as I'd stood before the fat old baron. The magic held, though I'd never tested my fellow soldiers with a public display of my issues.

Even more, I felt myself being drawn to the battle with an ache worse than my time. It was like the smell of food in the kitchen after two days of crumbs. The next time I pulled a weapon out, I knew it would not be to swat scullery maids.

Chapter Eight

Middle spring displayed its merry petals. They hid a little of the danger when I rode my horse down the cliff-side trail. By the ill-draw of twigs, I'd been lumped with Hobar and Horatio, though, as soon as we left camp, the pair informed me that Hobar led us. I decided that, instead of making a point of it, I'd yield and amuse myself with the results.

Yellow Eyes had better scout sense than either man. He couldn't make it this far away from his family, so I'd not seen him in a whole season. I'd tried to make friends with some of his relatives, but they proved shy. They worried about our war so close to their dens.

As for the patrol, I determined that it was going just fine, excepting that there were maybe as many as a half dozen enemy hidden right over the next ridge, and Hobar hadn't smelled any of them yet. I felt sure I'd see something interesting pretty soon.

"You stay in back. Watch our rear," Hobar commanded. He laughed. I fell back, knowing I'd see the results of his decisions better from behind.

I called up, "Hobar, perhaps—"

"Silence, you fool! And stay out of our way."

He'd said that louder than I'd been, so I slowed a little further. Hobar always told me that I didn't know anything, sometimes when it was important, and even when we both knew I was right.

The instructions were to never let ourselves be seen, and to come back as soon as we saw something. I suppose they assumed we'd always see them first. The whole army reacted in response to our information. We were sent somewhere else. That was the pattern.

Sir Randolf wanted all of the glory for himself. The only thing I'd used my sword for was practice and for trimming game we illegally chanced upon in what they called the rear area. I felt less than pleased with Sir Randolf, though he said he was winning his part of the war for the king and that he pushed Lacellor's green clothed soldiers all over the forest.

Just before Randolf sent his army after what we found, the holes we scouted next door filled up with the relocating enemy because they heard him coming. That made my job easier and harder, for Randolf accused us of misinforming him, while we had no trouble at all finding more enemy to report.

My solution for his suspicion was to sneak into the enemy camps and bring back souvenirs so Ankind had something to show Randolf. Randolf told Ankind that they weren't good enough to convince him, so one night I stole a whole suit of armor. Such wasn't easy because of the tinkling and clattering. That only made Randolf angrier, saying that such an act was less than chivalrous. I had no idea what that meant at first. Even after Ankind explained it to me, I thought he'd made it up.

Not that I didn't trust Ankind—much the opposite. In fact, I liked him a lot. He wasn't really tall, but, then again, he bore pretty muscles and fought well. I knew this from our training where I only had to cheat a little to let him win. His features weren't particularly dark, which I'd always been told meant handsome, and his almost hairless face cratered in spots, but I found him appealing in the moonlight.

He even taught me manners, something I'd never expected from a man. He took my side in arguments all the time and was as fine a leader as Sergeant Hadarm. He gave me my head in scouting, too, which meant he knew my worth. Only my mother and the crone had thought me worth much. Even Lady Lettoir had shown some reservations about me.

I looked at him often. And, he started catching me looking at him more than the normal amount. That was where we had our first serious disagreement. It was a hiss mostly, him not keen on anybody else knowing he was upset about the familiar looks I'd been giving.

I looked all over in my book for a special spell that would let him see me true and not let anybody else know, but it wasn't in there. Even if one existed, I wasn't sure I could trust him with the knowledge.

There was a love spell though. In fact, there seemed several. It was very confusing to me, once I sat long enough and thought about it. Could I use a love spell? Did I want to be stuck to a man and be put in some shack to raise his babies and plow his fields? Who would then keep him from being killed under the baron's brother's poor leadership? How was I to get into the battle, like the cursed extra soul inside of me kept telling me I had to do?

When he snarled at me, I pretended it was just his imagination that told him I'd been looking at him in a sinful manner. I didn't know how the coupling could work anyway. It was a miserable topic.

I have better eyes than anybody, so I waited until it got dark and the moon left before I looked at him. I made myself increasingly miserable doing it. It ached like times when I'd gone hungry to not do it, and almost as much when I did. I had to stop, and that led to me not talking to him much, which only made him wonder about my sexual nature even more, which I didn't want him doing, whichever way he unraveled it. I took care of that by going out on most of the patrols where I couldn't look at Sergeant Ankind at all.

This whole thing with Ankind was something that wasn't

meant to happen. I knew that. Something grand waited afoot for me, bigger than just making babies in a shack. I didn't know what it was, but it was as real as the three archers and four pike holders hiding over in the shrubs to the left side of the trail Hobar led us down at the moment.

I thought that maybe I'd let Hobar and Horatio go on in and get themselves killed. Goddess knows I hated them. I hadn't seen much real action either, but then I thought about Ankind again, and how much he trusted me to keep them safe, so I swore at Sho under my breath and galloped up to Horatio.

I told him, "This might be the perfect place for an ambush."

He didn't even turn to me, though he looked around some and saw none of nature's signs. Then he kicked his horse, catching up to Hobar. I waited for him to tell our fearless leader about my suspicions, but I'd not impressed Horatio with enough urgency, such as hitting him with a rock. He rode without mentioning a thing to his twin idiot.

Horatio left me no more moments. We'd pressed too closely, and only by being last did I find myself capable of diverting Ella from the disaster. I slid left through the pines which remained the last bit of cover.

My swift charge hit the archers from the rear. Ella's chest and legs rolled them over as I sliced a few minor cuts across their flailing arms and torsos.

I was supposed to scout them, not kill them, which seemed pretty naïve at times. I breezed by the first pikeman and only took off one of his hands. The hand clung to the spear as it fell into the bushes. The others came running, but I galloped clear across the trail and into the other pines before they could get a good angle and toss a couple of spears at my tail.

Later, when I had the time to think about it, I can't say I liked the vicious spirit that rose up from within me next. It left a bad taste in my mouth, the way I turned upon those farmer soldiers.

The spears fell too close. That angered me because one clipped Ella's flank. I plucked one of their spears out of the ground as I circled around and came at them again. What came next was not the work of Abi, for the spirit of a warrior crone took possession of my body.

One holding his last spear saw my spear coming at him. He acted so shocked that his arms and legs reached in both directions, leaving his body to take the spear right in the middle. He couldn't even fall over neatly when it came half the way through, toppling him over into a tree like he was a one legged chair. He wasn't dead right away, though his legs wouldn't work, and the blood came pumping out around the shaft. His hands gripped the thing that killed him. He pulled at it, but the pain kept him from moving it much, and then he weakened as he screamed himself to death in a series of yells that steadily quieted.

That was very interesting, and I had to go back and watch it after I'd put my blade through the collarbone of a second piker who was trying to pick up the other fellow's spear. I felt sorry for the man who had taken so long to die from my spearing, but he shouldn't have been my enemy.

When he quieted, I glanced around for the last unwounded footman. He had run out of sight, well down the path, racing for home. I tracked him with my horse. When I got close, I saw him look back. He sounded winded, and he staggered. His feet took him through bushes and saplings. When I got closer, he became faster for a minute, and then just fell over in the mud. I stood my horse over him while I scanned the area for other enemy, finding none. He caught his breath enough to roll over and fumbled backwards on his hands until he'd backed himself through some weeds up against a tree.

He wasn't pretty because he was just a thinly-fed serf, as

had been the other six. I wouldn't have known him for a soldier, had he not tossed a pike at me earlier. The running had soaked his pitiful rag of a shirt with sweat. He could barely breathe. Curious, I watched him, for I'd not been able to kill or speak to the enemy in all of my scouting.

Even though I had him well heeled, he showed a spark of courage. He grunted at me for watching him suffer. Then he said the unexpected: "Ah, I'm to be killed by a traitor. A traitor who has gored my friend. Oh, the horror of it. It's true. Traitors ain't got no souls!"

"Did Sho's priests teach you that we have no souls?" The question was first among a host of new wonders he'd raised within me.

"Don't you know that this war is about Sho, a miserable God if ever there was one." He spat before adding, "King Falstaff has sinned, setting one god above the others. His god is made of nothing. We … we suffer for nothing."

"He is not false. I have met him, though I agree with you that he is often distasteful." I spit my own wad upon his own.

"You ain't met him. He is falsehood, they say."

"Do I have a reason to lie to you here, now, like this, with my sword bloody and in my hand? Oh, to lie for a reason is sound enough, but I have no reason to lie to my enemy, whom I should slay without this conversation."

"Well then, perhaps he is a god like the others. Only a small one. One thinking too high on himself."

I laughed. The serf looked nervous though. To ease his mind, I said, "That is true. I know it for a fact, and he as much as confessed it to me as he negotiated for my soul while in a glen. He couldn't easily have it though, for I'd loaned it to the Goddess."

"You once worshiped this Goddess, you say. So now you deal with the dark one. I see you a traitor to yourself, as well a killer."

He was getting his wind back as he argued with me. I thought I'd have to slay him soon if I didn't want to run him to ground again.

"No, no, that isn't how it happened. I beat his champion fairly, and I am still the Goddess's servant, though I'd appreciate it if you kept that a secret."

"From who? Sho is listening? I confess. I included him in the gods I prayed to as I ran from your ugly horse. Now I unconfess it, traitor. I cannot risk my soul, if I am to die."

I decided I couldn't kill him, for he was only a peasant, and it is a rare peasant who speaks so well and with such conviction of thought. Yet, any more mention of treason would have me losing my generous mood. "I have to ask you to also stop calling me a traitor. I am in service to my king and baron, under loan of Lady Lettoir. Never have I changed sides in this battle."

"Then you are not one of the golden ones? You be not from the north?"

"I know nothing of northerners, though I can tell you much of ancient histories. Tell me about them." I leaned over my pommel, genuinely interested in any news I could spy out of the man and bring back to my sergeant.

"Why not? It is no secret. The Debrecians once fought your king. They say they will fight him again. In their own, I suppose. I hear they is enchanted and know no fear. When I saw you, I thought I seen one—a traitor one. Curse my ill luck. A Debrecian rightfully frightens us. Else, if we'd known you be nobody, I'd have fought better. Me friends, too."

He grew bolder and had his wind back, though I could tell by his posture that his side still stitched.

"Are there many of these Debazings?"

"Debrecians. Yes, there is many as the stars. They breed heartily. Only for warriors though. Thousands of magical warriors, all as tall as you. You'll see. They be descending on the bastards of Sho, showing their blazing swords of fire, and riding huge horses that no tire. I wish I be alive to see it!"

"You can if you do me one favor, for I see no need to kill you and have decided that your courage, though late, is handsome to me."

"For what service, lassie? Why spare this serf when we be at war? I will no give you my soul."

The term lassie left me speechless. He'd seen me as a woman. Ah, I'd forgotten to include the enemy in my spell this time, I realized. I suddenly had more questions for him, and yet I'd offered him only one bargain. I felt honor bound to continue, only I had to change my request completely around from the boast I'd intended to have him tell his friends: "Tell none of me. Say that you fell upon a score of troops, and have your fellows join in the lie. I wish no attention upon myself in this particular matter."

"Yes. That I can do to save all of us from our sergeant's wrath. To say that we were beaten. Ah, by one woman owning no skill …. They might drop us in the oubliettes and leave us whole to rot, or worse. I hear my Lord's pit walls come together in a point. They be no place for a man to put his feet."

"Then it is done between us. Keep your life as well as your soul. Also, you are right to be wary of Sho, for so am I. Go help your fellows. Some are carrion, but most are in need of someone to guide them home. I will see you on the battlefield, fine serf. If I make note of you, I will spare you again. If you are in my way, even Sho can't save you from my lacking skill."

That said, I rode away from him. My stomach churned to go back and kill him, for it wasn't in my warrior nature to be generous with an enemy, and this one had offended me several times with the worst kind of insults imaginable - those that are honest. There'd been that part about being a traitor, too. I'd felt it deep, and knew not why.

I had to work at pity and patience, I knew, as I rode my horse back past the carnage. I avoided the archers, some of whom might have recovered enough to take a shot at my flank.

When I met the trail, I found nothing but tracks. Hobar and Horatio had not come one step closer than where I'd last seen them. The trail wasn't fresh, so they'd not discussed my abandonment long, perhaps not even long enough to see me turn on the footmen a second time. Oddly, I felt better knowing that, not wanting them to see me as I was in a real, face-to-face fight. I'd played half a soldier among them in practice, and thought it best if I had my secrets.

Their hooves led straight toward home. Fools led the enemy back to their own camps. Of course, they didn't know that—I'd not taught it to them.

Other things troubled me more than those two. I had to think about how I was going to explain away making ourselves so obvious to the enemy.

Hobar would certainly claim that I'd led us into a trap, and then that I'd pointed us out by being hasty, and then that I'd killed them too much, and then maybe even that I hadn't killed all of them—the last half of which he wouldn't even know because he'd not been brave enough to linger.

So I had to worry over his lying—though nobody believed him much.

That only meant I'd have to talk to the sergeant, and I didn't want to talk to the sergeant because I felt like I needed to touch his body. It was a very uncomfortable subject, so I hoped he'd only need me to talk to him a little bit, and maybe do it when I was busy with something else to look at and rub on.

I had those thoughts racing around inside of me, and also the news about those Debrecians who the peasant had explained were tall warriors with the kind of skills I'd not seen much of among our men. I would surely like to fight one of those horsemen. The crone in me felt eager for a repeat of the big demon I'd met in the woods. I wondered if these Debrecians wore white. I hated the color white and itched to get at it.

I itched to get at the Debrecians, too, now that I'd heard of them. Something inside of me told me I had to go see them and put them in their place. It wasn't even thinking stuff, just feelings inside of me, like a part of my spirit telling me to go find them.

I'd need my teacher's sword to have a go at a bunch of those kinds of soldiers. In no time, I had it out and swirled it around in all the forms and fashions the crone ghost had taught me.

Getting off my horse, hidden right there in the woods between my lines and the enemy's, I summoned up the crone in broad daylight, and she came to me. She had a smile on her face so broad that I counted her missing teeth. It was strange seeing her so happy, but she couldn't tell me why she was so pleased with herself. Then we fought, and she wasn't easy on me, for she told me in my head that when I met the Debrecians, I'd have to unlearn all of the pretending I'd been doing in practice with the soldiers of Helfax. She said that I'd need all of the skill that I had just to fight off one of them. For her making me think that, I sliced her up into so many pieces that she retired for the day, and then I laughed at her for saying something stupid.

When I got to my horse, Ella kicked around in place. A pack of wolves stood on the surrounding ridges. I knew them for the ones who lived around in these parts of the woods, and I gave them a nod for the courtesy of not hiding their smell. No male leader walked out to say hello, for they were all bitches and older cubs. They just watched carefully as I left. Perhaps they were drawn by the blood on my britches and upon my horse's flanks, but it wasn't the kind of blood smell that would make any smart wolf hungry, so I had my doubts and ended up not knowing why they'd come to watch me at all.

Maybe they were drawn by my troubled mind, for I had yet another problem that I couldn't sort out as I aimed my horse into the lane set aside for us scouts. I looked into the eyes of those who watched me coming. They noticed the blood that dripped and lay dried on me and my horse as we took our time. I tested the looks to see if anybody else could see me as a woman. Maybe the spell had worn off. I wondered, but then I noticed that they were not dwelling on my serious face long. It must have been because the peasant was foreign that he recognized my womanhood.

The sergeant was angry, something I felt even before I saw him. He would be talking to me a long time. I aimed toward the roped off pasture, got down and took care of my horse first. That way I'd have something to look at and something to keep busy in my hands as he came over and started in on me.

"What have you been off to, Abe?" asked the sergeant. Everybody else wandered within earshot. Hobar and Horatio nudged closest.

"We were in the woods, scouting, Sergeant, when we came upon seven scouts on foot, three of them archers, and four pikers. They—"

"They were not a score or better?"

"No there were—"

"There were at least a score," lied Hobar. "We were about to turn back and report this, but then he—"

It was my turn to interrupt: "There were seven! Exactly! I sorted them all out, so I know the number. I had no choice but to take them quickly, as Hobar had decided to lead us into their trap—against my advice. Once I exposed them, these two fled. The only thing I am sorry for is saving them before the ambush was properly sprung."

"There were a score, and he nearly got us killed. He disobeyed my order to—"

"Enough! Most of us have the sense to let our scout do his work." Ankind backed Hobar off with his stance. "Let's leave it as a scouting squad of superior numbers." He glared at me and then the two idiots.

I started cleaning the blood off my horse's legs. There was only one among us with blood on his horse. Let the men think for themselves who was a liar. I sensed that the sergeant understood my message clearly. I dared not look at him.

"We were ambushed," said Hobar, going along with the sergeant's idea. "There were more of them than us. We were told to report back."

"That I can see. Now, no more word of it. I'll report it as an ambush that was won in our favor. It'll have to be enough. It might have been worse, and we can't expect to never be discovered in the course of our duties," said Sergeant Ankind.

"There is more." When he looked at me, I continued, "There is a new ally with Sir Lacellor. One of their footmen spoke of a tribe named Debrecian. He said they were not here in force but were scouting the situation and seeking a time in their favor to announce their alliance."

"The man was a liar!" Wistriff shouted from the pack of soldiers. Wistriff was our oldest soldier. He'd been professionally worn and led the other squad because of an even temperament.

I responded, "I didn't see him as a liar, and I have known many, having much practice in the craft, Wistriff."

"Well, he was a liar just the same. We lost half of our men in the last war, but we lost most of them putting down the Debrecians. There was only a company or two of them, but far fewer in their final retreat, for we'd come to want them all dead, each costing us dearly. We kept only a few as slave wives. They were demons in the night, worth any score of our own in a battle, and they were worse in the day. The man must have been lying."

"You can't wish a bad thing away, Wistriff," insisted our sergeant.

"I can wish whatever I want away, Ankind. I wish this away. See, it is done! Don't speak of this again within sight of my ears, Abe, for I am an old soldier, and there is a limit to what I can bear."

I found that most interesting, for I held no grudge against old Wistriff. I'd been on patrol with him, and though overly cautious, I'd never thought him a coward.

"We'll have to report this to Sir Randolf," said Sergeant Ankind.

"I don't favor seeing the man."

"Neither do I, but you are the one with the report, and I'll not go to the baron's brother without my source."

Thus, we came to be walking toward the nobles' portion of the camp. It was up on a hill a ways off, for we'd no place in any of the ranks. The captains of the pikers had no use for us because we had horses. The knights didn't think we were cavalry since we owned no armor and had no lands. As light cavalry, we most closely resembled Sho's White Shirts rodents, here a small but influential contingent. They hung around the nobles like tame ducks that were on the edge of pecking any children who came around while the adults were feeding them. All of this we waded through, in order of standing, on the way to Sir Randolf, brother of our baron.

On the way, we passed a man hanging off a rope. They'd hanged many from the beam they'd constructed just for hanging troops the nobles found wanting. They'd left his hands free so he could entertain them by clawing himself about the neck in his last minutes. The man had died a long time ago. His face was nearly black and his body bloated full as a plum. Nobody paid him much attention anymore, only hoping that they could cut him down soon, for he drew flies and smelled terrible. They'd already dug him a hole. They were probably hoping to cover him up as soon as they got word that the nobles were through giving us a lesson.

There, just under him, I broke the law against peasants reading and read a sign that said, *Killed for ravaging peasant lands*. In other words, he'd died trying to find some food. Sir Randolf almost never gave us anything to eat, and then he'd ordered that nobody could get their food from the local landholder's fields. Every so often, Randolf killed someone with a rope in order to prove that he was serious about asking everybody to starve themselves to death. I looked around at the pikers camped nearby, none of them law abiding and dead of no food yet, though some were trying, and there was no bark left on any of the near trees.

Living near the edge of camp, we were the worst of sinners and thriving. Ankind sent his messenger to his man near Helfax, paying for almost nothing but grain off the earnings for a stolen enemy horse at a time. He sent me to steal horses every few days, which I confess was some of the best fun I had there. I had no problem finding food in the woods and scrounged or illegally killed without troubling the peasants or enemy at all.

Of course, Randolf wouldn't see raiding or poaching as fair play, and he suspected us of breaking the rules more than anybody else. He always looked at his soldiers' bellies first off, to see if we were suspicious. Ankind always told him that we'd stumbled up on the enemy camp while they were cooking something grander than the gruel pot. It was an old excuse that worked all of the time because as curious as Randolf acted while regarding our meaty bodies, he seemed more eager to forget us and act like he'd never known us at all the next time we came to tell him something.

Randolf had us sit outside of the back door of his tent for most of the night while he ate and got drunk with his friends. Then he went to bed. In the morning the baron's guards came out to tell us that we were not supposed to be loitering around the tent of the baron's brother, so Ankind told them again that we were scouts who had come to report important information. It was midday when they said we could go in and tell him what we had found out.

We knelt, though I wasn't happy to do it because there were White Shirts in the tent with him. I noticed Sir Allen Wencor, second son to High Lord Wencor, second cousin to Baron Eron Prescott of Olan. His more soldierly minder kept him company. I suspected him of being a more dangerous man with a smaller name. Kneeling seemed a lot like offering my head, and my mood was such that I wanted my sword in my hand so I could paint the white sheets on the bodies before me.

Randolf had us rise. He looked at our bellies, but then he looked at the blood still on my britches and apparently decided to let Ankind give his report instead.

"We have come across scouts, my Lord, in the woods to the north. They were a superior force in ambush, so we couldn't avoid them, but they took many losses. We did not. One, near death, confessed that he heard the Debrecians intend to enter the fight on the side of Sir Lacellor. That is our report of the events one day past, this noon."

"And you took this long to report to your lord?" asked Sir Allen. His voice was a squeak behind a face that was too young to shave. I imagined giving him his first visit with the blade.

Ankind said, "We were asked to wait outside, my Lord."

"It matters not, at this point. We already know this information. In the future, Sergeant, report more timely." I supposed that Randolf had been delayed from his next meal.

"Then you know of the Debrecians, ser?" asked Ankind.

"Yes. I said you may go. Don't make me repeat myself."

The boy in white wasn't done with us though. He pointed at me. "It's you, the insubordinate one. I remember you from the road!"

"Is that so?" Sir Randolf bore down on me with his eyes.

"Yes, that's him," added the older White Shirt. Like I said, a most dangerous man.

"We can't have insolence," said the baron's brother. "What do you say for yourself?"

Ankind nudged forward. "Ser, Abe is my best scout. He is not used to nobles and meant no disrespect. He has been taught better manners since. I tutor him daily, as you can see by his kneeling, my Lord."

"Well, that is good," said Randolf, which told me that he'd not bothered to remember me from the first time Ankind had used that excuse in front of his brother.

"I must have at least a little satisfaction. A token," demanded the younger White Shirt.

"Very well then," said Randolf. "Guards, put this man in holding for the rest of the day. Release him chastened at nightfall so that he can get back to his duties. Maybe next time he'll find some useful information for a change."

They grabbed me. I'd not have put up with it had I not felt Ankind's hands on my other arm. It was like he was telling me to not fight the inconvenience.

"Oh, and let him keep his sword and knife as he is pitched in," said Randolf. "Let's have some sport, and see if he can keep them. I'm interested in hearing your report on how it goes when he is released, or dragged, from the prison."

Ankind stopped. "Ser, there may be blood in this. Should my man be blamed if—"

"Enough! Do you wish to join your man, Sergeant?"

"No, Ser. Come along, Abe. You must pay for your insolence toward these fair lords." He rushed me out with the help of the other guard.

I could have killed both of them and made a run for it, but I had no heart for killing a half starved guard and the sergeant I loved, so I let them lead me to the peasant's hut that had been boarded up and made into their prison. On the other hand, I was going to kill the young man in white and his minder as well. I would do so at my leisure, I decided, sometime after this inconvenience was forgotten. They wouldn't see it coming.

I saw the eyes of a squatting prisoner. He was blinded by the light when they swung open the heavy wooden door. The smell of urine assailed me, as did the heat of stale sweat and little air. The door guard pitched me to my knees onto a floor covered by a depth of straw. The prison was small, sunken and one room. The windows had been boarded over, making the room perpetually dark, though it was the heat of noon. I let my eyes adjust to the depths and corners, counted the eyes and imaged cutting them in half.

Only one prisoner sat at each of three corners. One corner remained bare for me, though they'd used that one for a piss pot. I shied along the wall over toward the large man who looked least trustworthy. I wanted him nearest to me so we'd be over with it soon. He didn't move though, nor, as my eyes adjusted, did he prove to be the most dangerous.

That was the woman across from me. She was the strangest woman I'd ever seen. She wore baggy britches under a half skirt. Her britches had been ripped away below the knees. The lost parts were bandages over a wound that still seeped blood near her ankle. The wound was serious, for the calf muscles had snapped loose and bunched behind her knee in a knot. I couldn't ignore her pain. I felt it in my mind. I didn't know why her pain caused this sensation within me when the pain of so many others had caused so little effect.

Beaten as well, she wasn't looking at me or anyone else, but seemed to be sleeping without breathing much or even closing her eyes. From the look of her face, she was dead, but I could hear her heart beating, measuring the moments like a mouse does when waiting to race away from Yellow Eyes as soon as the mouse finds out that staying still is not going to help.

I'd only once seen a wounded leg like that: one well scarred over and on the leg of my own mother.

My eyes finally picked out the details of my company. The men looked nervous about something. I didn't think I worried them, for they stared at the wounded woman lying by the wall. Their eyes were not good. I could tell that they looked for shadowy signs that she might shift. Both men wore scratches and bruises across their faces, as if they'd met with a bobcat and a board. I put one and one together, and laughed.

"What is so amusing?" asked the smaller man who was almost all the way across the room from me.

"I indulged my imagination. Is there ever a place where men forget the urge to breed?"

The big man beside me said, "It wasn't me. I know better than to try to mount a Debrecian, though in her tantrum, she took the occasion to beat on me as well. The room is not big enough to get out of the way of such a hellion, even wounded as she is. How some might want to take such foul women as slave wives is beyond me."

"She is to be a slave then?"

"Yes. The first we've seen—perhaps a spy. Her Debrecian blood is why they have cut her; so she won't run or kick. The men who want will take turns riding her until tame or dead. Though, if you were to ask me, I'd rather try bucking a team of wild boars. The nobles think it's sporting to see if any of our men can bring one to heel. The one who does gets her as his gift and is let go of his duty."

I watched her then with new interest. Her eyes stirred and seemed to see my shape just a little. They were warnings, though I detected a heightened curiosity as well.

My questions were many. "A Debrecian she is then. I'd be interested in knowing more about such a woman. They say that their soldiers are better than any in Lacellor's army. If their men are as fierce as this woman seems to be, it may be true. Do they bring their women to the battlefield like some of our lords do? Perhaps she is a noble's woman and feels that she is entitled better treatment? This does seem harsh. I don't favor treating her too poorly."

"More like, do they bring their men? I doubt there were many choices of treatment, once the nobles decided not to kill her outright and to make sport of her instead," the giant man said.

"She is as fierce as all that then?" I laughed again.

The woman spat quite accurately at me. "Are you what they call a whore?" Her accented words were far more clearly spoken than I'd expected. It was also apparent that my enemies saw me as a woman, this being the second of two who'd seen past my disguise. There was the flaw in my new spell.

"I am a warrior, like any other man here," I warned her. Just to make myself clear, I pulled my knife out and my sharpening stone as well. I slid the blade across the stone. Sparks briefly lit the darkened room.

The men took notice. Their eyes had not been good enough to see that I'd come into their jail with my weapons. As for the Debrecian woman, I could tell that her eyes were little better than theirs, though she hid her deficiencies better behind her careful and stalking nature.

The smaller man across from me said, "You should give me that knife. I am good with it, and I can help us break out with it when the guards are unaware."

He, I didn't like, so I walked across the room to him.

"Here, you may do better with this then, since you are the best among us with a blade." I pulled the hilt of my sword out of its sheath, banging him on the head with it. The bounce was good enough to send the sword right back into the sheath. He fell over, stunned.

"But, then again, maybe you are not so good," I told him as I returned to my wall.

The woman across from me laughed, though while choking. "You are not a whore then. You interest me. Why have they put you with us, so armed?"

"The baron's brother thinks it sporting. He imagines I might not leave here alive."

I pointed to the man across the way, though they probably didn't see my fingers. "That man is a fool to think he can escape with my weapon, for the guards have been tripled, and the whole camp is now betting on who will be alive among us by nightfall. As I see it, the only sport is not in who will emerge alive, but how many. As to who dies, I put my coppers on the White Shirt who inspired this insult."

"You think much of yourself. They will not like that," said the Debrecian.

"I have been destined by the Goddess to kill many. So far, the number is tiny, and so I know that my end is not near in this life."

"Invoking the Goddess? Are you daft?" asked the big man beside me.

I nicked his neck where I reached over and put my knife up close. He was so blinded by the darkness that he'd not even seen it coming. "Do you have a loose tongue? Did you not just hear me tell you that I was willing to leave here without killing you? All I ask is that you keep confidence, and mind your own business! After all, I'm just trying to have a conversation."

"I see your point. Uh, thank you."

He wasn't an overly bad man, I determined. I'd overreacted, as Ankind always told me I tended to do. I put my knife away.

"Are there others like you?" asked the Debrecian, as if we'd not even been interrupted.

"I am alone. They see me as a man and thus don't mistreat me more than they do themselves." I hoped that she'd caught my hint.

"How can this be? It is most curious. Sho's men are blind. Even in this darkness, I see you better."

I confided, "I can confirm that blindness. These are not Sho's men though. They are simple peasants who suffer from maltreatment, only to later return to lands that are barren. They will be short their taxes and not make next winter. It's Sho's men who put us here, and it is Sho's men who will pay—them and the well born—not these poor, suffering fools."

"Spoken with the weighing judgment and compassion of a queen's kin. Are you sure we don't know one another's spirit?" The Debrecian answered her own question: "No, of course not. I tend toward the angry nature of the shaman warlord. For all of your gloating, you did not kill the man across the way. There is something else within you. There is little generosity within shamans, save for the ill when she reaches for her bag of herbs and healing spells."

"So you have witches who know the value of herbs?"

"Our shaman knows some herb-craft and spells to aid us, but she is not a witch by trade. Witches live peaceful lives and have no place in the duties of our warriors. They are even in temperament and live for their herbs and study. No, our shaman leads us into battle. She carries her claws before us, and even your skills with all of your blades won't help you when her company falls upon you. Like I say, I tend toward her disposition nearly always and hope to be a shaman in my next life; that is why I am not good at conversation."

"On the contrary, I find your conversation agrees with me. It is too bad that we are enemies, and I must kill you," I told her.

"Please do kill me. I am in great pain, and when the pain eases, I have no desire to find myself broken and alive as their slave. Send me back to my tribe as newborn."

"I didn't mean that I should kill you in particular, for there is no honor in killing the wounded and the enemy's women. I meant only that you are the enemy in general, and when I meet the enemy in battle, I shall kill them, for this has become my only worth."

"That is curious. I feel your words, for I cannot see you in the darkness. Because of this, a part of me thinks what you say is true. A part of me thinks not."

That to mull over, we all sank into an appropriate malaise, as I suppose is the duty of the imprisoned.

Chapter Nine

In the end, Sergeant Ankind was terribly pleased that I had not killed anyone. This was true even though he'd bet a White Shirt, who'd gotten odds that nobody would get killed at all, which was both the case and insulting.

As soon as I got back to our camp and had some food and rest, I started puzzling over how I was going to go about murdering Sir Allen Wencor, second son to High Lord Wencor, second cousin to Baron Eron Prescott of Olan and his smaller named minder. It seemed that our paths never really crossed. The white knights made matters worse by hanging around the nobles where I'd be caught if I fought them.

My idea was to magically call them up in the woods like what had happened to the White Shirt knight who had been Sir Allen's equal. That was very fun in my memory. The Goddess remained scarce by staying invisible though. She only whispered into my imagination. I went wanting and grew impatient for blood.

I asked my sergeant about it, and he told me that I was out of my mind for even thinking it and, in particular, crazy to ask anybody about it—even him. So, I pressed Ankind on it because it riled him, and I wanted to watch him fuss.

"Abe, don't you know that you are a peasant? As high and mighty as you're ever likely to be is a sergeant like me. Every noble is bigger than you. Even the captains are knights and cousins of high nobles, and thus counted among them due to blood. You are nothing in their sight, and, if they are displeased by your words, they can hang you or something worse. I know I have spoken to you about this before."

He was across from me at the fire when he said this. The wood was green and full of smoke.

"I hear you, but it's not right. They know nothing about their own army, and all I can see of their worth is in their better food and clothing. Maybe they think they are better than us because they wear shiny metal, or maybe because they ride two horses. That sort of thing holds no coin with me, for the crone taught me that a person earns one's place, even if born to a different duty."

Sergeant Ankind tamped hard at the flames. "The crone was wrong about lots of things, it seems to me. What would the world be like if everybody was a noble? Don't you see the mess it would make? I think we have spoken enough on this."

I had to think about it some, for he had a point. I stirred the campfire flames with a stick, but then the solution hit me: "We could test them. If someone born a noble is found wanting, then we can kick them out of the castles and keeps. And, if they need more nobles, we can make the sergeants into captains and the captains into first cousins of the baron, and on up. And, the brother of the baron could be someone else, too."

Ankind's eyes narrowed. "Yes, Abe, that might work if there was no special problem with your idea, such as, who would do the testing and how would it be done. And then who would convince the baron to push his own kin out of the keep? Once gone, they'd have no idea how to breed horses, or even pigs and wheat. Which of the peasants would abandon their land for the new peasants from the keep? You should worry as well for their lady folk, who would have to find a place in the cabin for their fancy dresses and embroidery. Who would do that and where would they get the brightly dyed yarn? It is not good that we are even speaking of such, Abe. They would hang us both if they knew we were making up bad ideas about how our kin should rearrange themselves."

My sergeant's eyes wandered left and right. "Did I not talk to you about this before?"

"That you did." I thought some then asked, "I suppose I can't kill this Sir Allen Wencor, who has offended me more than I have in return, just because I talked to him in an unmannered way?"

"That's what I am saying. He is a noble, and you are not a noble. That is how God intended it to be, so we can sort out our lands and our kin and even our peace. We will not speak of this again."

I stood up as if to leave, but, as I spoke, I settled back on a smoother part of the log seat, a little farther from the flames. "That is a good idea, Sergeant, for it discourages me to think about it the way you say I must. My sin is envy, as I watch them so bold and selfish among us. It is not good for me to speak of it. Still, how is it that we know who the gods have told us are to be nobles and who they intend to be peasants?"

My sergeant kicked the largest burning log, showering the night with sparks. "I think I have said that we won't speak of this again, Abe. I know that it itches in your head. Speaking of it is dangerous and leads us to no end, but misery. Neither of us will ever be nobles, so what is the point?"

"The point is I don't like men who kill old women and who keep the women of great warriors as their slaves." I got up so that he wouldn't have to look down at me as I confessed a dislike for the mistreatment of 'mere' women. It was an error to tell him as much as that, for it would trouble him to know that there was more to my thoughts than my mean spirit bubbling out, which was what everybody always thought was the only thing that made me so hard to get along with.

The more I hated the nobles, the more I thought about the

duty of helping the Debrecian woman in our prison. After all, she was the enemy, so why did I want to help her at all? The moon that pulled me to do it was in the dark half of the sky. It was said that this meant trouble. Still, I was compelled, perhaps by the Goddess, to think about how I might pull such a senseless stunt off without raising a commotion, which was my usual way of doing things.

She reminded me of myself in that barn when I'd had no life before me. My, how it would annoy the baron's brother and his friends in white if she got away! War was boring the way we were fighting it. I could use the amusement. I determined to come up with a plan.

In the end, the plan was simple. I waited for a moonless night with clouds and some fog in the lowlands. A little drizzle made the guard's ears useless. I walked right down the main camp road. After all, I was a soldier like the rest, and only needed a cloak to disguise the exact nature of my Lord. When I got close, I snuck up behind the two guards. I used the crone's chant to make them sleepy, as they were nearly asleep anyway, and then I walked straight into the prison where there were the same two men and another one keeping the Debrecian company.

The woman's leg smelled rotten. She was wet with sickness and didn't know me. I told her I'd come back to help her, so she weakly murmured that it was good that I'd come to help her die.

This exchange impressed the men so much that even the new man didn't say anything. The big man said some prayers to Sho as I pushed away some straw and sat my little brazier of coals down on the dirt floor. There I heated my knife as I told her to go to sleep, "*Tpunwvw Own.*"

Her eyes widened with surprise upon hearing the magical words, though she couldn't see as well as I could in the dark room. Her eyes closed. When she was deep enough in her dreams, I said my prayers of health to the Goddess. Without waiting for an unlikely answer, I tied the limb up high then cut off half of her leg. With the flat of my knife, I burned the stump before dousing the wound with spirits and folding the skin over. I sewed the black and bleeding mess, leaving a small hole for seepage. My best poultice and chants finished the surgery. All of this wasn't as easy as written, taking much of my attention, particularly while sawing the bones.

When we were done, the men were in a trance almost as deep as the woman's. Hearing the sawing and sizzling had a way of making one reflective. Little amber reflections bounced off the cast iron pot, attracting their eyes and thoughts.

I told them, "If you are here without a chance of getting out, I will ask your help. If you are willing, then I won't leave you to your fate."

"What's to keep us from leaving on our own? If you can get out, so can we." These comments came from the man who'd goaded me the last time.

I picked the hot handle up on the stolen brazier pot, swung it in an arch and clipped the side of his head with its bottom. That adding another to the knot I'd left him the last time we'd met. He hadn't even seen well enough to raise his hands. The useless man fell over and slept as soundly as the Debrecian.

"I need some help," I repeated.

"I'll do it."

The big man and I walked out of the prison with her between us. Guards snored noisily as we passed them. I hoped they'd awaken before long, lest they fail to come up with a good excuse for letting their prisoners escape.

Some of the soldiers by the road might have seen us, or at least heard us pass, but it wasn't unusual for soldiers to help a drunken friend back to his tent.

I had the horses out in the woods. They were two little ones that the nobles used to pony around with but didn't really need. We put her on one, tying her with a rope to the saddle and over the horse's neck. The large man took off for the southern woods, since I didn't have a horse big enough for him. By the time I got on the other one, there came a fuss from back at the camp.

A plume of smoke rose above the prison hut. I grabbed the lead rope and took off toward the enemy camps a mile into the northern woods, hoping all the time that the Debrecian wouldn't fall off. She'd maybe hang herself in the ropes we'd tied to keep her safe.

I walked her into a small border camp of Sir Lacellor. A couple of guards watched my shadowy form tie her horse to a stump by some noble's tent. "Give this woman rest and soft food. There is tea and ointment in the horse's bag. If you don't treat her with care, I'll come back and have to kill you."

I nodded and then walked out before it got light enough for them to notice by my colors that I was their enemy.

Soon, I was halfway home and keeping company with the wolves who had come to find me a curiosity, probably because of how many times I wandered into their woods.

I told them, "You should howl a message to my friend, Yellow Eyes. He is a long ways off, but he is a grown wolf and a good leader, which you seem to need. He is as good a hunter as any wolf I've ever known, and he has a sense of humor, so he won't nip at you much." They were still too shy to say anything back, and I was growing tired of giving up advice to those not inclined to listen.

After changing my clothes and swatting my stolen horse away, I sneaked past our own guard and managed sleep before someone came around and told me that we were all supposed to make formation and account for ourselves.

A noble said, "Something has gone afoot in the camp."

I made it a point to grumble and complain about needing my sleep so they'd think I was normal.

The noble had come by to count us and to give a little speech about keeping an eye out for enemy miners and spies. "Some of them attacked the encampment, but they made a mistake and fired the prison. Nothing remains of our prisoners, but one badly charred foot and lower leg bone. The rest have been entirely consumed by the flames, though the guards repelled the enemy and kept them from murdering our leaders. For this we thank Sho and give him much praise."

Sergeant Ankind asked, "How do you know that there are spies involved, ser?"

"They got by all of the camp without raising notice. There may have been as many as a half score, for they overcame our guards and held them fast until the guards escaped and ran the spies off. I suspect disguises and even persons still in our midst, those vile enough to attack us from our very center. Witchery is certainly afoot, say the priests, but this is debated."

I wasn't in front, so I got away with a scowl. Others leaned in, as if the noble's story improved the more it insulted gifted women.

"These enemies don't even have respect enough for the rules of war, for even Sir Lacellor is learned enough to know that our leaders may not be touched, save in noble battle."

"I can see where that would raise a ruckus," I told the captain. "Ser."

Ankind quickly smothered my intended meaning by saying, "As you can see, Ser, we are all sickened by it and will raise our diligence, as well as bring our minds to deep thoughts regarding our service. It is a fearsome thing to think upon when an enemy hides among us and fails to offer proper respects. They will cross a line and find themselves paying for that disrespect some day, if they are not careful." He glanced at me as soon as the captain looked away.

"Why don't you get down and lick the jam from between his pink toes, Ankind?" I shot back quickly under my breath. If any of the soldiers around me had decent ears, they might have heard my whisper.

It all disappointed me in the end. I'd been counting on upsetting the nobles with news of the escape of the Debrecian woman. Instead, they weren't even going to go looking for the two prisoners who'd used the charcoal pot to burn down the prison in their haste to create a diversion. As good as that thinking had been, I was more impressed by the story offered up by the guards, and was pleased that they'd found a way out of their mess by being so good at lying.

* * * * *

It was quietly decided two days thereafter that we were to hunt the back roads for any prisoners who might have escaped in the confusion of the attack. The nobles were embarrassed to admit that the prisoners had not been burned to death in some kind of Sho vengeance. They'd sifted all of the ashes, having heard the advice of their cooks and blacksmith. No fire without a bellows and a whole day of cooking could have eaten up every bone except one lower leg. So it appeared in their minds that only the Debrecian had ended up cinders.

Thus Ankind and I found ourselves the lords' hounds, sniffing out the foxes. I had no heart for it. There was a big risk that the prisoners could recognize me, and much had been disclosed to them that I wished hidden. Worst of all, the dangerous minder of Lord Allen Wencor accompanied us. He quickly pointed out the way to go from the very spot I'd hidden the horses that night. He knew more than I wanted, apparently having some considerable witch tracking skills, though he dismissed entirely the many horse tracks leading toward the enemy.

"Those are the long gone leaders of the main enemy force. We can't reach them behind the safety of their lines," he told me when I mentioned the signs.

We were soon on the trail of the big man, toward whom I felt some obligation. The minder thought himself enough of an expert to work directly with me and my sergeant. We were his little company and under his temporary command. He made that clear every time he pointed us another way.

The minder was a minor noble named Barkar, and they called him captain, though he wore no rank beyond silver chain-mail over his hateful white blouse and britches. They'd been stained by the previous months of camp, but it was clear that some local woman worked hard to keep them mostly pure. He often went past me and led us, while behind us all, a stream of ten nobles picnicked and philosophized, often using the closest trails and roads as we scouts took the harder course through the woods. Ankind and I were continually backtracking messages to set them on new parallel road.

The nobles led pack ponies and at least one servant for each of them, making our party of horses nearly two score. Thus, pans banged, boxes rattled, armor clanged, and, at times, the gossip rose to laughing roars that carried across the whole landscape.

If I were the escaping prisoner, I'd never be tracked so easily. Ours, well he could have ridden a horse and left fewer tracks. If it were me, I'd have just eased away from the sound in one circle until they were tired of running around in a wheel upon their own tracks. Our big man wasn't as smart as all of that though, and, within less than two days time, his smell got too strong for comfort. Even the minder, Captain Barker, sensed him close. Each time the captain prayed in the woods, his head came up pointing in the right direction. His God cheated for him, which caused me anxiety because I was no stranger to suspicious eternal beings.

As all good trackers do, we moved increasingly slower as the large man's careless tracks got fresher so as to not chance upon him in a rush. Nobody wanted him to slip away, including Ankind, to whom I knew better than to confide my new crimes. The first to see an escaped prisoner would earn a gold. Ankind and I had no rank and were considered servants. Ankind had the idea that they'd spoken of it as a gentleman's bet accidentally in our presence.

Ankind was teaching me ways to say little and be even littler than lacking words, which might explain their mistakenly excluding us. I thought Ankind's an interesting tactic, and I practiced it as we tracked alongside the white clothed Captain Barker. He turned many times to see if I was there, often as I stood just behind him. I felt his heart leap and saw his scowl as if he suspected me of coming up to knife him in the back. This only encouraged me to learn the trick of silence better.

This, too, I was learning from Sergeant Ankind—not to think highly of the solution of killing everything I hated. This was harder than acting invisible, for the spirit of the crone plagued me.

Barker came to think of himself as my teacher. He whispered, "Stay back. I can sense that we draw near; see how this variety of broken twig is still full of its sap, and this track shows watery mud that has not yet settled." We crouched in the woods.

I nodded my head, making a serious and interested face, as if I'd just learned something new from a man of great and profound wisdom. Patronizing fools was one of Ankind's favorite tricks for looking invisible, and, from Barker's smile, I knew I'd completely fooled him at last.

I ran my fingers across the twig. "Yes, and from the moistness and size of his stride, I say we will overtake him within a quarter mile. I should go notify the party, for they'll be displeased if we come upon the prisoners without help. You should wait to go forward after you hear the clanging of pots and breaking of saplings behind us. That way you can gain the prize and have them as witness."

"Good idea, Abe. You may not be completely useless after all." Barker was skilled at giving compliments that sat ill in the stomach.

"I know that you dislike me for my rudeness, Ser. My sergeant has had me working on being more polite with my words and careful with my manners. I don't begrudge you winning the prize, Captain Barker. I consider it what I owe you for being insubordinate." I moved off toward the distant road full of wandering nobles as he stared at my back with a smug appearance of pleasure, hopefully thinking he'd made me a better lackey.

When I got past the first rise, I doubled back along a ridge. Just over a small hill, I heard the sound of a brook. The big man had stopped. Water made many animals feel safe.

"I will ask you to speak quietly, for half of the army is just over the rise. They seek to hang you." I knelt over a knee-tall ledge above the creek-side rocks. There he rested on his shirt.

He jumped up and twisted around, no more than a hand's length in front of my nose. "Oh, it's you." His muscles eased some.

"Yes. They'd have caught you a day earlier if not for me."

"Did I not help you before? Do you not owe me better?"

"I go where they tell me, for I'm a serf like you. Besides, there is a man of Sho whose god tells him your direction. He is right over the hill waiting for my word. Worse, a gold prize is on your head. They make sport of your misfortune."

"Do say. You ... the fools!"

"Quiet, idiot! Look, to start, stop leaving tracks all over the muddy trails and clean yourself; you stink. Walk in the muddy shore to the south, downstream a ways, and then double back, using the rocks under the water for footfalls. Walk as quietly as you can for five hundred long strides upstream, using the rocks to wash and hide your prints. Then flee to the mountains northwest. Don't sleep until you have counted to ten thousand and then only sleep until dawn. Can you count as high?"

"I can count. Which way is south?"

"You've been tracking east. There is nothing but more woods followed by swamps and headhunters. Everybody knows you must soon turn south, toward home."

"Then you propose that I move to the north where the enemy will take me?"

"Tell Lacellor that you've converted to the Goddess or some other god that they enjoy. The only one they seem to disfavor is Sho. They may put you into their army, but you'll be safe until our armies cross swords."

"It is blasphemy to denounce Sho." He shook his head.

"Sho's servant is over the hill, and, each time he prays, Sho sends him your smell. I've seen this with my own eyes. He prays, and then his eyes move to your direction like a forked twig toward well water. Trust me when I tell you I've seen Sho, and he is used to bartering for the small and insignificant souls of peasants."

"I don't know—"

"Know this: It isn't important to the gods which God you pick, just as long as you are wise enough to pick the one who finds you in favor. Knowing that you persist, even the gods mock you."

"Your sermon does not sound right. They say there is only one God."

"There is more than one."

"I am not so certain." He looked around as if the shade-darkened creek-bed hid a second option.

I poked his shoulder with the tip of my sword. "Perhaps I should kill you. I will earn the gold prize."

"No, the Goddess sounds lovely." He got busy putting down false tracks and then stumbled backwards up the brook. I handed him some bread as he passed me heading north. The last I saw, he'd left a trail of mud churning under the water. Even an idiot couldn't miss it. I followed him a ways, erasing what I could of his signs, and then backtracked in search of the nobles.

They all came rushing over in a mob with all of their horses under and behind them, maddened by the thought of winning what probably seemed a trinket to the likes of them.

Captain Barker was too upset upon hearing the commotion to remember that he was growing impatient with me for taking so long. He tried to keep ahead of them, but we were afoot at the moment, and they charged on all flanks. Even the thick overhanging limbs on the trees were no obstacle to their heavy armor and beastly horses. Soon we met at the creek. All tracking signs were obliterated by horseshoe marks, and even the smell swirled like a cook's spoon racing around in a pot. Torches were lit as night fell. Captain Barker found the tracks leading southward.

I came up beside him and put my fingers into the dirt, bringing the mud up to my nose and giving it a smell as if the technique was somehow useful. "It is certain that he has passed this way and well about time. Sooner or later the man had to turn south, lest he never get home. It is cunning of him to use the creek for a highway."

The nobles standing around gave me nods of agreement, which felt momentarily odd. Then they eyed one another with suspicious grins. All at once, they broke for their horses like someone had flashed an invisible signal. The gaggle went charging down the creek, making sure that even I couldn't make out any more tracks. The racing continued until they'd frothed up the lips on their horses and left the creek entirely in defeat.

In truth, only the falling of the moon caused them to give up. We left the creek and our mad charge in order to set up a camp. I found Ella in the pack train, the poor horse having been run hard by the servants, all of them betting on their own particular master's luck. There was probably more money bet among the servant train than the gold itself, I learned, not to mention that it meant far more to their lot in life, so they were quite serious about it.

Ankind and Barker were thoroughly annoyed at how it had all turned out, and I joined them in my disgust regarding how poorly the last hours of our expedition had gone.

"There was nothing professional about it. They should have left it to our captain. He'd have known better than to tear up the tracks." My face was a pasted mask of misery, I hoped.

Captain Barker nodded. Ankind gave me a curious look. He probably wondered what I was plotting behind so many flowers. When he asked me about it later, I told him I was practicing his art of being invisible, though his curious look didn't falter as we parted for our own blankets.

Our next morning was long in the camp. They'd bruised and battered the horses, and everyone was eager to have the scouts go back to the creek and pick up the trail more properly. Meanwhile, the nobles' own servants surveyed to the west for a better road and a village where they could claim rights for food more befitting their station than days-old travel fare.

I took a more active lead. Barker was so glad of my complimentary nature that he made the mistake of trusting me instead of troubling his god. It helped that there were no tracks for Barker to follow anyway. I got us wandering down the creek and then back to the southwest where the fields allowed tracking on our horses. Finally we ended up on a road leading toward Helfax. There, as I'd expected, I picked up the smell of the two other prisoners.

They mostly used the road. Their footmarks were mixed in with all of the rest. It didn't matter because I didn't know their foot signatures anyway. It was on that road that Captain Barker had us stop.

"You have no idea where the track is, do you?"

"I've found his trail again. Don't be troubled by it."

"Look, we've moved too far and too fast. He's afoot. We should have overtaken him a half day back. If he had wings he couldn't have gotten this far. You know, the Lord guides me, and Sho has told me that we go in the wrong direction. The man we track is north. Sho is perfect, having given me this blessing." He turned his horse around.

"Then I confess!"

He turned his horse back toward me, apparently eager to hear it.

Ankind drew closer as well.

"The man passed, by chance, the footprints of the other two. I know that we must have passed the first man by, as you say, but I have taken up the cause of capturing the others instead."

Ankind spit.

"And why is that?" Captain Barker asked.

"Well, because two is better than one. It is twice the success."

"But I don't know these signs," complained the Captain. "How are you assured that this new pair of prints belongs to our prisoners? At least with the one man, we knew we were on a right trail."

"They are our prisoners. Of this I have no doubt. There were signs of charred clothing. And, where the paths crossed, the three may have chosen that place as a rendezvous. They probably missed each other, but these two continued along the road."

"That's a honey dipper's bucket of crap," said Captain Barker.

"Is this true, Abe, or are you pretending to know?" asked Sergeant Ankind.

"It's true, Sergeant. I'll have the convicts in front of you prior to noon meal. Also, this time we won't alert the other nobles, and, instead, let our friend, Captain Barker, take the winnings. After all, it is rightfully his, for he has led us this far; it is only by chance that I have been blessed to make these last minute observations."

"I'd give him till then, Ser," suggested my sergeant, though I could sense his disgust with me because of his lack of trust in my newly found and overly kind disposition. I'd been more secretive with him over this than any other thing I'd done.

"Ah! It is unfortunately the only chance we have. We've lost too much time to backtrack. Very well, let's see what comes of this—on your head, Abe, and only until the sun is straight above," conceded the knight of Sho.

It was with some relief that I'd drawn the concession, so I took off alone at a gallop, which I'm sure Captain Barker hadn't expected. At a woodcutter's path, I angled into the woodland. The smell of the convicts was almost strong enough to touch. In the same direction, smoke rose into the air from a place far from any village. Thus, all I had to do was bear in the direction of the coming wind.

Ella and I soon looked toward the pair's paltry camp and a roasting pair of mice. They were in a field of spindly, new-growth trees that strained forth, probably rejuvenation from some forest fire years back. The new trees were thin and spaced well apart. Tiny plumes of green fought the competition for sunlight, three times my height above. Sunlight burst through in holes, as if also tree trunks.

The prisoners took one look at my horse bearing down on them and grabbed some wood spears they'd apparently thought to bring with them. It would be a bad idea to throw one in the trees, I thought, given all of the obstruction. I stopped short of throwing distance, my own small shield and iron tipped spear at the ready as I wound through the maze of tree trunks.

The men drew aside, so I mirrored them with Ella, slowly driving them at an angle toward the roadway. After some time, they managed to back all of the way to the road where they apparently thought they'd have a better throw.

I circled down the road, taking a stand on it just as Ankind and Barker came over a rise on the other side of the escapees. The two convicts sized up the odds and came my way to fight a way clear, so I backed off as fast as they came at me leaving them frustrated. Our horses were faster than their feet, so there was no lasting gain in the maneuvering as even the pack of nobles started to understand the situation and came up behind Barker and Ankind.

The chief noble handed Barker his golden coin. I saw it sparkle between their fingers and then I saw the smile on Captain Barker's face.

For the moment, I'd even lost interest in my animosity toward the minder. No, that fight was meant for some other place, I decided. For the last of this, I chose to be invisible, taking it as a test of my new skills. Ankind had been right; there was much that was worthy in the talent, for, by pretending to sleep, my enemy grew less wary.

They came upon the prisoners in a rush of hooves that froze the doomed men in their tracks. The useless spears were dropped into the road's muddy furrows. I'd have fought for my life, a fitting way to die, but perhaps they sensed some sign of mercy that I didn't credit the nobles giving them. The men fell to the dirt, praying and looking up at Captain Barker, seeing his white uniform and professing their love for Sho.

"We ask Sho's protection, for we are innocent of the charges and didn't escape out of fear of battle. Put us in front in the next charge," was the gist of their complaint.

I thought such a gesture from Sho would be in keeping with the promises of the priests regarding taking up countenance with the least of God's people. Besides, any man on the first row of a battle block was certain to die anyway. This, of course, I couldn't say, for I was least among them, in particular because the prisoners knew nothing about me other than my voice.

It was with personal shame that I stood back and watched them hang, for as evil as they might have been, I saw less that I liked in the ones passing judgment.

The nobles milled about. The hanging men struggled for air, futilely kicking their heels. Each noble offered the rump of his horse so the men could stand on one leg and catch a half breath of air. As one horse's rump wandered off, it was slowly replaced by the rump of another. Both knights and servants laughed in roars. This joke went on until I couldn't stomach any more. I slipped away to find a brook where I stripped to my skin and cleaned myself of the sin of the worst work I'd ever done.

Chapter Ten

That year Redwater's plains didn't flood, not even during late spring. Light rainfall left our fords open for the whole of Sir Lacellor's army to cross and engage us in open fields. We had less than a quarter of the king's available soldiers. It was ideal for Lacellor, for his only chance at fighting us was by doing so in pieces. The nobles who led us either didn't know it or were incapable of preventing it. I thought perhaps both, as I sat on Ella and watched the battle unfold.

Smoke from campfires, torched arrows and oiled rocks lit by the catapults' braziers streamed across the windy field of rich, black soil. Tiny pricks of yellow stalks sprung up from the brown matt of last fall's reaping. The winter's wheat had gone unplanted. The tenants of these border fiefdoms were almost all either at war or near the duke's city Dorne where they learned new crafts such as fletching, ditching and the endless cutting of pikes.

Upon the next year, half of the nearby peasants would die of disease and starvation, the price to be paid, several times that likely on the battlefield that day. Not a word of the suffering beyond the battle will make the history books, I knew, having held so many and read no mention.

Back on a rise where he oversaw almost all of the formations, the duke rode a mighty horse bedecked in shiny plates. The horse's armor left barely enough room for him to piss. The morning sun flashed off the animal enough to make my eyes hurt. Messengers raced up and down the hill, also pointing him out by the direction of their haste.

By his side, men waved flags telling us where to go and how many of us to put here or there. We had a man with a flag of our own telling the duke where we were going, though our messenger still raced.

The duke's standard flew a head higher than that of our baron's. The baron was second in command while his brother joined two other relatives of high blood, all five contributing soldiers and counting as our five generals.

The duke only managed to rush a score of mounted knights to this, supplementing our armored cavalry to three score. Being light and peasants, we were not counted among that armored force. The rest of his personal forces were days away. It was said that the duke's legion marched to our aid, though I doubted it meant any more than they'd enjoy a second battle after this deed was done.

The baron had marched us four days to get here with our eighty score of foot, joining the small company of a lesser noble who had spotted their scouts and called the alarm. Other nobles came from close fiefdoms bringing pikers in various stages of training. Some peasant soldiers had been swept up in the movement. They were no more than farmers, old men and boys, some foot soldiers for less than a day. The swell was now four ragged blocks of roughly six hundred men apiece. The boys and old men had been put up front, so they couldn't run. We were not the Sapatians of my history readings, for our men up front also had no idea how to fight.

Our blocks were formed, twenty deep and thirty to the side, with great gaps between the blocks so they could be moved and could match the enemy's four block formations as well.

We, again, were an afterthought. Up behind the rightmost block, we sat far to the rear of Lady Lettoir's first fifty pikers, who stood in the fifth and sixth ranks of the block before us.

Their uniforms were grayish-brown tunics. Their countenance bore the look of professionals compared to most of the others. They had no sergeant with them, and, for what they were going to be wasted on, I doubted they'd need one.

When they'd seen me in camp, none knew me, including Kitchor Ranglson, who had finally become, for me, no more than an ugly part of an old and fading life. My soul had twisted into something different in the past year, seeing old wounds are small. Oh, to be sure, I still owed Kitchor a debt because of his betrayal of my crone, but I thought our lives long, and his life so tiny to me that I judged him easy later pickings.

When we'd seen Lettoir's first pikers come to our camp, they'd looked up to us as if we were gods. Only Hobar and Horatio took to this with any vigor, so Ankind made them their minders for the purpose of quartering and marching, and, in general, minding their place. They had only to do what they were told, go where they were directed, and, in general, pretend they were cows. To me, it seemed a lot like telling a condemned man how to sit backwards on a horse so he could get the hemp necklace on easier and then watching the man shimmy right up with a smile on his face.

I looked out at them in their rows, clearly the two neatest in the baron's block. The most motherly feeling in my life came over me, a feeling that I truly hated because I knew it diminished my ability to fight by the degree of the distraction.

Lacellor was our mirror, though his blocks appeared deeper, maybe as many as thirty by thirty. He'd put a few detached columns out to his right, matching a company of soldiers the duke had ordered into our left woods the night before. They were supposed to be hiding. I figured that, upon the battle, they meant to come in and hack at the side of the closest block, disrupting their order and rolling them up. I knew the tactic from my illegal history readings. They were too few to do anything, and, though the duke's hiding fools shifted on their knees from bush to bush, I doubted if there was a single soldier who hadn't seen some of them up on the small, wooded rise. Lacellor surely had, and whatever tiny battle they had over there would not likely matter.

Our block hung out on the other end, our duke's far right. Farther to our right, there was nothing but more black fields and then some weeded hills. Since the direction was downwind, I felt nervous about it because my other senses were entangled by the smoke and the many noisy bodies, and, I'll admit, a wee bit of excitement.

The small contingent of White Shirts doubled our tiny and mostly unarmored cavalry. They comprised Lettoir's left flank. This put me Ankind, the very young and untested Sir Allen Wencor and his minder, Captain Barker, in the center where our roughly equal force of horsemen met. Altogether, we were eighteen long and two deep.

In theory, Allan Wencor was our leader. He kept sending irrelevant messengers back and forth to the baron's brother. This was always after a whisper to do so from Barker, who also outranked us because he had blood in his veins, and we had something closer to water.

Barker kept looking at me strangely. I didn't know if he wanted me with him still, or if the god he served was telling on me. As I've noted, he and his fellow nobleman had once plotted to kill me in the confusion of first battle. What I have not said is how they sought to recruit me to their guard after the incident of tracking down the two escaped prisoners. It was almost a sin to refuse, and I dared not accept, lest I find myself one step further removed from the leanings of my heart.

My heart grew less and less attached to these allies. I fought for nobles I hated, for a God I saw as childish and beside men who thought me strange. I didn't even have the luxury to be who I was born to be while in their presence. Those in my own troop had mostly learned to respect my instincts in scouting and skirmishes, but we didn't share more than a few words around our fires, for I had much to hide, wasn't good at manly banter and felt awkward in their company.

Worst of all, I found myself attracted to the look of many of their bodies, which they were not reluctant to show one another as if beasts on display. They thought me prudish when I found other duties to attend while this went on. Some even came to the irritating conclusion that I was destined to be a white priest by my manner—seemingly against all nakedness. How odd, given that my retiring looks away were due to liking it too much.

While we watched over the coming battle, Sergeant Ankind remarked, "It is a grand and horrible day. I have never felt such closeness of death." His lips barely moved as he looked across the field.

The first of Lacellor's three catapults were letting loose a new round of blazing boulders. We'd assembled in too much haste to have any of our own. The shooting stars of oil and pitch landed well to our rear where the archers stood waiting. The catapult aim was terrible, and not apt to get better, as we were now too close. Smoke trails lingered, hellish arches moving softly to the right in the wind above us.

"That it is. Grand indeed," I said, pulling my teacher's sword out and kissing its blade to show my affection. I could wear my hidden sword today. With all of the things to look at, nobody was apt to notice the finer craftsmanship. Besides, Ankind would think I'd stolen it from some enemy knight, which was the sort of talent that better equipped us all.

I looked over to see all three of the leaders glaring at me strangely.

"You could die this very day. What is the grandeur in that?"

Ankind spoke as if his words had not been considered.

I'd gotten to the point where I could look at him and not go pity-pat in the heart. I suppose my love for him had been just an infatuation, or perhaps something that happened to women at certain times of the month. In any event, he was getting on my nerves the way he always told me what I wasn't allowed to think about or say to him. It had become his overbearing nature to do almost exclusively that since we'd rounded up the prisoners.

"I don't think I will," I told him flatly.

Captain Barker differed. "It can happen. I've seen the best soldiers die in battle under the very first volley of arrows. Nobody is outside of the laws of fate, and, if Sho determines, we will go to our reward. As for you, soldier Abe, twice I have asked you to accept the commitment to our order, and twice you have walked away, saying only that you will think upon it. We who ride under his protection are more likely to survive this battle."

"That is true," said Ankind.

I couldn't believe how easily my sergeant had fallen into that. Perhaps it was fear of the battle that had his mind so vulnerable to the White Shirts' trap.

"So, a little prayer to Sho should help you better stick your lance and swing your sword, is it?" I asked Ankind.

"It wouldn't hurt, though I will be more worried about where the others are sticking theirs." Ankind knew me all too well, and, thus, he knew how much it hurt for me to hear him say such foolishness. Others around us murmured their agreement, including of course, Sir Allen Wencor and Captain Barker.

I had one better tale to tell. I said, "I am not ill disposed among God. I have heard a prophecy. I am meant to kill many men before I die. When I ride this day, I do so with no fear of the outcome."

"That is bold of you, but foolish," replied Ankind. I think that he thought it best that he scold me quickly, lest the White Shirts take exception to my tongue.

Sir Allen added, "Well said, Sergeant. Consider this, soldier Abe. There are many men before you. You will have to kill some just to justify the loan of your horse. Then, if you die, the prophecy you speak of so often has taken its course and is fulfilled, assuming you die later than the first piker in battle."

Of course, I hated him, but, after a moment's thought, I at least had to admire how he'd spoken so eloquently upon the subject of battle, given I could almost taste the fear churning his stomach. Thus I conceded, "Perhaps. Yet, I don't think there are enough men on this little battlefield to fulfill the prophecy as I saw it."

That brought a chuckle from the ranks behind and to the side. The man on my right even reached over and slapped me on the arm, showing admiration for my courage and wit. It may have been wit, but it was certainly not courage. I knew nothing of such things. The fact was that the experience of my life had long taught me that life wasn't meant to be pleasant, and, therefore, the only issue with life was in making sure its death was grand. After all, hadn't the crone shown me that in her very last lesson? I'd never seen her so joyful.

While I thought of her, I looked out over the many rolls of the earth. Though his army was on our side of the shallow and rocky ford, I spotted Sir Lacellor's nobles as they peered down from a hill on the other side of Redwater River. The few in armor over there were less heavy than ours, and the company Sir Lacellor kept was both few and informal. They had no battle flags at all, though their messengers were plenty. Instead of flags, a steady beat of drums pulsed over the river plain.

The biggest thing that concerned me was the fact that only a handful of horse troops were visible around the great and rebellious lord. That was trouble. My scouting had proven that they had them, for I couldn't steal all of their horses. They could be anywhere, even to our rear. The enemy cavalry were certain to hit our pikemen at the least opportune moment, and I had no faith in the duke's ability to employ his own in a timely fashion. This thought fell neatly into the category of how easily our nobles starved and deprived the common soldiers that were pressed into service by forced levy.

I could imagine the duke up there on his hill, plotting that the whole contest might be worth the deaths of every foot soldier, assuming he got the enemy's cavalry knotted up in a slaughter. Without enough armored cavalry, Sir Lacellor was certain to be outmaneuvered in the next battle, but such wouldn't do the common footmen much good.

I couldn't take my eyes off the distant hills. I sought the sign of rising dust or the head of a lurking scout. Somewhere over there, beyond some hill, I knew Lacellor's armored horses waited for us to get similarly entangled.

Then, almost directly in front of us, three outriders materialized. They were well to Lacellor's left, our right, two hills over, hidden by a few trees, but, as I focused, I saw them pointing. I imagined their words to one another. The three held a proud bearing. They had hair that was thickly tied on top but which flowed above the single top knot. Of course, I couldn't see them clearly, for they were twenty bow shots beyond us, but, when they moved, I gleaned what I could from the change of their profiles. The three had no metal armor on them or their horses. I sensed a free spirit about them, and then I felt an oddness in my heart that I can only describe as love.

Words came to me, as if singing in the air: *Love for the battlefield. Love for the queen. Love, for I shall soon tell my children that the time is ripe to loose the Princess of Battle.*

It had been several weeks since I'd heard the words of the Goddess. While waiting for war on my horse, I finally heard her speak—of love. Her words came as clearly as if one of Ankind's rebukes. It wasn't just words I heard either, but a stirring inside as real as the hate from my ghost. There came no less of a wind inside of me than that which blew the catapult trails above.

The earth stood still for just a while, long enough to see Sho walking, not far from the three on horseback. He didn't speak to them at all, nor did they seem to see him. Still, he stood there facing them, then me, from the impossible distance. The god started to talk as if I sat right in front of him and not from a dozen fields on the other side of the river.

Be of good spirit. My child, I forgive you for killing my champion. Do not trouble yourself. A year has passed, and I see your repentance. It gladdens me to have you here. You shall serve me better this day than my champion could ever have in his mortal lifetime.

The Goddess materialized near to him, but she didn't stand too close to Sho. I knew she didn't like him. She didn't look at me but, instead, stared at Sho and laughed. She did so without the need for breath, as the laughter lingered longer than possible from a mortal. I couldn't make sense of it. Both seemed happy. Was everybody over there on the other side of the river happy? Such did not bode well for our chances.

"It's going to be all right. Just follow me," said Ankind from my side. I glanced over and noticed his face. He seemed overly concerned as he looked at me. "You looked like you'd gone into a trance, Abe. Don't let fear freeze you at the wrong moment. It'll be all right, I tell you. Just keep me on your left."

The footmen in front of us had already started forward, and, in fact, were only a few strides from crashing into the block of enemy. Some time had been lost to me. I looked up at the distant hill far across the river, but it was empty of the three outriders and the two gods. We'd been left alone to kill one another in peace.

Outbound arrows rained over while Sir Lacellor's answered, some reaching a few of the men in the back ranks of our block. Shields went up like hats, save for those held by the front ranks. We, however, held our ground as the battle moved away and forward in front of us.

Soldiers, downed by arrow hits, started to trickle out from under the feet of the last men. Few of them were dead. Arrows are almost never enough to kill a man without sufficient suffering.

As if mindless, the two blocks of soldiers met in a crash of shields and the scrape of pikes or short swords that slid across them. Rows behind pressed those in the lead until some had no recourse but to shove their way into their enemy's spears. Men yelled individually and in masses, perhaps hoping to terrify their foes. Others screamed out songs of horror, always followed by the call of suffering. Overhead, shrieking balls of flame that were shot from the catapults spoke as well, one or two landing in the swell.

The sounds of battle were like nothing I'd ever imagined. There was nothing of glory in it.

I looked along the line and marked the other three pairs of blocks as they met. Arrows continued into the back ranks of each. It was like four little wars, each a world of its own. I was glad I wasn't in it, for the fate of those dying was in the hands of whatever pressed upon them the most, and, thus, skill had less to do with it than order and pain. It struck me as the perfect war for Sho, who I suspected didn't like free and mobile soldiers like those in the guard of Lady Lettoir. We were not restrained by his shining armor, and we didn't stand facing the tyranny of untutored service like stalks of grain ready to be reaped by the next pike or short sword passing through the wavering walls of shields.

Next, something happened that our duke had not expected. Lacellor's drum beats altered. The last six ranks of Lacellor's four blocks marched to their left, and then in column turned to race alongside their own block. They did this to each of the four groups, soon clashing at the edges of our four orders. Turning inward, the enemy started to roll up the sides of each of outer rank.

Our men in the wedges were caught by two flanks. Under the press of all sides, they marched into the plow-shear of the enemy's corner where they were, one by one, stabbed, pushed to ground by the press and trampled under a hundred feet. One shield was useless in the jaws where Lacellor's pikes came at our men from two sides. The enemy had used a tactic as simple, old and deadly as Hektar.

The slow churning might have lasted a half day, had they not outmaneuvered us. When the enemy took our flank, our soldiers started falling at many times the old rate. Enemy soldiers stopped falling, for at the point of attack the enemy always held the advantage of two against our one. Down went one, then two, then another, until it mattered a good deal.

Captain Barker and Sir Wencor kept looking up at our duke's hill for instructions, but none came. Up there, they were all looking over at our far left flank where the hidden men had come out and been met by Lacellor's small contingent. Well to the back of our lines, coming over the farthest hill, the heavy armor of the duke rode to the aid of that meaningless push way over there on the other side of the planet, as far as I was concerned. Lacellor was destined to lose all of his men over there, but such foolishness had nothing to do with the main battle.

We waited, still not counted as knights, telling me our

leaders had little thought regarding our proper use beyond setting the right anchor. More importantly, Lacellor's knights proved very patient, remained hidden, and told me much of the enemy lord's discipline.

I looked around at Ankind and saw him fidget. He was looking around to see if the enemy's armor was going to add to the disaster before we could be put to any effect on our side of the battle. We still didn't see any sign of them. More importantly, we still didn't move. The duke continued to be distracted by his shining nobles on the left. I started to think he had no regard for our light cavalry at all. I had a thought. *We can do something; we can save one of the blocks and, with it, maybe roll up enough of the next to save a complete disaster.* The duke and baron must have thought otherwise, but I suspected they thought of us not at all.

Finally, a flag waved our way, and Sir Wencor passed down the command to move forward two score paces. We moved where the flag suggested. Sir Wencor waved, signaling that we should wait.

I couldn't believe it. We'd been moved within reach of the enemy archers, and still our soldiers fell before us while we watched. I could toss one of my spears and easily run one of the flanking enemy through from where I sat making an arrow's target of myself.

I reached forward with my shield, catching an arrow meant for my horse's head. It stuck out of my shield, a good, straight arrow with a metal point and decently trimmed fletching.

When I turned to show it to Sergeant Ankind, he was holding a shaft near his chest. It had rained down upon him, angling down into and through his bowels. It was so deep that at first I thought it was just some spare fletching on a broken arrow that he jokingly held against himself.

Almost immediately, Sergeant Ankind weakened. We'd had

our spats of late, but all of that was forgotten as I watched my only friend in the world lean to the far side of his horse. I reached to catch him, but I couldn't get more than his boot. I did catch the look on his face though, as he went over the other side of his horse. He was shaking his head, telling me this was a complete mess and that he'd become a dead man for nothing.

The heart I thought I'd lost in the crone's burning cabin sank with him under the hooves of our waiting horses.

Captain Barker apparently felt the sergeant hit his horse, and looked to see it as he, too, missed a grip upon the falling soldier. He shook his head with the sadness of a man who'd just gotten a good look at his own death and knew the pointless meaning of it as well as had the sergeant. For the first time ever, our eyes met, and we were one thought.

I shifted, finding my sergeant on the ground. The sky reflected off his open eyes. There was no blood around the wound, all of it trapped and swelling inside his body. How could a man such as Ankind die without the ample showing of a mighty warrior's blood? It seemed a grave insult to us all, though I don't know why, other than it was something to latch onto as I felt the sorrow of his senseless loss stir the core of me into rage.

I screamed with pain and fury. Then I looked up at another incoming flight of arrows, and both the smell and the noise of the battlefield ceased to touch my senses. What needed to be done became crystal clear.

"We have to move. It's no good standing out like this!" I edged my horse forward.

Sir Wencor's face pleaded up toward the duke's hill. We'd all be dead by the time our leaders up there noticed our losses. Wencor was bound to their every issue, I realized, as my shield caught another arrow. Three of our company's horses fell over or dodged away with arrows sticking out of them.

"On me!" I kicked Ella forward a couple of strides and then around to face the men. "Right wedge on me!"

I'd always been beside Ankind in our exercises, well to the front, so there was little to learn. The closest man drew his horse up a step, forming the start of a wing. I turned Ella, hoping everyone followed.

I swung out from under the next rain of arrows, and took us to our left so that we could bear down on the back side of the enemy after we'd rounded the whole block. This gave us the use of our right hands as we grazed into the backs of the last ranks of enemy troops.

I lost my spear through the shoulder of the first man I hit. My horse did the work of running down two more before I got my sword clear and sliced the head half off the last man in the rank.

We immediately turned a fast left wheel. All of our soldiers followed, including Captain Barker and Sir Wencor, who'd found themselves too busy to replace me at the fore. The White Shirts were not well schooled in our maneuvers, but they only needed to follow our example.

We hit the backs of the flanking ranks next, breaking their backs before sliding off and hitting that group a second time. That flank comprised few ranks and found itself suddenly thin.

Some of us made the mistake of sticking the enemy with our swords, losing the weapons to the tug of the meat, but I kept my blows to slices, caring less about killing them than dissuading their pikes and letting my horse batter them to the ground where they were trampled by the hooves of following horses. Four such passes took out the entire flank of the enemy.

We kept at it, though half of my cavalry fell on the field or rode back up the rise because of wounds. The archers were so terrified that we'd turn on them that they started shooting directly at us from across a field They hit many of their own men in the backs. It was the footmen's flanks we had our sights on, though, so I turned us into it three more times before we withdrew back up the hill.

My arms were tired. Blood bathed the side of Ella, and no few slashes scarred her. They'd tried to kill her while they were ducking away from our stampede but were not good enough. Only a dozen of us remained in formation. The count included Captain Barker and Sir Wencor, ole' Wistriff, Hobar and even Horatio. Others were down, dead or wounded, or leaning over their horse necks at various stations around the battlefield. As we waited, some got up. They crawled up onto their horses or limped back leading them. These few filed past us, up the hill and to greater safety. Some went out to get those having trouble, saving another half score. We took horses and weapons, too, because we were continually resourceful.

One White Shirt leaned over a horse near the right block where an occasional piker came out and poked him full of new holes. Archers ran forward piling arrows into his body, though to no effect. He was somehow pinned and would not fall until the animal died, bringing them both down in a heap. A hundred holes and another hundred arrows had been wasted in the attempt to kill a dead man.

The clashing block before us had a new shape. No longer were we flanked, and no longer were we the smaller group. Stragglers from our foot reformed. They battered at the edges of the smaller enemy, clamping them into traps.

The men of Lettoir were in rows five and six, at the front by then, the first hundred of our block dead and churning under the feet of the crash that took on the qualities of a hill near its center. Our men had enjoyed a few weeks of training under Sergeant Hadarm, and it made them many times better than most of the other footmen on the battlefield. Keeping our best men from the front ranks was now paying off, though mostly by the accident of our intervention, I determined, as I watched the tide turn in the battle of the right flank of our army.

Over to the far left of the carnage, our armor had killed the small contingent and stumbled their way into the far left block. Pikers killed some of our horses. The nobles fell into the crowd with the crash of tin where other enemy footmen beat on them with stones and shields until the ringing itself murdered the knights. Those stupid enough to wade in deeply got surrounded and were poked to death through the cracks in their armor. The crowd parted in places where the designated axe-man was given room to split the armor of a fallen noble. Some were dead before they found the room to fall off their horses. Still, through the sheer weight of the armor, we were barely winning the far left block by as much as our flurry allowed victory on the far right one.

The ends were the only parts of this battle that were going well. When won, we'd have only small forces left on the flanks to attack the huge blocks of enemy dominating the middle.

The duke and his generals had moved all the way over on the left, getting a closer look at their knight friends. They were so distracted by their successes over there that I doubted they'd even seen our charge, or worried about the middle.

In the center, two blocks were losing badly. Over half of our men were dead already, or dying under the rising heap of Lacellor's soldiers. Finding themselves outnumbered by four to one, and increasingly outflanked on at least three sides, the rate of the loss quickened. Those who could flee were a trickle, and that was the best of the news as I saw it. The end of them was close, and the enemy had nearly as many remaining there as when they'd started. The back half of their blocks were even in decent formation. Turned now with pikes outward, they were alerted against feints like the ones we'd mustered on the right.

Out at the horizons, Sir Lacellor's armor remained hidden.

If the armor came now and hit us nearly anywhere, the field would be lost, and the duke would be forced to ask for terms. Fleeing now was his better option. After all, I knew he'd call the partial losses in Lacellor's army a victory of attrition. The duke would even win the praise of his brother, the king, for the good deed of reducing the rebel's ranks. I'd lived among them too long to not know that much about their politics.

If they struck where we stood, we few horsemen were no force to oppose them. We'd lose outright. Three of the four battles would roll up quickly, leaving Lacellor with enough troops to overwhelm any force the duke could muster out of what was remaining on the left. If he struck the duke's armor instead, while they were tied up with the pikemen, the duke's armor would perish, leaving our field to be run over by Sir Lacellor's heavy cavalry. This I saw right away. I could only hope that the duke knew this, or even saw it as it came on, and would send signals to disengage his armor so they could reform and meet the almost certain threat solidly enough for the able third of his army to escape.

We waited, just out of bow range, catching air for our bodies and rest for our horses, shielding our retreating friends. A few more of our small force escaped, though the numbers fell to nothing. This we all watched over without speaking, the necessity of some patience and oversight apparent.

All of us were too winded and worn to talk. Almost everybody had some poke or cut that bled and needed tending. Hems were torn, making do for bandages while still ahorse. Even Captain Barker and Sir Wencor mended themselves in determined haste.

I thought we could go down and kill another two score before we perished, but the right block seemed to be doing well on its own now, and the others in the center were beyond the repair of two handfuls of light horsemen. The difference between a wounded half score of light cavalry and a healthy two score seemed all of the weight in the world.

Two or three of our worst wounded joined up. Blood was seeping out of them so fast that I thought it might be best if we attacked right away while they still lived. I held knowing we had no mission, and one might reveal itself soon enough.

Signal flags waved, and the duke's armored cavalry disengaged. They safely formed up on the far left, much to my relief that they were no longer entangled.

Then the signal flags waved, and the duke's armor once again charged into the mass of the last two hundred in the far left block. Crush them they did, but not without getting stuck in the mass by the few enemy pikers who were resilient. My relief vanished.

That's when Lacellor's heavy armor chose to reveal themselves. He came through the same woods that had hidden the duke's ruse. It was no more than two score, but the duke had wasted half of his, and the other half languished, bogged down in the block. Worst of all, they faced away from the threat, apparently not even seeing it.

When Lacellor's knights struck, nearly half of our remaining knights fell without a single enemy loss. In the time it took for them to turn and properly meet the enemy knights, less than fifteen of the duke's heavy cavalry were visible. Those had driven hard since the beginning of the fight. Now they fought for their lives just to break free of the mess so they could apply themselves in more than pairs. They retreated in order to do so, but their efforts didn't allow any force to form, for they were few. The previously winning block of our leftmost foot fell back with them, and they were all soon running, the last ranks getting cut down by knights as they fled.

I yelled, "On me!" And we raced into the closest block again, cleaving necks and shoulders off the back and side ranks of the enemy pikers. There was less than a hundred of the enemy left there, so we had good effect for so few horsemen. We raced down the edge, and then when the enemy broke, I drove us into the center of the fight, waving our own footmen back.

Our own troops were not eager to go. They yelled that they were close to winning the battle, obviously judging only from as much as they could see. None at the level of the ground knew the whole story of this battle, nor did they know how little time they had to disengage. They pleaded to pursue, exacting revenge upon the enemy before them, but I turned our horses toward our own men threateningly. They obeyed the command of our weight and rank, and the men soon turned and marched with some order up the rise where they were safer.

I'd driven my force right through the center of the right block's fighting, scattering all the enemy footmen. Even the archers were in retreat because of the lack of a proper shield of pikes. We were suddenly alone there. Our horses drove over bodies of enemy and allies alike. It was a churned mess of both living and dying flesh under our hooves and surrounding our portion of the battlefield with only us left to witness it.

The next block over suffered a different fate. The enemy had hundreds, and though we could still see the flash of pikes and the sound of battle, I saw none of the duke's men on the outside ranks of soldiers. We didn't have the force to even get close, as a double wall of soldiers, thirty wide, were turned our way. They braced the hilts of their pikes solidly into the dirt, awaiting our challenge.

Captain Barker came up beside me, putting his hand on my shoulder. He said, "It's time to leave the field, soldier Abe. We can do no more than what we have, saving one part in five of the army. It will have to be enough."

I nodded, knowing he was right. Then I found two of my

friends, and we went up the hill a little where we put the body of our sergeant over a horse. I set the rest of Lettoir's horsemen to the task of rounding up more horses and any swords they could get close to without injury. Our cavalry left the field as the armor of Lacellor roared around the two center blocks, killing any that hoped to join us. Hundreds fled in all directions from that brutal killing.

We backed through our own camp, picking up whatever stores, blankets and tents we could roll into a bundle and toss onto a horse's back. Each of our remaining horsemen towed at least two animals that bulged with the poorly packed spoils of our own camp.

Servants ran every which way, with great fear, some trying to mount our horses to the dissuasion of our spears. Many were forced back only after persuasive wounds. There were almost as many servants in the train as fighting men, and I had no patience for them because they were the mere pets of nobles. They should never have been there, and we didn't have time at all to abide their interests. Let the enemy make use of them, for all I cared.

Surprisingly, most of a score of knights joined us as we fled along the road. Everyone riding a horse was used to barking out orders and helping build enough order to make an army of us as we raced, then walked, and finally staggered in file away from the pillage of our own camp.

I counted fifty score footmen. It was astonishing that so many survived, though two score died before we finished the march to the duke's main force, two days distant.

As for the duke and our generals, we saw no sign by first nightfall. Word passed that they'd fled to the Duke's castle at Dorne, early and untouched by battle. Even the few surviving knights who'd helped us organize eventually raced ahead, leaving the footmen to our care. We marched nearly the whole distance led by our light cavalry and the highest rank of sergeant, though there were two battered captains, Barker and Wincor, to whom we occasionally reported those things we'd already done. The better the group for the baseborn order of rank, in my opinion.

Half a day's march beyond the field of battle, the drums of Lacellor stopped.

Chapter Eleven

"We have a score and a half of Lettoir's foot. We have nearly as many horses." I rode beside Wistriff, the only remaining squad leader. We were all shaken, but mostly we were too tired to notice. The men we were with, the bulk of the army, dragged more than marched a half night distant from the duke's castle. I worried about the leadership we'd find there, for we had nearly none of our own.

"I am tired and sore from wounds. Don't press, Abe." Wistriff did not even turn to look at me.

"I'm as tired as you are. Still, we should regroup. If we are orderly, the noble dogs will likely leave us as before. If not, Lady Lettoir's foot will be put into the command of yet another idiot noble and wasted."

"Sergeant Ankind was often angry regarding your ill-chosen words. The nobles are our lords and we their subjects."

Wistriff wasn't a bad soldier, but he didn't have a mind for deep thinking. Ah, why had Ankind died, leaving me with this? "Yes, yes. Now, which words should I forget—the ones about the nobles or the ones about saving the lady's men?"

Abe, let us get to camp. They will put us in order. It is not our place to make decisions. Certainly not yours." He took a swig of his water skin and winced from an arm wound.

There was no getting through to him; he'd been a common soldier too long and thought everything was put into order by somebody else. Such was never the case, I suspected, or at least not for me.

"Well then, I loved our sergeant and his body has started to swell. I will see him into his grave, and any noble who dislikes that can meet me on a field with his sword." I stifled a tear.

"Sho, save us from your mouth." Wistriff grunted. "Tell me what you plan."

"To bury him in the low hills where the soil is soft. He would want to be buried in such a place. One or two of us wish to say words." Our sergeant was the only dead man being carried to Dorne. The noble dead had been driven forward with their own kin. I fought to hide my emotions for Ankind, but for the nobles I felt nothing.

"All right then. He was more your friend. See to it. I'll remain and oversee this portion of the march. Catch up before we make camp, or I'll report you missing." Wistriff closed his eyes and returned to sleeping in his saddle as I stopped. He rode on, rocking like a load of beans.

I told each of the men we'd been given the order to go bury our sergeant. They eagerly pulled out of the ranks. When I got to the footmen, I saw how mingled our troops had gotten among the others in the ranks. It took a lot of time to gather those who still appeared able to fight. Those I steered onto a low hill.

In the end, eight horsemen and seventeen of our footmen gathered, all from the fiefdom of our lady. By the time I'd finished organizing the foot, some of the horsemen had already dug the hole. The moon shone upon my friend's shrouded body. I looked at him, knowing I could have been looking at my husband, had fate been different and put that hex on me. That was not for me, but I still missed him as if we'd been connected. A good part of me felt dying in pace with his rotting corpse.

I held my palms up for silence, then bit my lip until I bled, holding back my emotions. "When I look out onto the battlefield, I ask, 'Why am I here?' Though I hunger for the fight, I still do not know why we are at war. The arguments often seem grander than our own views."

"Yes," said an older soldier.

"Now we go back to join another army. We will be sent to new battlefields by those we do not trust. I will look over at my sergeant's ghost on that field of glory, and I will not let him down, for I knew him well, spoke to him often, and loved him greatly."

Many of the men nodded, though some remained still.

"If you did not love him, you did not know him. Still, you must have loved someone. You cannot help but feel this pain. Many of our friends are gone. Let this body stand for all of those we think upon tonight. May their God keep them safe."

One of the men clapped me on the back as I stopped my speech. I put my head down, silently shedding my tears. It was dark. I wanted none to see, though I was not alone. Men had lost friends, and, even if they did not like him, Ankind was the symbol sparking our shared remorse. Ankind was eventually lowered. Dirt fell over his earthly flesh.

"Now I wonder whom I will fight beside when we meet the next battle. Will it be a stranger? Will it be nobody? We of the Lady's guard know one another as horsemen and are not eager to allow others into our ranks, others untrained and who have not earned our trust."

"That is true," said one of the older men.

"And yet, if we march into the duke's camp as less than a half score, we will be pieced out or stripped of our horses and put into the footmen. Eight or nine is no force, and they'll be eager to see it wasted, for they expect little from the likes of us and hope to prove themselves right. It will be the end of us all. Our foot will also have no sergeant."

"Should you be speaking this way?" asked Hobar.

I cast him an angry stare and continued. "We will be put

into the front with the weak and condemned. I ask each and every man here: Do we remain the cavalry of Lady Lettoir, or do we follow our sergeant, having died the death of neglect for reasons we cannot fathom? This is not the time to be overly proud of our station. This is the time to plan before someone does the planning for us. I know Sergeant Ankind. I know what he would tell you."

"Not me. I do as I'm told, as is my place." Hobar drew a nod from two of the younger horsemen.

"Good." I walked over to his horse and stripped a pack off it with two knife swipes on the roping.

Hobar stood in the way of my doing more than that, but he knew better than to challenge me to a fight. I loved the feeling of shoving him aside and facing the men as if he did not exist.

"Are there any more volunteers for the foot? Surely, such is the result of stupidity!" My knife remained in my fist. I sensed Hobar leaning another foot from my reach.

One of the older horsemen spoke up. "Hobar is foolish! Yet, let him keep his horse. You have kept us from death, so it is right what you say. Without horses, we are doomed. We will take count."

"Good." I smelled Hobar's stink near my back and smiled.

I went back to the grave where I took count. Every one of the footmen stepped forward, including Kitchor Ranglson.

"Then we are all horsemen. Each pair of you, take a mentor among the experienced. We start now. Know that we are put above you in the ranks in all that you do and are charged to be harsh so you'll learn.

Hobar made his way around me, perhaps enchanted by the idea of leading others.

"The first chore is to break the loads. We'll need to share provisions and rebind them tightly so the horses can be mounted with at least blankets for saddles until we can find the leather and give a good appearance of order. We have ten extra swords, and the rest of you will bear iron tipped pikes. No soldier rides without steel. You must look like you belong. And, remember, when Wistriff sees you, he will not be pleased."

Many words were shared as men went to their tasks. Even Hobar found two mates after he made it known that I was out of line and foolish. He retrieved his fallen packs and got to work breaking them apart. I went around and helped tear all the packs off the other animals. My own gear was already tightly bound, and I planned on sharing nothing because half the company's gear consisted of things I'd stolen anyway.

We soon had blankets and tents rolled tightly around our individual goods, and, when bound back to the horses, we looked half as burdened for the tightness. Only three animals were left for pack. Neatly folded blankets went on the horses without saddles, and some of the horsemen even shared out their spears, with holders. There were only seven without swords and six without saddles. We rode out of the woods, over a score strong, looking nearly as bold a force as when we'd marched out of our lady's gate.

Our new company made up time in the dark morning hours. We passed the slow and lumbering foot. When we passed the remaining five White Shirts of Sho, Captain Barker nodded in my direction as if he knew everything.

Wistriff wasn't as attentive when we eased in behind him. He was sleeping his way into dawn. I marveled at how he could do it without falling off his animal. It was a skill known only to old soldiers. The rest of us suffered.

When the sun came up, Wistriff noticed he had a whole half company of horsemen to tend. "Ah, what fool thing have you done now?"

I looked at him and shrugged. Luckily, Wistriff didn't seem to have much energy left in his old body for an investigation.

Thus, we made the outskirts of Dorne without further comment.

Our tents were pitched outside the ring of the back moat but still in the shadow of the duke's castle. The grounds were grand, and many standards flew from the parapets. There were six turrets pushing out from the curtain walls and a keep within that was four times the size of the baron's. A moat of running water surrounded the walls, and the only way over was on a bridge. We'd been told that we weren't worthy enough to enter the ramparts.

To one side of the castle, the bustling city of Dorne brewed with rumors that Sir Lacellor was on the heels of our battered forty-seven score. Our broken army had awoken the whole city when we filled the main road. The town-folk lined the gate road. Their faces said they thought we were more trouble than use. Only half of the footmen had pikes, and few had kit. The foot, starving, looked long into the shop windows and, at one point, rushed a bakery where they stripped the place bare. They were pushed back by a contingent of the duke's own guard. His better fed men were not merciful in their slaughter. I found it hard to not hate all of them, footmen, peasants and lords.

We were quick at finding our lonely spot beyond the city and to the rear of the castle, lest we end up in the midst of the disease and infection that rode our army.

As it was, we had plenty of infection of our own. I kept busy in the forest, finding the roots, bark, flowers and leaves I needed to make herbal remedies. It was a sure sign of a witch to overly use the magic of plants in healing. Still, men turned the other way whenever I walked in and out of the woods. They each ripped up at least one set of clothing for boiling as dressings. Only a few did not end up wearing my poultice. It was illegal to hunt in the duke's own preserve as well, but the men did that even without my help, allowing me the time to be their witch.

* * * * *

Sir Lacellor didn't come. I knew he wouldn't. His army had won a great victory, but he'd suffered the loss of almost half of his footmen in doing so. Storming the duke's castle with the army he had left was unthinkable, given our continually reinforced ranks were soon three times what we'd started with, and the walls of the duke's castle were far too strong for only three little catapults. Even our armor had swelled to four score and kept growing as knights came from all over the kingdom.

In truth, we killed ourselves faster than Lacellor could have. We did this through starvation, disease and the folly that comes with too many men in too small a place. Here the nobles only thought enough of us to put every minor offense to the law, adding to our attrition.

In time, I escaped the madness by volunteering to scout all the way to the ford. I led four others, using the road we'd just travelled. I was assigned all new men because Wistriff wanted me to teach them scouting skills. These men included Kitchor Ranglson. I thought to do something mean, but it didn't seem right to kill him outright.

Our army had dropped enough stores in our retreat to provision ten score troops. I had to send one of the men back to get wagons, lest the peasants reap the wares right out from under our feet. The remaining four of us scouted on, right up to our old camp, which had been stripped so clean that the only way I found it was by the smell of old campfires and latrines. Over across the ford, chimney smoke rose over an outpost, obviously housing much less than a company. Outside, four messenger horses grazed.

Between us and them, half of two armies rotted under the sun.

Our dead soldiers were naked, while the enemy's were only half disrobed of tunics and those things useful. A few were buried right on the field. So few buried attested to a job barely begun, and in haste, judging from how many of the shallow graves showed where animals had dug-up body parts. It had apparently proven too great of a task for a victorious army so sorely battered. A thousand vultures flew overhead, while twice as many settled into meals, feeding mostly on the far fewer horses.

The men with me were fearful that someone from the outpost might venture forth, but I rode us right onto the field looking for spare saddles, swords and pikes. The field had been stripped bare of the necessities.

Across Redwater River, the small enemy company stirred when a guard came out of the trees. Several of them emerged from the cabin and watched us with interest. One went for a horse, so I walked Ella right up to the edge of the river and drew my sword. We waited. I rested the tip of the teacher's sword on my pommel. I was an arrow's shot across from where they stood, but I saw no archers readying arrows.

A captain held his hand up, stopping his men. This caused the rider to pause after he'd only dipped his horse's front hooves into the ford. The captain seemed to study me from afar.

I shouted across, "A good day to you! It is a waste, is it not? I commend your lord. He appears to have fared better than ours! Looking upon the dead though, I profess I cannot tell ours from the others. There is a heap of both left for the birds!"

The captain cupped his lips. "My Lord shall fare even better the next time if you persist. I see Sho's king has come to the bottom and now sends women!"

"Would you care for a test? I need to bring terror to your camp when they hear of me."

"Nay. There is no sport in killing our enemy's women, for you will soon be among our fondling spoils. I would be mocked, even should I best you in combat, and be perhaps forever ridiculed for wasting one so pretty." He smirked after his own boast.

"I heard otherwise from some serfs I bested a moon back. One of them confided that Lady Lacellor herself awaits salvation from men who travel with their brides. Debrecians, I hear."

"We have no women so armed." He said that after a moment of hesitation. I liked him, for he wasn't a good liar.

The others in my troop heard our references to women, but the men in Lettoir's guard often poked fun at one another in such ways. My movements had long been suspected as feminine, too, and stories of my longing for Ankind were rumors none told to my face.

"Is that the truth? Well, I confess confusion, for I've had great sport killing warriors easily mistaken for ladies. I thought I noticed the method of sweeping floors in the way they fumbled with their pikes."

A sergeant walked up to his captain, and they conferred. The captain had a changed demeanor when he spoke next. "It seems a few of us have been told ... by a likely ally ... to watch for a noteworthy woman fighting for Farstand. Do you know why you are sought by our ally? Would you be the one?"

"Now that is a better attitude, but I'd cease your jesting regarding my sex if I were you." My body itched with the thought of my enemies fearing me beyond measure.

The captain nodded. "Well, I will need your name. We can offer you truce. Our leaders and allies are curious. You need only answer some questions. I am afforded the duty of guaranteeing your safety."

I wanted no more of this banter, preferring either silence or battle. Something about meeting those Debrecians brought a fear surfacing from within me, too. I had no idea where from, other than perhaps my very soul

I nudged my horse and rode back past the bodies, leading my men into the woods where we camped. I had designs on the night, our mission of scouting done, and, as I saw it, our mission of provisioning for Lady Lettoir next at hand.

"Have we done enough, Abe?" asked one of the men as we camped without a fire.

Another bumped his friend on the shoulder. "Maybe the war is over? Their army seems to have gone home."

"I'm not satisfied. There is more here."

"What is left?" the first man asked. They all fidgeted. Out beyond the boundaries of our camp, a wolf pack prowled, rustling the leaves. Everybody's eyes and noses were useless to them, for they looked about with startled eyes, perhaps imagining the wolves the enemy. I'd heard their thoughts and knew the wolves were only curious. One or two of them followed at distance almost everywhere I went.

"Listen to me. War is not so much about killing the enemy as it is about eating well, avoiding the attention of the nobles and riding into battle well enough provisioned to survive it. Our mission for the duke has ended, but we are poor soldiers when we neglect our mission to Lady Lettoir. Such a mission presents itself." I shrugged in the direction of the river.

Kitchor Ranglson complained: "Now I know why Sergeant Wistriff is uneasy within sight of you."

"I propose to go across the Redwater and steal horses, saddles, and, if they will let us, some swords so we will all be armed and ready for the next battle."

"That's madness!" all three of them exclaimed, though the exact words varied.

"It's a trap," said Kitchor.

"Or so they imagine. It's as if they aim to give their goods to me. All I see is an outpost blinded by the night."

"Lady Lettoir has not asked us to do this. The whore is too

far off." Kitchor laughed.

I put my face up to his. "Watch your mouth, Kitchor! No man lives who befouls her good name? Ah, what's your problem? Did she short you a copper and a black potato?" I wanted to stick him, but determined to do it after I'd gotten good and fed up.

I continued, "Ankind spoke for her, Kitchor. Now my words are as good as hers. I've taken from the enemy often, and we'd all be naked without it. Do you think the duke is going to give us saddles and swords? They would rather take our horses and put us in the foot."

One asked, "You have a right to ask this of us?"

"Sure, I can tell you what I want. I can tell you to go jump in the river and drown yourselves. Will you do it?"

"No."

"Well then, there you have it." I got up on Ella's back. I tied my darkest cloak around myself. "Don't go anywhere. The wolves will not eat you, but, if you are found straggling, they will be tempted."

"You mean to do this alone?" One of the braver of them stepped near the horses as if willing to go.

"I have the eyes for it. You are new and probably too noisy." I kneed my horse, and we parted the limbs.

Once I was clear of the men, the wolves fell in around me. I noticed a young grey whose eyes were golden. He was not yet full sized, but he'd grown much in the past month and itched to declare himself the leader. He came at my horse and nipped before darting away. Doing this three times was a grave insult, so I stopped, even though I'd come to the river's edge. I turned and rode toward the place he'd scampered.

"Is this how you greet a friend?"

He wasn't shy telling me in my head that I smelled a lot like the bloated corpses littering the river plain.

"You'll have to think of better ways to prove yourself. What you're doing may waste a friend."

He snarled a little bit, but the bitches came around and persuaded him to behave.

They fell behind, and I made shore downwind of the outpost. The captain I'd spoken to didn't seem as much a fool as most of the nobles I knew. I'd seen some movement down the western portion of the river, but he still worried me a little. I determined it was best to put my horse in a stand of trees nicely away and east of my objective.

I grabbed my staff because it was silent, and I'd grown comfortable with it in my youth. Then I waited a while to see if anyone had seen my crossing. I wasn't confident I'd made my crossing unnoticed. The moon remained ample and the clouds sparse. Sure enough, as I let the minutes pass, I sensed someone coming close. He was in the water, closing along the bank. The trees were too tight around me for my staff, so I readied my knife and found a good place to get a jump on the sentry as he passed.

It surprised me to see Kitchor wading near. The man looked right at me as he passed and didn't see a thing. He continued toward the enemy a step before I said, "Don't move, or they'll see you."

He splashed and turned but still didn't see me. "Abe? It's me, Kitchor."

"Well, I can see that. What are you doing here?"

"You need my help. I can't have you taking all the credit. When we return to our camp, they'll say we were cowards." He stepped a little closer.

"I don't believe you. Why does a Ranglson stick his neck out?" My palm sweated around the knife's grip.

"From where do I know you?" His eyes danced all around in my general direction.

"I'm kneeling above you with my knife. Now, why have you followed me? And, no more foolishness."

"The comment about a copper and a black potato is from a saying I used back home. Phrases like that. Mannerisms, too, persuade me you're familiar."

"There are plenty of coppers and plenty of potatoes. To speak of them is nothing special."

"It's more than that. It's like we're kin."

"Not likely. I'm a bastard. I have only one kin, and she is not like you in any way. Don't think on it. Let's think how we are going to do this mission instead." I desperately wanted to tell him I'd killed his brother and watched him squirm. My darkest instinct was to slit his throat. It seemed a treasonous thing to do to Lady Lettoir though. She'd become the center of my ethos.

"You're not serious about going on?"

"Perhaps it's best you go back. I'm too busy to argue with a Ranglson. Besides, we're unlikely to encounter women and unarmed merchants."

"That is an insult to my family name. I'll have it out, if that's what you want." He stood several feet away, still in the river and looking up at me. I noticed his eyes had adjusted just enough to roughly see where I crouched in the shadows.

"You have a sword in hand and I a knife. Take this chance or leave it. I won't suffer worrying over a blade in the back." The grip on my knife hardened. Thoughts no longer lingered on the mission of stealing horses.

The sword he'd started to draw slid back into its sheath. "It need not come to blood. I have heard enough from you and from what the others say. Your manner is short tempered. I give it allowances, and I'll hold no grudge. We are on the same side. It's said you have no equal in war. This a man respects."

It wasn't what I'd expected him to say. I doubted the pledge would last long if he knew I was Abi, the girl who'd killed his brother. That was a stain I still didn't regret, though I now knew the boy to have been virtually defenseless against my might. Then again, maybe I did regret it. The boy was nothing — why not let him live? Somewhere inside, I was not right.

All of that was a distraction, so I decided to let the matter pass until another time.

"You can make use of yourself by shuffling a load across the ford."

"Why not go with you?"

"Horses are noisy and can't make sense of being stolen. Me, I know exactly what I am doing."

"But I—"

"Unlike you."

I left him to stew and found another spot to wait out any hidden sentries. That blind was close enough to the enemy horses to make one of them whinny. Of the four, there were only two horses left. There were no sentries out in the reaches. It seemed the only man out of the cabin was a sentry doing his shift by sitting lazily on the other side of a fire in the cleared yard. Every so often, he got up and walked around the cabin, but it was almost as if he avoided the horses and had chosen to limit his search to places lit by the flames. For a company at war, set to guard a crossing that had proven the apex of the biggest battle, I thought the lone sentry fatally posted.

When I was sure he was alone, I took off as fast as I could right into the fire. I leapt over it straight at the sentry. As I emerged from the smoke and flames, he saw me, and his eyes sparkled from the reflection of the fire. I flew my staff, twirling it and crashing it into his skull. He dropped dangerously close to the pit, so I pulled him clear and even propped him up by a log to make it look like he was just dozing.

There were no saddles and no swords other than the short

one strapped to the sentry, so I took it and the horses back to the river bank. Kitchor was gone. I feared he'd taken Ella, but she was still where I'd put her, and so I tied them all together and went back to the cabin to see what else I could find before the sentry woke up with his headache.

The cabin had one window made of poured glass. I looked in and saw the shape of two men sleeping and another sitting at a table. The one at the table shifted in an overly nervous manner. He wavered between nodding off, bouncing his head up, as if poised to strike at the door within a moment's notice. His attempts at wariness raised my suspicion. Still, I was hesitant to let the chance pass. I looked in again, and noticed that the door was unlatched; its heavy brace leaned by the door.

Going around, I knocked lightly and then slowly opened the door before I walked in and made my presence known.

The man regarded me as if expecting a friend when I walked in carefully. He saw my face and gave a gasp. He stood and pulled his sword out. It hit my shaft with a glancing blow. A thin sliver of wood flew like a feather between us. I popped him in the crotch and then rounded on his elbow. The sword loosened in his hand as he leaned over in pain.

A second man lunged from his bed and swung a short sword as I ducked aside. The cabin's fire was too dim for a waking man to make sense of his surroundings. As he raced past, I popped him on the head with the end of the staff that rested a hand's width from my fist. He fell over the first soldier, both of them down in a pile. The last man was slower still, sitting up. I cracked him across the chin and then gave him a headache bad enough to keep him in bed a little longer.

The first man untangled himself from the fellow who'd fallen. He came at me, but I had his sword by then, and I slid the blade down his. I parted the meeting of metal long enough to get past his hilt. My blade sliced a neat row of cuts to the bones of his four fingers. On the same back swing, I caught his guard, lifting his sword from the damaged hand.

He froze at the point of my sword.

"Go back to bed. In the morning, find a good hedge witch and, if she's good, the Goddess might let you keep your fingers." I stepped over his second friend to get my third and fourth sword prizes, though three of the four blades were short and not much good to a horseman. He cradled his hand as he backed toward the far corner of his bed with nervous glances at me and the door.

I went through their war provisions, bundling the best of them into a couple of cloth sacks, including some of the better jerky and flour. Four swords in total and a fairly robust pouch of coppers were there for the taking in that camp. A light saddle sat by the door, and I took it as well, though I could barely hold my staff as I backed toward the door with both hands struggling with my new spoils.

That's when I saw the book by the door. It rested just inside a bag that was made of fancy patches of cloth, as if on display. I fancied the book and its bag, taking those, too.

"You best not follow me, or I'll not be so generous with your lives the next time." I nodded. I waited for a reply. I nodded again.

One of the soldiers thought it best to nod back, so I backed out of the cabin and raced back over the fire, the leap much burdened by my load.

I took the time to saddle one of the horses and went right to tying the burdens of goods onto the stolen pair, knowing that, as soon as I started across the river, I might be in need of all the haste I could muster. I put my staff into my own bundle.

Over by the cabin, the soldiers fussed. They were running in the opposite direction and yelling out alarms. It hardly mattered; I was ready to leave.

Then I heard a yell. Curiosity overcame me. I went back to see Kitchor pulling his blade out of the belly of the man with the wounded fingers. The man he'd killed was unarmed. Back behind the cabin, the tree limbs were still swinging from where the others had taken off into the safety of the woods. I watched as Kitchor went through the pocket of the dying man. Kitchor wasn't even waiting for the man to fall. The dying man moaned. He sank to his knees as Kitchor stole his purse.

I tried to tell myself I'd taken a purse, too, but knew it was different. I'd not killed an unarmed man solely for his own coin, but, instead, I spared him and the other one in a lawful raid on the enemy's stores. I'd left them their lives and made a bargain for their trouble. Now, here was Kitchor, and, with our horses behind us, we were easy pickings for any enemy who might find them unguarded.

I pulled out my sword and walked toward the fire. My legs were not my own. I had no sense of control at all. A pair of fighting souls possessed me, one swelling like a tornado of rage, the other turning her back, allowing it to happen. I chanted words with each step, the words coming to my mouth without even a thought. It felt as if the Goddess herself possessed my lips:

"I am who I am.

I am the angel of death.

I am the taker of life.

I am Abi, the sister of the crone.

I am Abi, daughter of my mother.

I need hide from no man!

Let the gift of death fly before me now.

Thank the Goddess for it.

So we might take the soul of the enemy before us."

"Tpunwvw Own,"

I walked right through the fire and felt no pain.

Kitchor stuttered my name, "Abi!" His eyes must have seen a demon. He fell back across the body that moaned and bled beneath his feet. Kitchor kicked himself away from the man he'd killed. Then he found just enough room to get up. He held his bloody sword out before him, inexpertly, like the amateur soldier he was.

I came possessed and with the added strength of a mighty spell swelling my muscles.

I came down on his poorly made sword, cleaving it in two.

I came down on it again, cleaving the stub of it in two.

I spun in place, and, with the full force of my rotation, cut his head off him, even the bony spine. The head flew, spinning out threads of blood. The body below it still stood. I caught his hair, spit on his face and turned it so he could see his own body fall.

I confessed, "I killed your brother! Now I have killed you!" even before his eyes glossed over in death. Then I tossed the useless head into the fire where it belonged.

When I was done, I gave the stub of Kitchor's sword to the bloody fingers of the corpse of the man he'd murdered. The soldier clutched it in an enormous pool of two men's blood. Then I left that unholy place, collecting my horses.

Their captain had been busy setting a trap for me, and I'd seen some of his movements earlier. He and the others had been standing watch over the wrong end of the river where the forging wasn't deep. They were coming on the wind I smelled though. I crossed the deep, downwind side of the river as they arrived at their camp.

I knew eyes were upon me as I rose up the distant shore. It felt as if some of those eyes saw into my soul. I didn't know if it was clean or filthy in there, but I'd determined to claim myself as my own, regardless. I was Abi, shaman warrior. I heard the crone's words clearly now, though I didn't know the title's meaning beyond the wrath of the warrior who fought in there. That battle raged deep within the body. The warrior was winning, though I was not yet old enough to be troubled by it much.

Chapter Twelve

I led the string of horses to our camp where it was too quiet to be believed.

The camp was littered with footprints, but my last two soldiers were a clearing away. One was on the ground, spread out in an almost ceremonial death pose. The other hung by both hands, palms pinned to two trunks by arrows.

I broke the shafts and slid him off. He was breathing and pink but had been severely beaten. After dousing him with water, I left him to recover while I checked tracks and found two new sets of horse prints to go with the two horses they'd stolen. My enemy apparently shared my inspiration for theft.

The men's weapons and packs remained hidden behind some brush. Perhaps they'd beaten my man for nothing, since the horse was obvious, and they'd taken nothing else.

"Markel? What happened?"

I leaned too close. The moon had risen, lighting my face as I hovered above. All at once, his eyes shifted to my chin, and he cringed back against the ground. "Don't kill me!"

"It's me, Abe."

"You're one of those Debrecians!"

"Your eyes are playing tricks." I dipped my face and leaned closer so he'd not see my features in the faint light.

His breathing eased, but he stayed tense. "I didn't recognize you. Your voice—it seems different."

"It sounds that way because your ears have been battered. Enough with this foolishness. Tell me what happened."

"Two of them. They were just women but also warriors like I've never seen. The first I knew of them was an arrow. It impaled my hand on that tree. I screamed a warning to Jasuah. He screamed and fell nearly at my feet.

"One of the demon women came. She held my other hand to the other tree. Her friend shot it. I had no choice. She shaved hair off my arm with a knife while I screamed. I was their puppet, and they beat me, too, asking about you."

I was stunned. What was I to them when there were swords and saddles so free to be taken with a simple enquiry?

"And what did you tell these women?"

"Everything I knew of you, I suppose. It didn't seem one of those important secrets, so I was not slow in spilling even the gossip. I'm sorry, Abe. But what is the sense in it? Who of us don't know you are a decent scout, though you are no one in rank. You are just a bastard with no blood in your veins. I told them that, too, -- for you." Markel licked his lips, so I tilted the water skin, missing his mouth mostly.

"Ah, it is true I have no royal blood in me. Did you tell them I had no blood in me at all?"

He didn't answer, though his heart quickened.

I should have been angry with him for telling so much to the enemy, but there was much more to the story than me. Besides, he was right; what was I but an open tale? Then again, I was anything but, I told myself. All of it adding so much to my wonder and worry.

Markel said something else, which I didn't at first hear because my brain was working over the facts and could find no footing. He repeated, "They didn't believe me about the blood."

"What else didn't they believe?" I got up from kneeling. I needed to do something about my powerful disguise spell before the sun came up. It would be best to not be too close to Markel until I could manage it, I was thinking as I looked around.

"They said you were a woman and that they had seen this from across the river. I said we weren't led by a woman but by a man named Abe. They wouldn't believe me and beat me until I told them you were a woman. I am sorry, but what was I to do? I would have told them my own father was an ale hag if it caused them to stop." The man turned to the ground, beaten. There he wept.

"Hey!" I nudged him with a foot. "I would have called you my sister as well had it been me. There is no shame in it, for you survived it. The same can't be said for your friends."

"It is a hard lesson." He tried to sit up.

"It will be harder still, for we have two long days of riding, and you'll need to do some of it before we can properly tend your wounds in a safe camp."

"Yes. Let's get out of here." He suddenly found the strength to get up. I took the shirt off his friend's body and tore strips off it, tossing them to him so he could wrap his wounds. Then I packed the horses.

"Ride into the moon, straight through the woods. Don't go to the road. Only when you can no longer see the moon in the sky should you stop and rest. I'll be with you shortly if your course doesn't waver. Otherwise, you'll be lost, and the forest will eat you." I tied the extra horses onto his. I laughed at my joke and gave his horse's rump a quick swat.

Golden Eyes was still standing at the edge of our small clearing, looking at me as if he thought I was unaware of him. I didn't think he was mad at me; still, he wasn't friendly either.

"Well, if you come with me, you'll learn something better than staring at my horse with spit dripping off your lips." He pretended to go away, but he'd only gone as far away as he thought I could see.

The tracks took me back across the river. Over there, they

vanished on a creek bed of hardened rock. That I saw as no accident on the part of the scouts as my respect for them swelled. There was sure to be a new ambush up ahead. I climbed the creek bed's bank and, following a parallel course to their tracks, kept as much downwind as possible.

When I got close, I backtracked, hiding Ella. I didn't see them when I crept up closer, but their four horses were easy to spot. They tried, but they couldn't hide their smell either. I was careful, lest they leave their smelly laundry about to distract my nose. To be sure of it, I backed off, keeping my distance until I knew them better. One came into sight. She moved slowly, right toward where I'd previously been watching. She paused; then, she stood in the exact spot I'd occupied and looked down into her own camp. I imagined her thinking that a good spot for a scout to see them from.

I was very impressed by it. She was the most diligent soldier I'd ever observed, and she was just a woman.

The Debrecian woman wore riding boots with hard leather on the outside and soft soles underneath. Her britches were like a man's, though she also wore a short skirt. At her hip hung a sword and a long knife right beside it, the sheaths bound together in a bundle. Across her back rested a short bow with a small quiver of arrows bound right to the wood. I would not be so comfortable with so many weapons, but she wore them as if they'd been there all of her life.

A necklace danced between her breasts. Two coins winked at the coming dawn. It was the only distraction to her dark and colorless clothing, and I longed to see the coins closer because it reminded me of the wolf coin I wore between my own breasts. The loose seam of her brown shirt showed her breasts as she moved, though she acted comfortable that way. The woman moved unlike anyone I'd ever seen, one with the land, and, at the same time, as free with herself as a fox in a field of rodents.

Though young, her hair was the color of the snow on top of the mountains. She bound it with a knot tight at the back of her head. Hair spilled from there in a fountain.

Her spirit sang the song of a building storm patiently rising along the northern horizon.

The woman was tall, too, almost the same as me in so many ways that I eased the branch back, hiding more of my face from her quick and eager glances about. I knew I couldn't walk into her camp, even in the dark, for she was magnificent to watch as she moved with wary stealth in spite of her mighty stature.

Young Golden Eyes sat down on an exposed boulder near me then, having picked just that moment to decide upon a trusting friendship. His body was in plain sight to all of us as the sun came up. He apparently decided it was a good place to rest, falling asleep on the rock. That demonstrated his newfound trust. The woman turned to see all around again and paused, looking right up at him. She watched him for signs that he was too lazy to give. After she got her fill of curiosity, she went on, circling around and back to her camp. No doubt she'd tell her sister she'd seen a grey wolf lounging in plain sight like he had no sense. They were earthy women, possibly witches, so the sign of my wolf would likely be an important omen to them.

The horses, inviting spoils to me just a moment ago, couldn't be taken from these women, nor would I get close enough to learn more than I had.

I went back to Ella and took the round path back to the river, crossing at a place that forced Ella to swim. I felt I'd learned nothing. As I went, I invoked my charms and returned to my old disguise of Abe for the benefit of the men serving the king.

After paralleling the river, I passed near the ford. Across from there, on the enemy's side of Redwater, the captain and his sergeant noticed my passage. I showed my palm and kept a safe distance before galloping off to find Markel, whose finding was simple.

* * * * *

It took us three days to get back to the city of Dorne and the duke's castle because of Markel's fever and aches. I didn't regret the delay; there was much ill news to convey. I felt a failure for losing half of us to such a small force and with no more horses and only a little more gear in our possession than we'd left with. With a shared feeling of failure, we went around the castle and into the field where I expected to find our camp. It was occupied by footmen.

Up on a hill, I looked around for horses, finding Lady Lettoir's soldiers mingled in among a larger group of the duke's and the baron's assorted light horsemen. Our troops had been moved to their own third of these grounds, clearly made a part of some new order. The hated White Shirts were mingled with us, having been reinforced to nearly a score. The rest were messengers. At the center were Sir Wencor's tents, large, white and with circled crosses marking their dedication to Sho. I paused before the combined camp, disgusted to see it.

First I found Wistriff. He'd sewn a sergeant's chevron on his sleeve.

Next, out of our largest tent, Sergeant Hadarm emerged, apparently having arrived from the fiefdom at last. He took one look at me. Before I could even get off my horse, my old sergeant said, "Abe. Right away. We have to talk."

Hadarm ducked in, obviously expecting me to follow. He put his head back out saying to Wistriff, "Alone."

I looked at Wistriff, who appeared to be enjoying the idea of exclusion. He sternly nodded to me before I ducked in.

Sergeant Hadarm started the moment I entered. "Sergeant Wistriff has told me you took up matters above your station."

I took a seat on one of the new barrels of oats that lined one side of the tent. "I didn't notice it troubling him much. Besides, if I'd not, Wistriff wouldn't be here to complain about it."

"There are several versions of that." Hadarm smacked his small table with his palm. "Now, to start, what about the idea you had of putting our new foot on horses?"

"I serve Lady Lettoir. She wouldn't be pleased to see her subjects fed into the slaughter as simple footmen. If you'd been there, Sergeant Hadarm, you'd have seen it for the folly it was. I thought to save both our men and our horses. Ankind had a good head about the problems we faced in keeping our steeds under us and not under some noble in need of animals to bear his comforts. Wistriff is a good man, but he doesn't see far on matters of importance."

"And have you thought about how we'll pay them? A footman collects four coppers a month. We pay our horsemen two silvers. Provisions are also nearly five times the sum paid foot. That is five times the sum twice, Abe. Did you think upon that, for I can assure you our new Sergeant Wistriff reminded me."

I once revered Sergeant Hadarm for his knowledge of the minor issues that amounted to so much we guardsmen took for granted, but I was weary. "It's a trivial concern, Sergeant. If they want to return to the foot, let them. If they intend to stay on horses for the duration of the war at four copper, let them do that as well. As for the provisions, we get none from the baron, and it's nearly impossible to steal what we need without our animals."

"You have a mouth that you need to better manage, Abe!" My sergeant stood, though he couldn't do it properly with the low ceiling.

"And, now that you're here, you have a company that is in need of attending, Sergeant Hadarm!" I stood just as poorly.

He cast a threatening stare. After we traded stares, he sat back down. "Would that I could. Sir Wencor has taken command of the reorganized light cavalry. That, at least, settles your concern that none speak for us in the order. As for your mouth, you're already in trouble for it. There's an enquiry into the battle. In the process of laying blame for the lacking victory, things whittled down in your direction. I'm to take you to the baron's brother for judgment."

"Who is he to judge me?" I nearly laughed at the idea.

"He is the baron's brother. That stands him as tall as a mountain next to the swamp, you insolent bastard!"

"I gather you put stock in that, but I've come to wonder about such things. We shall see how his judgment passes." I had no idea why I felt such confidence, but it had come rushing into me as if I were a bowl under the rain drenched eaves of a cottage.

"Where do you get such thoughts?" His voice felt resigned as if he'd come to some conclusion that saddened him.

"Do you really want to know?"

"Surely. Tell me."

"The gods. They speak to me daily now, as if I'm a battlefield upon which both Sho and the Goddess play for sport. They confuse me often, Sergeant, but one thing is not so confusing to me: The baron isn't much in their eyes and his brother less. They shall say and do what they will, and then I shall move on to the next thing the gods have planned for me."

"God's plan for you? God does not determine our path, for he has given us our choices, and yours are not wise." He shook his head.

"The gods shoves us off cliffs and convinces us on the way down that we have many ways to scream and flail the air."

He looked at me blankly. "I'm almost afraid to ask you about the mission."

"Then I shall shorten it. The enemy has left the field guarded by only a half score. I raided their camp. Before I returned, two Debrecian scouts raided ours, killing one man. These two enemies were only their women. They are far better at killing than any of us and beautiful to behold as they go about their tasks. Oh, and I killed Kitchor Ranglson for murdering an unarmed man while stealing three coppers out of his pocket. I'd appreciate it if that went unmentioned."

"God be merciful," he breathed.

"Unlikely, for the birds were eating our corpses by the hundreds, though they favored the taste of the horses."

"If you speak like this before Sir Randolf, he shall hang you for sure. I cannot protect you in this."

I decided not to say anything to that.

"Better. Now, Sir Wencor's man, Captain Barker, has offered to stand beside you in the inquiry. He was there at the battle, and he is respected in the circle of Sir Randolf, so it's an advantageous offer for you. Find your best tunic. Someone else will tend your horse. We go as soon as I fetch Sir Wencor." Sergeant Hadarm waved toward the flap of his tent.

* * * * *

This was the first time I'd been allowed within the walls because of my low rank. Now, the blame for the duke's poor leadership had rolled all of the way around and finally to the lowest soldier they could find. It had taken more than two weeks, so I had to admire the drama involved in finding me. I was sad to know I'd heard none of the rumors in it though. They must have raced exclusively from noble to noble, story upon story. Strangely, I felt honored to be the king's brother's excuse, given he'd proven such a bad leader.

That is not to say I wasn't nervous appearing before so many who looked down upon my unfortunate birth. I was nobody to the likes of the king's own brother, so the duke had determined to let my head noble, Sir Randolf of Helfax, sit in judgment. It was an ill omen; I knew Randolf to be even worse at managing his men than his battles, for he was the one starving so many and hanging those who were not good at poaching. Already I'd been in trouble before him, once by usurping the command of his brother's chamberlain, and again when I'd been put into his prison so he could wager bets on my survival. The Goddess will be furious with him if he persists, I thought, wondering if even that was true, given her remote loft and estranged quality.

I came through the grand hall door beside Captain Barker. Behind us, Sergeant Hadarm was escorted in beside Sir Wencor. The grand hall was unlike anything I'd ever seen before, and I determined to not miss a bit of it as I looked all around and up and at the walls and ceiling. The windows were panels of colored glass with stained pictures of men and horses fighting. One showed a lady, not unlike the Goddess, standing with her palms up as if she were giving us something she didn't have in her hands. That one seemed the most honest window to me at the time, given I had seen how poorly the knights fought on their horses, and how I felt at that moment, as if the Goddess were offering up nothing in the way of help.

Guards in puffed up sleeves, striped and baggy britches and long silvery staffs stopped us from walking on while the nobles on the other end of the room mulled over other business.

Noble women and men watched the entertainment of judging. They filled the spaces around the wide aisle. The men were in front and the women behind, the women mostly standing. Some of the women were doing small and large stitchings. Well turned out girls of waiting were there just to hold up the yarn. It must have been an official chore for the noble women, for some of them must have made the carpet. It was red and thick and covered the whole floor up to the central aisle, all the way to the duke's ornate chair and the baron's brother's smaller one. I imagined someone's whole life spent spinning and weaving the floor drape and nothing else.

We came up when called. There were guards on each side, all looking down upon us with straight heads and trailing eyes. I guess I was supposed to be a criminal, though I came in with Lady Lettoir's colors, my best black shirt and my sword and knife dangling in their sheaths. I was a soldier still, until they deemed me otherwise. When we got close, we all bowed, touching our foreheads to the floor as if we were offering our skulls to be stepped on.

They were rude to us, leaving all four of us like that until they got tired of it, and Sir Randolf told us to get up to our knees. It was from down there that I assessed the duke in his chair and Sir Randolf in one almost as nice beside him. They gossiped as if on some kind of break between jousting events. I heard all of the words, but they only reiterated the lies that had brought us before them.

Beside the pair of them stood a number of other finely dressed nobles, including an old friend, the tax collector, Sir Irstan. When our eyes met, it was a surprise to us both. After a time of being on our knees, Sir Randolf noticed Sir Wencor and Captain Barker, and had them get up all the way, leaving me and the sergeant to enjoy the stone work under our knee bones.

It was painful and a good reminder of the hospitality these higher beings afforded those who served them, even unto forfeiture of our lives in battle. The soul of the old woman inside of me yelled for me to get up and kill every last one of the fat and useless nobles sitting and standing on the stage before me. We'd have no fairness in our conversation if I were left looking at their ankles. Still, the dead Sergeant Ankind's many words echoed in my head, telling me to hold my temper and see what came of it. Then, of course, if things went badly, I could leap up suddenly and kill them with a clean conscience. That last part, of course, was not the sergeant's advice, for I heard the crone's last swordplay clanging in my ears.

The duke didn't know how close to death he sat when he said to Randolf, "I have decided to let you judge your own man, Sir Randolf."

Now I knew, of course, that Randolf had an obligation to please his duke with his ruling, and, also, I assumed, to please the many in the court with a good show of it. He said, "Is this the soldier Abe about whom I have heard some rumor?" I looked up, and he added, "Ah, I think I know your face, but I cannot place it. Yes, I am sure of it, for it is an unusual face in some way that I cannot note."

I prepared to do my chant, so he could see it more clearly before I stuck him like a pig. Instead, Sir Barker intervened on my behalf: "This man is well known among the low in birth, my Lord. He is known for his unusual bravery and great skill at scouting, which he does tirelessly, wearing upon the enemy camps. As well, the escaped prisoners, regarding whom I did serve to help capture, were tracked with the considerable help of soldier Abe. He was always obediently at my side. I will touch upon this later, if it pleases the court. All I wish to tell you, as an introduction, is he has proven a good soldier for the king. Any determination by this court that finds Abe in ill light is a fair and different consideration, but I plea only that when judgment is met out, mercy finds room, kind Sers."

"So heard by your Lords," said the duke.

Sir Randolf began, "Yet, this is a serious matter before us, a matter that has troubled the court for many days. Though the victory was solid enough, and I've just learned the enemy has fled the field entirely, proving it so, there was an instance when the right flank was loosed untimely, leaving us with no reserve. It has come to the court's attention that a common soldier led a charge that was unwarranted and proved costly to our heroic knights. Without the reserve, we had no defense to call upon when the enemy armor fell upon our rear. It is a grave matter that we lost many good friends that day, caused by the lack of discipline. It would do the army good to make an example of such nonsense, once and for all."

The court mumbled its approval, particularly the women, who had shrill voices and who aimed to please their men with the sound of them.

Sir Barker said, "It was this solder, minutes ago, who brought back news that the enemy has fled the field. He came back with two of the enemy's horses, and much of his gear, having single handedly killed the men who rode them. He sent word back for wagons to collect stores tossed aside by the peasant levies on their march to our duke's castle. These arms and clothes supply many men at arms. As you have well stated, Sir Randolf, an example should be made, but the example should be made in a wise manner befitting the words of the Lord Sho regarding his best servants. For God does not ask that his servants be perfect, only that they serve him diligently, always seeking to serve his interests."

The duke interrupted again, his interest apparently piqued. "Do you repent your poor judgment, boy?"

Do I repent? What kind of question was that? Yet, I had to say something, so I said, "I don't repent killing the enemy who killed my sergeant, if that is what you mean... my Lord."

The ladies gasped, and nobles frowned. I studied this, finding it curious. Was killing the enemy not why I was here?

"Ser, may I speak," Sergeant Hadarm said behind me.

"Yes," said Sir Randolf, for the interest of all of the nobles was high, even to the point that I could hear all the needle-points cease their clicking.

"Ser, Abe is from a loan of land well back in the woods, and he has no social understanding. He belongs in the woods, smelling out the enemy, not at court, where he is certain to sound a fool every time his mouth opens."

There was a roar of laughter around the room. I guess I was supposed to appreciate that, but, at the moment, I was doing all that I could to keep the crone's spirit from bursting out of my chest and spilling heads all over the floor.

From behind the duke, I saw Sir Irstan lean over and say, "This I know to be true from an experience I had on the road with Lady Lettoir, my Lord. The man stands out as having no social sense, and yet he seems most sincere in his service. For two days, he nearly outran our horses."

Just to make the insults worse, Captain Barker added, "This is exactly the case, my Lord Duke and Sir Randolf. Abe is a servant of the Lord, not unlike Jonie the Baptista, who also made grave errors of judgment, and who was uncivil in court. It is said he had no manners. Do not let it end as did that story, for the Baptista had his head cleaved when his service before the court was misunderstood for disloyalty. The very king who ordered his death did also grieve that loss, for he lost the ear of God through it, as you well know from the Gostic."

The court murmured with many conversations due to that, forcing the duke to take over the proceedings. He shouted, "Do you contend that God himself is interested in this matter?"

"Let us reason is all I am suggesting, my Lord. While the court's many wise councilors have run this story from ear to ear for weeks, little has been said about the hundreds of soldiers saved by the charge Abe led. His sergeant was killed early. There was much confusion. We all know that battles are full of confusion. While we all regret the loss of so many knights, could it reasonably be said that light cavalry, clear on the other side of the battlefield, and mostly dead from sitting idle under a hail of arrows, could have raced so far fast enough to save more than two or three? These are not trained knights; they are common soldiers who bear no armor. As well, they have little training, the idle minds of common birth, and no understanding of tactics. Claim this to the demons of confusion, and then all we have left to consider is the will of God."

"Pah! The will of God, you say!" scoffed Sir Randolf.

Behind me, I heard the voice of young Sir Wencor speak up without asking permission. "Yes! It is the very will of God that we speak of, Lord Randolf and honorable Duke Crestlin of Falstaff, true blood, and second only to the king. Captain Barker has spoken to me about the way Abe helped find those prisoners. Few men can track as Abe does, often without prints or common signs. God points his way. Many speak of it as if a great mystery. I do not like Abe. He is not friendly and does not know his place. So, with this dislike in my mind, I sought the guidance of Sho. Without hesitation, Sho sent me a vision. He spoke as clearly as the words spoken in this hall. He said, 'This is My servant. I will have no harm come to him through your hands until this is finished. If you do not obey, I shall give you unto his hands! He is mighty and serves My will!' Thus armed with this vision from God, I have tried for three weeks to persuade Abe to come into the fold of the holy guards of Sho, though to this moment I have told no man why."

There was a great shuffle of feet and voices, which a man in armor hushed by banging his staff on the shiny rock floor.

Why didn't they just put me in some prison again, and take bets on which prisoner would live, I wondered? I didn't like their attention one bit!

The duke asked, "Did you just say that Sho wills this man to live among you so he may taunt you?"

Sir Wencor answered, "It seemed to me that God said I should not fight him. If I do, and win, I'll be in God's disfavor, though God does not seem optimistic with my chances. I have known fear but will not cower at my duty, my Lords. I will fight any man I must, but I will not fight the will of God, for that is a sin against us all."

"This I had not expected," said the duke. He sat down, though I'd not seen him rise as my concentration had been on all of the gasping people.

Sir Randolf couldn't have been pleased, but he knew his judgment of me had to shift with the countenance of the duke. "There seems to be only one recourse in this matter. First, I have decided that this soldier is guilty of all charges laid before him. The only matter before the court is one of disposition. I believe God even works his will through animals and rocks, so why not this, our lowest soldier? We should wait and see what comes of it, as God wills. In the meantime, we cannot have this soldier unattended and untutored in the ways of soldiering, nor in the ways of God. As punishment, I remand him into the hands of Sir Wencor. Let him make no orders and lead no charges, lest they come through you, Sir Wencor. Take charge of this man, so he does no more harm. This way we correct the error of having those of low birth leading our companies into ill conceived charges. Does this suit the will of the duke?"

Duke Crestlin nodded, and then said, "This does not set well with those who have lost fine knighted husbands, sons and fathers. Yet, even their deaths are the will of God in some way. Let us content ourselves by knowing it was the enemy who murdered them. God has said his will, so let us stop our thoughts and turn them to the true enemy of the king. Vengeance will be found only on the battlefield where it properly belongs. So spoken, this matter is done!"

The armored soldier banged the floor with his pike, and so we got up and were ushered toward the side door. I didn't like the idea of being put under the awful White Shirts, nor did I like the idea that they'd gotten the main point affixed that I'd been the cause of the duke's idiotic failures on the battlefield. Still, I was walking out and could decide on how to manage it later. As humiliated as I felt, I was undecided about whether it might have been better if I'd just finished it all with some gut poking and head cleaving before the guards took me.

When we were only halfway out of there, a soldier ran into the great hall. He scurried forward with some haste. Everybody turned to see what the matter was. We shifted to the side, making a third row of ourselves behind the nobles and women. The soldier fell to his knees.

He was one of the duke's own men, a court guard by the looks of his useless, but pretty uniform. His cheek was bleeding, as was his knee, though he put his knees to the stone without much of a flinch. With his head all of the way onto the floor, he took a breath and said the first thing I could understand in the echo burdened room:

"There is a delegation from Sir Lacellor, my Duke. The ambassadors were not seen until they stood at the very entrance of this castle. When I asked them to wait, one of them beat at me such that I had to summon half of the castle's company! They didn't seem pleased to be here, and yet they insisted that I call them to your attention directly, my Lord."

"How many?" asked the duke.

"Two."

"Two? Just two?" The duke could see the blood on the man as well as I could. It was humiliating just to look at him.

"Two great warriors, my Lord. We, of course, didn't have the luxury of killing them, for they held the white flag of truce and declared themselves ambassadors, my Lord. One, is uh…"

"Is what. Spit it out, man," shouted Sir Randolf.

"A woman, Ser!"

I had to bite my fist, lest I laugh.

The high duke sighed, but then waved to the man to get up

and bring the ambassadors before the court.

All of us wanted to see it. Not a word was spoken as we found places along the wall, near enough to the side exit door that none would begrudge our loitering. I wasn't comfortable being in the presence of enemies who were not under my spell, allowing them to see me as a woman, so I shuffled behind the big hair and bustle of an overweight woman knitting a large picture of ducks on a pond. She wasn't knitting at that moment, of course (her attention was fixed upon the unusual excitement of court), but it was enough that she held the cloth up, adding even more width to my hiding place.

Two tall and muscular ambassadors brushed aside one of the guards with the fancy pikes, sending him tumbling. They walked up before the duke, the guards never quite catching up. Only the guards bowed. The ambassadors stood unblinking while the duke waved the door guards back to their posts by the grand entrance.

The man was broad shouldered with clear eyes and interesting dimples. Some parts of the dimples were hidden by a well trimmed and brown beard that went ear to ear. The beard also hid a handsome jaw. He wore finely tailored clothing of purple and green, clearly that of a noble and warrior, worthy, but not fancy with frill. He looked right into the duke's eyes, almost as if the elevated deck upon which the duke stood had sunk into quicksand.

The woman was another matter entirely. She looked around the room continually. Her attention was rarely on the duke and his entourage. It was as if she meant to see into every face in the room. As for dress, she had a cloth shirt under a leather vest. Dark linen britches showed under a knee length skirt. She wore a sword over her back, the handle leather-bound and well-worn. In her belt, she carried two knives, both short and aged. She was blonde as the sun. Her pale blue eyes were the sky. They shone probing, knowing and without any fear or sense that as a woman she need know her place. I ducked behind the enormous woman when her eyes drifted by my hiding spot.

"So, what does the coward and traitor, Sir Lacellor, propose to the mighty king of Farstand?" asked the duke.

"Ser, I am unaware of the king's presence. He seems to be missing. Might we then do well to wait for him before proceeding?" asked the knight.

"Do not try me, traitorous knight. I have had setbacks enough for one day. Now, you well know me to be the brother of the king, and I shall speak for him until I can no longer do so. When that time comes, we shall send word to His Majesty and see what comes of it. So far, we have not even made proper introductions, so I see no point in this," declared the duke.

"Forgive me, Lord Crestlin. I did not mean to offend. I am Sir Daren Drake, and I speak for Sir Lacellor. Beside me is Representative Beckli Kahnsa. She is a member of the largest gathering of Debrecian tribes, to our north. We have dealt with her tribe in trade, and we know her word to be authoritative in matters related not only to her tribe but also regarding the general disposition of the many united tribes of Debrecian culture."

The duke asked, "Does she bear no title beyond that of Representative?"

The Debrecian's eyes had been wandering around the court as if disinterested, but at the question her head snapped to the duke, and she responded with a sharp, but pleasant voice, "I am no princess. I'll bear no duties as queen, nor as shaman, though I am known to have many gifts. My gifts are my title, though I will not trouble you, nor will I show the tokens of my titles resting between my breasts. These gifts are for the people and not shared among strangers."

Randolf interrupted, "I can see you have gifts, woman, and

you may show your breasts to us if it pleases you." His eyes roamed her body.

The crowd laughed.

All of a sudden it was as if I could feel the Debrecian ambassador's hidden emotions; I ducked behind the big woman again, wondering how many people this tall woman was going to kill before I could find the door. When the laughing died, and nobody screamed, I looked back. I don't know which was more impressive, the way she scowled at the baron's brother, or the fact that she'd not cut him into pieces small enough to feed to the hounds. She remained unshaken and didn't even twitch her hands toward her knives or sword.

I thought of Ankind, and what he'd taught me about patience with fools, and then I saw it in her, and the oddest thought hit me square in the head: I wanted to be just like her. Not just a warrior who was a tool to my own anger, but also a woman who could stand before kings and one who would not flinch from a greater duty when the princes and jesters spat upon me for being the lesser sex.

"I have the gift of knowing, Sir Randolf. I know that in battle you will rely upon your large body, so I shall not directly take on your claymore. When you pass, I shall cut you, and then we shall parry once again, upon which time you shall make the same mistake, over and over again, thinking the bigger warrior in battle is the one who is destined to win, as if the gods will it. Even as you lay bleeding the last of your blood into the soil from my many fine cuts, you'll toss your sword at me, thinking that all of your might can reach way across to where I prepare to mount my horse. I will have forgotten the fight by the time your sword falls useless between us, and I will have moved on to something much more interesting to me by then, though my vision does not show me the distraction at this moment," said the woman.

"What foul threats are these? Did you come to our court to insult those with whom you have chosen to negotiate, vile heathen?" said Sir Randolf.

She waved his comment away. "I was reluctant to tell you that I have the gift of prophecy, Lord Randolf, but it was you who insulted me. Otherwise, I'd have kept it to myself. We all know that the gods wish us to determine things for ourselves. I have done you a disservice by speaking my vision as it came to me, but some things are predestined. Let us turn to the things that we can change." She walked closer to the duke.

The crowd was full of hisses. Some booed and surged at the edges, threatening to get at her. They were held only by the protocol of embassy and a few pretty guards.

"What can we change then?" asked the impatient duke.

Beckli turned to the hostile crowd and walked a ways down, looking at as many faces as she could. Clearly she was looking for someone among the nobles. Their open hostility had no effect upon her. Then she said to them, as if they were the duke, "We can end this war. We can do it here and now. It is simple, and it is bloodless for us all if we do so. I have been given the authority to sign for all of the tribes."

"How so?" asked the duke.

"Great Duke, I remind you that the Debrecian tribes are not yet at war with your king. And, as you know, Sir Lacellor does not have the number of men that you can muster. Oh, he will fight on, but he will lose without our help." She turned to the duke, and then added, "This is not a prophecy. It is merely speculation based upon my training in the matters of war."

"Then there seems to be no point in this negotiation."

"Oh, but there is, Lord Crestlin. You see, we Debrecians were defeated by your king some twenty years back. We do not forgive such insults easily, and our memory is long. In fact, the list of insults is nearly beyond forgiveness. You did, for example, slaughter women captured in battle. Our own queen was cut and tormented into slavery. A tribe without its queen lives for nothing other than revenge... or considerable restitution, the sum of which I have not even considered. At the time, I think you thought little of the insult. We think much upon it and have not forgotten. We, the chosen people of the Goddess, pray every day for resolution."

"Then you have tossed your lot in with both the traitor Lacellor and a false God. We have nothing to give you, and we are not disposed to do so. The king will not pay bounty to those who should be his willing subjects," declared the duke.

"We do not reside within the borders of your king, nor is it bounty we seek."

The chatter grew. Even the huge woman moved to gossip with a friend, forcing me to hide another step to the side.

The duke said, "It does not matter what you ask. We will not compromise with traitors."

The Debrecian was truly an ambassador, for she went on as if rejection wasn't an option. "Sir Drake has accompanied me here. He is, if I may speak for him this moment, granted permission to negotiate a surrender of Sir Lacellor's loyalty. Should I succeed, Duke Crestlin, you will personally be able to assure the king of Lacellor's return to the kingdom, along with restitutions for the hardships of war upon the kingdom. You see, I come with an offering of bounty. I ask no gold from the king."

The crowd finally lost control upon hearing those words. It seemed that the war was to be over, and with Sir Lacellor's full restitution. It was a complete victory.

Sir Drake scowled, but he didn't contradict the Debrecian's claims.

The duke leaned forward, his interest suddenly peaked. "Tell me again what it is you want, Ambassador Kahnsa, for I would like to win this war for my brother."

"We want our queen back!" she said. She walked briskly back up to the duke.

"How say you?" enquired the duke as if he'd not heard her correctly. "I don't know if we can find this woman you speak of. The war was a score some years ago. As I recall, we have no knowledge of a captured queen. I don't know which women we condemned or which my soldiers took as slave wives. What if she has died in the meantime? Are we to scour the whole land for a dead woman we never knew?"

"She is not far. I can sense it, as can many of us with the right gift of spiritual sight. It is said, even among the most powerful of the shamans of our tribes that she may not have aged since her capture. Many go as far as to claim that she rides with you and is undefeatable. Others have dreamed of seeing her in your camps, magically still young and full of herself, as if hidden among the soldiers in plain sight."

"If she is with us, how do you explain it, woman?" asked Randolf.

"She is a queen without her people. This is not the same as a warrior, or even a shaman. The shaman is wild by nature, but the queen is our rock, as are we hers. Without our companionship and protection, she is driven to the land; madness is said to come quickly. This is how I explain it to myself, for I have seen the signs in young princesses who lose themselves along the paths during their trials before the Goddess. One cannot predict the outcome of an unattended queen," explained Beckli Kahnsa. Her hands flew into the air and then upon her head, as if she meant to show the court the difference between a shaman and a queen.

Randolf laughed, "We would know if such a woman was among us."

"We have been among you. You do not know this."

Randolf scoffed, "That is an idle boast, woman. No women roam among us unnoticed. This old queen in our camps—the very idea is amusing."

Beckli Kahnsa wasn't pleased to hear his words. For once she appeared rattled. She roamed the aisle, appealing to all of the nobles. "Do you not understand me? She will be tall and proud and beyond any man's authority. Her hair is fair, as is her spirit in the wild. She talks to the gods. She leads you when you do not wish it. This you will easily see! I am telling you that I believe this. She is here; I know that she is close. If you do not find her, the queens of the lesser tribes will wash their hands of it, sending their shamans forth to command at the Goddess's most ill-tempered pleasure. The shaman is a healer. In war, her debt of healing is repaid so she may once again grow strong in healing. It is a terrible thing to see. Our shamans cannot come home until their thirst is sated."

While the great ambassador spoke of the queen, I felt my head spinning with the many details. Also, the better her description, the more I felt my eyes lifting up toward the tall stained glass windows.

Up in one window, the colorful glass lady was still showing her hands to me. The glass woman appeared to come to life, as if breathing in a way that matched my own. Perhaps it was just the light, but I couldn't help but notice how the glass lady moved in rhythm with many of the words uttered by the great ambassador as well.

And, when Beckli Kahnsa was finished describing the queen, I found that the Goddess in the glass window was also done dancing, and somehow I couldn't find the description of the queen at all in any part of my mind, other than the broader knowledge that she was among us and should be found.

In its place were the words from the Goddess, "You shall seek the queen with all of your heart and all of your nose and with every organ of your body, save the one between your ears."

"Ha!" I whispered back to the Goddess, "That should be plenty. None are better at tracking with the senses than I." As I have noted, it is a good thing that I had these gifts, for when Beckli Kahnsa was done telling us how we'd know the queen, I remembered nearly nothing of her words until many months later. Clearly, the Goddess was interested in testing my tracking skills without the hindrance of hints.

The fat lady in front of me didn't turn, but I heard her lips say, "Shush!"

"There will be war until she feels the balance," continued Beckli Kahnsa, as if the Goddess had not interrupted at all.

The ambassador added, "Sir Lacellor knows he cannot beat your great king if King Falstaff brings all of his men to one or two battles. However, he will be heartened by his new ally and persist if we go unsatisfied and enter on his side. Many will die quickly and with great violence! Then this war will linger, and so many will die that it hardly matters who wins it in the end, for we have grown strong and many. We have given birth to warriors until our wombs have burst, seeing this day through the eyes of the prophets!"

"You've already decided, have you not?" asked Sir Randolf. "Did you not say that you prophesied my very death in this war that you threaten to rain upon us all?"

"Prophecies can be changed by bold men doing bold things that gain the attention of the gods," said Beckli.

"Ah, of course, the way out for all witches and soothsayers," scoffed Sir Randolf. He sat back down, as if to say that nothing more was of interest.

The duke conceded what he could. He said, "All of my holy men will search for your queen. We have a reinforced contingent of Sho guards. Their tracking skills are most admirable, I've just been reminded. If we find her, we shall return her unscathed and avoid this war. If not, then I imagine I'll soon see both your heads on pikes. Now, the matter is done. Return to your lords and await my reply."

Beckli Kahnsa didn't look pleased to be leaving empty handed. Sir Daren Drake, on the other hand, beamed a smile that stretched ear to ear. Clearly, Sir Drake was a warrior at heart, and he didn't much like the sound of surrender, nor had he been as comfortable as Ambassador Kahnsa during the proceedings. I didn't want my eyes to leave his beautiful face, but then I couldn't make my eyes leave the great Beckli Kahnsa either. I watched their every step as they left the great hall by the front door. The guards shifted well to the side, terrified that they'd be humiliated again before the whole court. None spoke behind them. For that moment, the assembly had been stunned into silence and was busy taking a long last look as well.

We left by the tiny exit before our lingering was noticed, already aware that the duke would be sending a messenger telling us of our new mission.

I wished to be the first to find this queen, for I wanted to know all that I could about how she hid so well among us and about what she knew of the elusive Goddess that I and the Debrecians shared. I was a good tracker, and I knew none could beat me at the chore of what I saw as an easy search, for the camp was large, but not as big as the whole kingdom.

There was, of course, one serious problem with my plan. The crone twisted inside of me, not at all pleased to know that the war was so easily ended. The White Shirts had woken her, and she would not be so easily put to rest. I, too, thought of the prophecy that I'd kill many men before my sword. What was to be made of such contradiction I wondered all of the way back to our camp.

Chapter Thirteen

Searching for the queen took up all of my waking moments. This was in spite of the fact that a full score of White Shirts helped me, and I had the run of the camp. Not even captains could stop me from barging into their tents and looking behind their chests or under their wagons. Of course, Captain Barker was almost always at my side, and when it wasn't he, it was some other hated White Shirt who accompanied me.

Captain Barker, of course, had his own skills at tracking. His troops considered him so skilled that nothing could avoid his view, so it was no small thing to note our failure. Sho wouldn't help him see beyond the feeling of closeness, he told me, neither of us knowing why.

Sir Randolf came and asked about our progress every few days, going away pleased that he could report our failure. He could also report fairly to the duke that we worked tirelessly.

It was the duke's pleasure that we never cease our search, and the duke he couldn't ignore, but Randolf was soon convinced that the elusive queen was a figment of the Debrecian's imagination. Kahnsa's fallibility pleased Randolf as much as the search's failure, given she had also reported his own demise.

I grew to know Sir Randolf better with each visit. He was a man of violence and burdened with muscles, loud proclamations, and no wisdom. The baron's brother did have one use. He held the high baron's lands secure; thus, he was the man most feared in the baronage of my birth. No man opposed him, and, even on the duke's other lands, he was obeyed by all but a few, ranking second in the duke's combined armies.

And every woman was his to breed. He had a reputation of taking his noble right on many wedding nights to prove it. Sir Randolf made up for not being baron by throwing more tantrums, bedding more women and killing more sinners against the endless edicts than anybody I knew.

War was his ultimate chance to show his might, both against the enemy and against the soldiers he commanded. Thus, while his brother tended the accounts and served the interests of the lower nobles and merchants, Sir Randolf enjoyed all of the amusements of rank. I thought that, if we found the great queen, we'd do well to bring her straight to the duke and not to Randolf. Captain Barker agreed to this.

Oddly, I felt the queen everywhere I went. I'd thought to sense her best by comparing her to the body and soul smell of the ambassador. I wanted to meet her in the worst way. When I failed to turn her up, I asked the Goddess for a better sign, but she found me out of favor, spending the summer avoiding me.

This could have been because of my treason.

The first thing upon our return from the duke's castle, Sir Wencor gave me a white shirt. He'd said that I was to wear it, as it was both the duke's and Sho's very commandments that I do so. The sight of it made my stomach turn.

Then I thought about the great and noble Beckli Kahnsa, and how she'd offered to surrender all of the complaints of her people and even that of the rebellious Lord Lacellor just for the worthiness of peace. She'd stood there as the proudest person in the castle even as she said that she would humble herself before her enemy. All that she'd held foul, she'd welcomed in the pursuit of something bigger than her. I didn't know anything bigger than myself yet, though I thought that perhaps there was such a thing in store for me if the Goddess had gone to all of the trouble of introducing me to my mother, the crone and the unbelievable Beckli Kahnsa.

If I ever met the queen, I was sure she'd help me find an even greater entity within myself. The only way to do that, it seemed, was to wear the shirt of my greatest enemy.

There in the middle of our camp, I took up the shirt and put it on.

As soon as I did, the Goddess woke up the angry wind inside of me, and it was so strong it lifted me off my feet. I hovered, circling in the air. While this happened, the sun decided to point through a cloud and in my direction.

Soldiers as well as servants stopped their duties and quickly called their friends to see the embarrassing phenomenon. A host of men, many bodies deep, surrounded the knoll over which I floated.

Then, after a full minute of that, I fell to the ground in a heap. Even down there, the world spun as if it were a big top. I put my head on the ground. Even as low as I had it, it felt as if my head was going to float right off me.

"It is a sign from God. Did we not all see the levitation?" said one of the replacement White Shirts.

Sir Wencor agreed: "I did not expect such a powerful vision from the Lord. Sho has smitten him just as he did the Apostle Paulus." He fell to his knees and cupped his hands in prayer. Captain Barker was second to fall. All of the rest of the men surrounding me did the same, for it seemed even the lowest among them could feel the presence of a god's attention. Men who were passing us stopped, even those who'd missed the levitation, some of them joining in humbling themselves, though we were strangers to many. There seemed several score who bore witness, as if they'd been drawn to the occasion even before the event.

While all of the worship went on around me, I tried to catch my breath and keep the world from spinning away. Sweat poured out of me. My skin grew cold. When some of the spinning passed, I got to my feet and ran to my tent, barely able to run a straight line. There, I got into my blankets and pulled my books out, searching for guidance.

The new one I'd stolen wouldn't let me open it. A great magical ward was upon it, so I put it back, still knowing nothing of its contents. Since the gods didn't even want me to read, I wrestled myself to sleep in the middle of the day, hoping all of this would pass as a bad dream.

The next day, I got up and nobody said anything about my spell and great laziness. Instead, they all looked at me as if convinced the ravings of Sir Wencor had been true. I was no saint in their eyes, but I stood as a sign to them that their God was with them in their quests.

I could find anything, I'd come to believe, but I didn't find the queen. It had to be the shirt I wore that opposed me, for it must have highly offended the Goddess that I had to wear it. Only she could bedevil my senses so gravely. I knew the shirt plagued me because, whenever I took it off, I felt much relieved, but not so relieved that the Goddess saw fit to forgive me with a nose for the queen.

Time dragged on. Still, Sir Lacellor didn't show himself. I knew he'd sent his men home to till the land and bring in the fastest crop they could before returning. The duke didn't share this common sense, so the whole army wasted a planting season. Thousands would die from famine, including many among us.

Time passed, and Beckli Kahnsa was to become my enemy, it seemed, though I didn't feel right about it. We hadn't found the queen, and war was not to be avoided, though our duke waited upon the pleasure of his enemy. Instead of unleashing his forces upon the unguarded border, Duke Crestlin spoke to

the massed troops about some code of chivalry that bound him
to meet Randolf in a mighty clash of thousands. I thought this
idiotic. The crone and I both knew war was a matter of
opportunity.

By late summer, I had my fill of being a member of Sho's
guard. It was a steaming night when I rode into the woods to
think about what was happening to me. I had grown to dislike
even myself for the color I wore. Bearing no fruits for my
sacrifice, I thought the humiliation had been for nothing. I
hadn't found this queen who surrounded me, and yet I'd been
tricked into thinking the cost worthwhile. What if wearing the
shirt had not been a sacrifice, but rather, Sho's trick to tear the
heart out of me?

Still, the moon was full, and I thought I felt the Goddess
pulling at me, though she wouldn't show herself.

I needed to get into the woods where I could perform the
rituals of cleansing. I took my books and staff, leaving my
sword behind so I'd come before the Goddess with at least
token humility. The thirst for battle overwhelmed me nearly
always now. I had to discipline myself, for there was conflict
enough inside of my soul. Was I only a warrior, and who did I
truly hate?

Ella was as happy to be out of the dusty camp as I was. All
of the grass in the camp was gone, and Ella thought it unfit for
the horses to live there. Once we'd cleared the camp road and
gone to the trails, we stopped every few steps. Ella insisted
upon tasting every weed in sight. Not even the flowers were
safe from her lips.

I rode toward the enemy. They were several days to the
northeast, but I wasn't going that far. I knew the woods in that
direction, stopping far enough away from our own camp to
avoid all of the other soldiers that were out foraging illegally
and poaching to stay alive.

I looked into my book of spells, finding nothing useful for the occasion of contrition. Putting it back into my saddle bag, I retrieved the second book; it was the one I'd stolen at the enemy camp across the great ford. I itched to open the treasure, but, every time I reached to pull the cover open, my body filled with a sense of dread. It was no ordinary book; I'd learned this fact months back when I'd first tried to open it. Perhaps I'd find a time to ask the Goddess about the ward that protected it when she decided me worthy enough to talk to. I put it into my saddlebag unopened.

I took the white shirt off, and then the harsh binding that held my breasts squished against me. Finally, the rest of my clothing went into my saddlebags.

I even took my necklace off. I didn't feel naked until I'd freed my neck of the golden wolf coin. The coin was all that I had to remind me of my mother. It seemed the Goddess commanded me to come to her with nothing more than my person. This at least started feeling like penance. I'd not understood that I'd gotten so attached to the wolf coin.

Easing off Ella, I put my feet into a cool creek while Ella finished drinking her bellyful. There I took a sliver of my best made lye and scoured the sinful smell of the white shirt off my skin until I was red. Dripping, I left Ella under a pear tree where she could only reach a couple of pears and wonder about the rest.

I wandered up the creek into the wildest parts of the forest, having to use my best eyesight to make my way through the gloom to where the Goddess led me.

The tiny creek widened at a clearing. The moon blasted through, inviting me to stay. There, under the Goddess's light, I stretched, shrugging my body and breasts for all of nature to see. I was no longer that small-breasted girl that the Ranglsons had scoffed at. I was a woman, wide of hips and strong in body and as beautiful as one of the duke's statues under the moon.

This, I realized, was what the Goddess had brought me here to see—myself. She finally spoke directly to me, telling me that the flesh I'd been born with was nothing that I should be ashamed of. In fact, it was the world that called upon me to hide it. It was the world that had sinned. And, it was the world that should be full of shame for asking such a high price of a person. I felt her forgiveness for all I had done to hide myself. I fell to my knees under her light with tears of understanding. I had not sinned against the Goddess, but against myself.

"I need your help, Goddess," I said to the light above me. When I said this, she walked over from the dark side of the moon and took a seat upon its top, looking down at me as if she were my sister. The expression on her face was one of great curiosity.

Golden Eyes walked out of the woods from where he watched and sat down beside me. He found my behavior of looking at the moon curious.

I was determined to pay him no mind, going on with my conversation with the Goddess.

"I have a duty to Lady Lettoir. I have a duty to the baron and duke. I have my duty to the great crone and to my mother. The vile murdering White Shirts have stolen me, but it is for the task of finding the queen of a great tribe. All of this confuses me, my Goddess. Can you tell me the right thing to do?"

"Why do you ask me these things when you can ask Sho? He listens to everything you say to him now."

I could not read her face when she said this riddle.

"He listens to nothing," I told her. "He is like the others. He sees what he wants to see of my skin and knows not my heart. Do you not know him and how shallow he is about those under him? Those who can't think well for themselves love him the most. They set up mountainous temples in his name and utter oaths to him with their dying breath so there is barely room for the subject at hand. He is mad with power and the desire for idle worship beyond all utility. His soldiers starve, and his women suffer. What would he think of me if I came to him as I am this night? What would he say to me if he saw me dancing naked and happy under your moon, for he measures us by how much happiness we give up in sacrifice to him? Would he send me a man and put me in a cabin full of babies, thinking him done with me then? Or, would he show me mercy by burning me at some stake for being something he can't understand?"

"You do his service."

"What is your will that I do, my Goddess?"

She laughed; her face was full of delight that I didn't share. I could never account for her shifting moods. "I will have you seek the queen. I am not really angry about your service to Sho, for it is mere testing. You must go back and seek, my child."

"I can't find her. I feel her everywhere among us, but she is a worthy witch, and none can find her face, not even myself. I know of such illusions, for I pass as a man with the same kind of spell. When you hid your favor from me, you took away my ability to smell her out."

"I did no such thing to you, my trouble. Oh, surely I have done things to you, but I have not changed your skills. In time you will see why all of this difficulty is necessary, but your service with the duke's army is not quite done. Let me tell you this much: I truly do not see fault in the service you pay to Sho. I give voice to it only because it is ironic, and I find it useful to tease you for it. Truly it amuses me when I see him fancying you as his warrior, for he shall not always have you." She smiled down upon my confusion.

"And the queen?" I asked.

"When you are ready, a tiny cloud will lift, and she will show herself plain as the sun," the Goddess answered.

Golden Eyes walked in front of me then, and he whined. He seemed most anxious, but I was busy and shooed him away with my hand.

"I am ready to meet her now!" I screamed at Goddess.

"Then, if you are ready, you have already found her, my child. Oh, I see my answer does not please you. Then perhaps we are not as ready as we imagine. I will not lift this cloud from where I have put it. For now, do not be troubled."

Such puzzles I didn't want to hear, and the last sentence seemed even a spell that left my head spinning as badly as when I'd been levitated. Thankfully, the spinning eased almost as quickly as it came.

I told the Goddess, "War will come if we don't find her. I cannot say that battle does not attract me, but to have so many innocent peasants die for the pleasure of Sho and his nobles seems wrong, even to a warrior in love with her sword. I would rather fight the nobles over something as petty as my pride. They fancy themselves worthy of my steel and are at least well fed."

Such was my state that I pounded the earth and lifted a fist in the direction of the duke's castle.

I felt pain in my arm as Golden Eyes bit me. He tugged at me to leave the place, all of this adding to my animation. I bled where he bit. Turning my head to get his attention, I growled at him, convincing him to back off while I was talking to the Goddess.

"I have a book—" I began, but, before I could finish, the Goddess interrupted.

"Let us see what comes of this," the Goddess said.

She grew quiet, though she still sat upon the moon. Her eyes wandered off as if distracted by another mystery of the universe. I wondered if she was always busy with many conversations.

Golden Eyes rushed off into the woods. As he went, he told me in his head that I wasn't a good wolf for letting three humans sneak up on me in spite of his many warnings. Even a tiny pup could smell them, he complained, and, of course, he was right.

What he didn't tell me was that they were all women. I could smell the difference, and I'd never known a woman whom I feared.

I didn't need to turn in order to sense that two of them were behind me with strung bows. When their leader walked out of the woods in front of me, I told her, "You can put your bows away. I have not come for battle, and you can't easily kill me with your little arrows."

The one before me looked at me appraisingly, but she didn't gesture for her friends to let down their guard. "You don't fear us?"

"No. I lost the emotion in a cabin," I told her.

"I heard you praying to your God, girl. Do you not have a better place to worship your God than here in these woods where danger lurks? The wolves might have had you, had we not grown curious."

I measured her. She wasn't as tall as the other Debrecians I'd seen. Her hair and eyes were brown, not blonde and blue. She bore her sword on her back. A knife was worn on a hilt buckled around the top of a boot. Leaves were stuck to her hair, telling me she'd crept through the forest in some haste to get to me at just that moment.

"There is no better place to discuss things with the Goddess than the place where she leads me. Perhaps you should ask yourself why she permits your attendance at our private conversation. Is it not apparent that we've gone to great trouble to find a lonely place?" I got to my feet.

"You pretend to speak directly to the Goddess. Foreign

breeders are not worthy of such an honor." I saw her face redden.

"Can't you see her for yourself, sitting on the moon? I had something else very important to ask her, and now she has decided to attend to other things because of your interruption. I humble myself for her and her alone, so she might know my repentance. It is not the idle habit of wonder or even worship. As for breeding, that is my business." I strode up to the warrior. Our faces were soon close.

"You are naked and unarmed, or I would kill you for insolence before a warrior. What is your business with the Goddess then, peasant breeder of my enemies?"

"I seek the missing queen and the reasons behind certain mysteries. And, if I were armed, I'd thump you across the head so the fleas may feast upon you all night and breed up your behind!"

This bought me a shove, though I didn't lose my feet. Behind me the other two were laughing. That got the woman before me even angrier. "How do you intend to find the missing queen out here in the wilderness? Do you imagine your naked peasant body will seduce her? The Goddess has no use for whores, and the queen has even less."

"I don't know why she wants me here, or how she thinks I will find the queen. That is what I was asking the Goddess, among other things. She thinks I'll find her in my own way and in my own time, though she wasn't specific." I turned as if to leave but decided instead to turn back. I shoved the warrior, as was her due. She stumbled back, falling over a bush.

She got up, yanking her sword out of her sheath as she recovered. Behind me, one of the other warriors stepped past, coming between us. The new warrior was still laughing, as was her friend behind us. "That is enough, Catrina! The breeder is full of fire; that is all. Do you not know we are all bound to honor courage? Besides, she worships the same God as we. Let the Goddess sort out who does it correctly."

Catrina looked at me hard and then put her sword away. She said, "I don't like her. Now we will have to find a new camp because she's wandered into our woods. How can it be a coincidence that she came to this isolated place? Their men are weak, and they use their breeders as spies."

"She can't be all of this. Can't you see she is just a naked and unarmed peasant?"

"She has more muscles than seems right for a breeder. Also, no peasant would be put to the test of seeking out our queen. What do you say to that, Gerta?" asked Catrina.

"They may have set a bounty prize to be claimed by any. Did we not ask them to find our queen?" replied Gerta.

I interrupted, saying, "There is no bounty. I have been told to seek her—that is all. There are reasons why I'd like to find her for myself. I want the Goddess's aid in this, but she refuses me any special consideration."

Gerta replied, "There is no reason for one such as you to speak with our queen, so, of course, the Goddess won't aid you. In her glory, a queen would spit upon you for stumbling into her presence. Only warriors of the true Debrecian tribe may approach her openly. Besides, crazy breeder, you would need the gift of seeing people as they are in order to find her after all of this time. Such a long time away from the tribe will have addled her brain and made her appear common. It is the tribe that feeds her. So, you see, it is not enough to look upon her to know her. That is why I think your people have failed in your quest to find her. In your eyes she will appear as nothing."

"And you two warriors have this gift of finding the queen?" I asked.

The look on their faces told me otherwise, and more -- that now both of them didn't like me. I gained nothing by being such a brat in their presence. These women were different from the women I knew, not so easily cowed by a temper. I had to make allowances for it. In a way, I was an ambassador to them, much as had been Beckli to us, I reasoned.

I said as an apology, "Which is it then? Will she appear common to me, or be so full of herself that none may speak to her? This sounds like two women, not one. If I sound surly, don't take offense. I think you mean the best, but you've been too long without her to advise me on this, and she has been away too long to find her own way back. That is why I believe only the Goddess regarding these things. Yet, I will have to think about this gift of inner sight that you speak of. You are kind to tell me of it. It interests me, given your great queen has managed to elude my nose."

Gerta accepted my explanation, losing her frown before answering, "It's not a gift commonly given to women outside of the tribes."

"I don't think myself so limited."

Catrina said, "Ah, don't speak to her, Gerta. She has the art of argument. Let her chant to the moon if she wishes. I see now that I was wrong in confronting her, for she is crazy in love with her delusions."

"Yes, you are right. She may be a witch, for it is their habit to speak gibberish and dance naked under the moonlight. Men in Sir Lacellor's camp have said that all witches are from the darkness, but we know they are also harmless and sometimes useful with herb-craft. The men in this land, however, burn them up when they catch them. She has enough trouble. Let's leave her alone and be on with our work," agreed Gerta.

The three of them wandered away. As she moved past, I saw the third one. She was a young girl somewhere near the age of fourteen, though she moved catlike in the meadow as if she had spent twenty years in the wild. I saw her look over her shoulder at me as she departed. There was a sparkle in her eye that told of the great curiosity of youth. I was glad I'd not had to fight one so young and eager to see the world. She was the last one looking out at the glen when Golden Eyes came walking up beside me to nuzzle my hand. I smiled at the young warrior, and then I nodded my respect as the young Debrecian girl merged into the woods behind her sisters.

* * * * *

I didn't go straight back to that decimated camp. Instead, I took my time salting beef from an old cow I stole from a monastery. It pleased me to steal it from the priests, for they got most of their livestock as offerings from the peasants. I considered that to be one fool giving unto another fool, and then into my needful hands. Besides, the best thing that could happen to us all would be the priests starving to death and leaving us in peace to prosper without the burden of sacrifice.

Golden Eyes thought it amusing sport the way I led the cow away so willingly. I seemed to him a god for the ease of convincing the cow to come along. He was so impressed that he didn't ask for more than the entrails and a few meaty bones, all of which I had no use for anyway, given I had no stew pot with me. He proudly stomped away into the weeds with a bone the length of his whole hind half. He'd be a hero, soon leading the pack back to cart off the rest of the spoils.

My horse dragged the mess of beef to the edge of our camp. Each man from the cavalry of Lettoir stole away into the forest for their share. They hid the treasure from noble eyes as quickly as they could grab it.

I reported to the White Shirt camp because they now thought me their charge. Captain Barker, not knowing of the larger fortune, took a beef offering of repentance from me for having become lost in the woods for two days, which was a serious crime. I knew as long as the two nobles were fed, all was well, for such was their kind's greed.

This wasn't to be the case, however. Captain Barker and Sir Wencor thought they owned my every moment. "It is God who orders us to watch over you, Abe. Now tell me: What have you done these two days and three whole nights," insisted the young Sir Wencor.

Such enquiry caught me without a good excuse. What I needed was the best lie I could come up with. Wencor, Barker and several of the white shirted soldiers examined me with interest while I lingered.

"Well, out with it, Abe!" shouted the impatient Captain Barker. This brought the attention of some of the men of Lettoir, Sergeant Hadarm among them.

My head finally filled with the best lie I'd ever come up with, which, in this case, was the truth. I explained, "I went out into the deepest woods to look up at the moon. There was a lady out there looking down and talking to me, though I didn't understand some of what she said. You see, I was naked from washing away a taint and.... Do you wish for me to be more detailed about this part?"

Sir Wencor said, "Nay. Skip that and get on with it."

"Well, all right then. So, as soon as she finished, three other women showed up. One was short and on me in an instant. The next was much prettier, taller and very fair of skin. She argued for my favor and kept the shorter one from pressing upon me too severely. They were most insistent that I be forthcoming, however. I was as if their prisoner, or I'd have attempted an escape. There was a third one, but I had no time for her. She was too timid anyway and preferred to watch the more experienced and learn from it. Do you wish that I go into this with a fine comb, Sir Wencor?"

"No. That will suffice. Just get past the illicit part," he commanded.

"Well, I know little about illicit things. I've had no experience and was at their mercy. All here can attest to my lack of certain kinds of worldly—"

"I can attest to that myself," interrupted Sergeant Hadarm. The men of Lettoir behind him laughed their agreement.

Nodding my thanks, I went on: "So, anyway, as you might suspect, this took some time; I have only a little more time to account. Don't you know that time shortens after such close escapes. I went to find my clothing, which a woman had left in a remote part of the woods far from me. It would not do to return without my britches, you see, and this took even more of my time since she'd hidden them beside an overgrown creek bank."

I brushed my hands against my shirt and britches, as if removing leaves.

"Yes, yes, Abe," said Sir Wencor impatiently.

"This is where it gets more interesting, Sir Wencor. I would have asked your advice, had you been there, for you and Captain Barker are more experienced than I about such things. You see, the very next place I came to after my escape had several demure men in long skirts. They were inclined to want even more of me than the women in the woods. They were as succubae, seeking to feed on my very soul. It was only after they'd turned their eyes from me a few seconds that I was able to escape from them as well, taking with me the provisions I have recently given over to you. I figured they owed the provisions to us for delaying my return and for their inclination toward taking advantage of my vulnerability, Ser."

"That is an amazing story." Sir Wencor put his hands together and looked up. "It might have been a vision. We all know Sho has smitten you blind before with his mighty hand. I shall write these words down and see if they lead us to some kind of later understanding."

"I am inclined to believe it's a mud dipper's tale," said Captain Barker.

I quickly added, "Well then, in that case, I won't tell you about the large male animal with a big bone who also escaped from those in the flowing gowns." The giggling stopped. I could see all the men were trying to puzzle the meaning to that part out.

"Enough already, Abe!" said Captain Barker. "I can stand no more. Just go back to your tent and set your things in order. This is for all of you: The duke received a challenge from Sir Lacellor, so we must put the camp behind us and make ready for what might be the main battle."

"My thoughts exactly, Ser. I have no desire to recall such troubling events more than once and am eager to get on with whatever God has set before us on the field of battle." I departed for my tent. When I crawled in there, I determined to make myself ready but went directly to sleep until Sergeant Hadarm kicked my tent.

Chapter Fourteen

Four days later, we waited over a wheat field. Our mounts had rags loosely tied over their lips to keep them from eating the grains and foundering. The army was stomping most of the wheat into padding for our horse's hooves. Peasants scrambled around the edges of the summer harvest, hoping to avoid the attention of the soldiers as they reaped what little they could salvage. Every so often, a captain or sergeant yelled, sending some of the peasants stumbling out of the field in terror.

I plucked casually at the seeded stalks that surrounded my horse, filling a pair of coarsely sewn sacks I'd retrieved from my saddle bags. It was a leisurely thing I did to pass the time— sitting in my saddle and waiting for one army or the other to make a move that would start the killing in earnest. We'd been nearly at the same spot, on or off our horses for two days.

Officially reserves, we horsemen of Lettoir shifted our position to the left or right, up or back, even at angles. Each wee move followed the tiny orders of the signal flags in the duke's and baron's brother's ranks to our immediate right.

Behind the duke's party were a few old nobles in decorative armor, some servants, squires and pages, and even a few ladies in delicate tin breastplates who were young enough to want to see the business of their new husbands. As well, the ever present contingent of priests rode in white gowns, purple sashes and pointy hats. Flags, standards, planks and other symbols of their worship were in abundance.

In all, the nobles amounted to less than a dozen real warriors out of the mess of them.

Our two flanks guarded the nobles and amounted to around two and a half -score each. We were like wings stretched out from our body of betters. We were light, and only half of us truly knew our business while mounted on our animals. Over on the far right side sat the White Shirts. I was glad they were over there and not alongside the men of Lettoir. Looking the other way, I saw Sergeant Hadarm out there at our farthest left wing tip. Since the lady's men had no nobles to lead us, and all we had was our sergeant, Sir Barker lent himself to the chore. He and I perched on the far right of this left group. This put us within shouting distance of the duke, the baron's brother and assorted decorative members of court.

All of the archers, catapults and duke's heavy cavalry were well ahead of us. This time the generals were making sure our peasant cavalry couldn't steal the victory out from under their defeat.

Up in the distance, some hidden by the slow roll of the reasonably flat farmland, were eight thousand pikemen, over half raised from the duke's own lands. They were formed into four-wide blocks, not unlike in the first battle, but, behind them, the duke had learned to place four smaller blocks of reserves. They were ready to fill any gap and put the weight of the duke's soldiers into any breach.

It was only with my good eyes that I could see the lay of the enemy. They were far fewer than us this time, causing me to wonder why Sir Lacellor persisted in this war.

I hadn't seen Lacellor's heavy cavalry yet, but he liked to hide. I felt sure they were over the horizon or in one of the many stands of trees to our flanks. As for the duke, he showed his heavy armor at each side of the footmen, as if daring Lacellor to attack in anything but a straightforward fashion. The knights showed every color and reflective metal imaginable.

They made the greater number of dingy footmen seem like cattle crawling over the mud and weeds.

The duke was doing better, I thought, though his heavy cavalry and footmen had no mobility beyond the set field. Given he didn't know how to use swiftness anyway, and was too far from his men to do so, I thought that a small mistake. On the other hand, we, on his deep rear flanks, were mobile, though we might never see battle from as far back as we stood.

"You can't bear that grain into battle, Abe. It will slow your horse," instructed Sir Barker from Ella's right.

"I intend to drop the sacks as soon as they are through piddling with us. When the battle is over, I'll come back for them. They amount to enough for a hundred loaves, and I'm tired of being hungry for grain. Besides, my hands itch to be about some task. I've told my hands, 'You can't kill those around us, don't you know. You will have to wait and wait some more.'"

"Can you be that eager for the killing, Abe?"

"I am full of the desire, Captain Barker. I don't know the reason for it, but my soul has been full of the want of it for two years now. Ever since my friend was killed by those not entirely unlike you, I confess. It is best that I leave my hands to their idle chores, lest they become aware of the similarities."

"Do you hate us then? Are we not serving the same master?" enquired the captain.

That was a question I'd felt gnawing on me ever since I'd joined the baron's army. Serving Lady Lettoir had seemed a good thing to me, a long and trying year ago. This ... I hid from dwelling upon overly much. I asked, "Do you remember the first day we met, Captain Barker? Do you remember the look in my eyes? Ah, you didn't like me much. Now, do you also remember your own heart when you first saw me? Did you hear your God speaking? I know your God. I have heard his voice.

There is vengeance in the mind of heaven."

"Vengence?"

"Your God has had many changes of heart since that day, so don't be troubled. He now imagines me his very arm. He has told me this himself. Even I wonder how many of my feelings were imposed upon me by the gods. Are we all victims of their whims? I mention these secrets only as curiosities, since you asked about my feelings. Then again, perhaps the best way to know my feelings is to know your own, Sir Barker. Did you not once hate me?"

"I did, and I confess finding your ways often hard to bear. Such as this very—"

"It was God speaking to me that day, I can assure you. God told me not to kill you. There was yet a third and more settling soul inside of me, however. She did not want to listen. If it were not for God, you would have felt my blade. For quite surely, not a one of you would be here had that warring spirit taken me. No, don't fear that I will stab you in the back on the field of battle. I have learned to not hate you, in spite of the war in the heavens. And, there is no reason for my conversion but that I have learned to think with my own heart. Where I managed to find it, I am not sure, but, if it is possible for a person to have two souls, you are looking at it. These sorts of things may be why my God has seen fit for me to linger in the wilderness."

Sir Barker searched my face. "I do not well understand all of your rambling, nor do I much like your thoughts."

"If we knew everything in one another's hearts, would any of us like the other? I am guilty of the sin of truth. And the greater sin of having hid it so well."

Captain Barker did not react the way I'd imagined he might. "Sometimes I envy Sir Wencor's purity of heart. It is much younger than either of ours. I do not think he has as many experiences turning it into something ugly, as is the case with you and me."

"And yet he is an idiot. As hard as he works to overcome his fear, and as well schooled in the nobleman's craft of swordplay as he is, he would not last a minute in or out of battle without his minder. This, of course, does not speak to his gullibility in belief." I didn't mention that I was younger than Sir Wencor.

"If I were doing my duty, I'd have you flogged for those words." He glanced to his right, apparently checking for signals from the nobles. "But, then again, we are looking into one another's hearts as we look over a battlefield that will be the death of so many. Such a place is a special place, is it not?"

"That it is. The burdened half of me hates it. The free half of me lives for the moment I am unleashed upon it, for it has been prophesized that I shall kill many men, and there are nearly enough here this day, Sir Barker." This time I sensed the captain shudder beside me upon hearing those words of providence.

There were times when I spoke to him in lies and times when I spoke in riddles—and those things we said that day.

"That story ... about the three nights of fornication: What is the likelihood any of it is true?"

I looked at him, and decided the truce before battle merited some truth: "In its own way it was as I claimed. The women I spoke of, however, were not wanton women, as I led you to assume. None of those I mentioned desired my flesh. The three were Debrecian warriors, Sir Barker. They were most upset that I'd ventured into their hidden camp. It was most fortunate that they caught me while naked, humbled and speaking to God, for they saw me as no threat and didn't know my true nature, nor could I easily fight them."

"Our scouts have seen no signs of Debrecians, Abe. They've given up their quest for their queen and determined there is nothing left to be done about it." Captain Barker looked at me with eyes that suggested wisdom.

"I have seen many signs. There are at least four camps of them, each two to four in number. They are good scouts, keeping their tracks hidden, their numbers small and their excursions under the cover of moonless hours."

"You mentioned nothing of this. You admire these women then? It is not proper to admire your enemy and not tell what you have found."

"I think not. I must admire my enemy. That has been one of my better lessons."

He didn't reply, so I continued, "As you've admitted, Captain, you and all of your scouts haven't seen them. Perhaps I am mistaken and have only dreamed of their camps. Anyway, without their queen, only God can save us from their wrath should they determine us unworthy of their forbearance and worthy of something else. It seems their queen is the center of their soul and, without her decision, they linger undecided."

"Give them credit for being contrary women and no more, Abe. Tales of savage warriors in skirts are somewhat true, but, like most tales, they are overly stated."

I nodded, mostly because I didn't want to argue with him when he was pretending to be my teacher. There was no point in it. Nobles expected to always have the last word, so why not end it when they'd uttered the most absurd thoughts possible.

Signal flags flew from among the flickering silver and tin assembly a stone's throw to our right.

I dropped the two bags of grain from the rump of my horse and made myself light. The waiting had ended. The catapults unleashed their smoking trails of flaming rock.

The aim on one of ours was true right away, killing a dozen of the enemy archers with a single rock. Men raced out from the area of that impact like sparks from a campfire. This aim, of course, forced Sir Lacellor to call his forces to the advance. Pikes met shields and bodies; the first yells from the clash were one, then two, then many faint echoes across the distant fields.

Next, the whole lay of the land before us was one solid scream with tumbling masses of bodies and pikes. The men dying across the landscape were so tiny that I imagined them a part of some other kingdom's affairs. Belying this, the smell of smoking trails linked our distant world to theirs.

Halfway to our blocks, catapulted fire thumped destruction upon our archers who parted like slow tides before the boulders' lumbering falls. The archers recovered, making the best lines they could before sending fresh, arching showers of arrows into the back ranks of distant advancing footmen. I had no stomach for such warfare, for I'd never see the enemy's eyes while standing under such a rain, pressed in by so many at my shoulders that my instincts would be useless. I learned that the stiffness of these ranks was the reason many could not avoid the fall of the enemy's comets.

Next came Lacellor's heavy cavalry to our front-left. They rode forward at a pace so slow that I thought it an illusion provoked by the great distance. There were not many of them, perhaps less than a score, though they aimed their horses right at the three score of our knights on the duke's left. Perhaps with a charge they might have broken through the first ranks, but I saw no reasoning behind trotting inferior numbers of knights up to bigger numbers and patting swords.

Then two of them broke to the front, and they charged at the duke's horsemen. These two lowered long tournament quality lances and split our ranks with them. One of their lances impaled a rider's tin, while the other glanced off several better made breastplates, knocking one of ours off his mount. Then, of course, the lances were burdens, and the pair of heroes quickly got rid of them. They drew their swords even as they turned to escape the knights who gathered around them while hacking. An axe cleaved a shoulder plate and got stuck. Blood slashed out of the steel. The second knight fell from his horse, a victim of several swords, one carefully struck under the gap at his neck.

This changed everything. Lacellor's armor turned tail. Our blood was up, though, and the leader of the left flank of cavalry called a charge. He took the whole force of three score horses after them. All of those knights raced off to the far left woods.

I'd been so distracted by that change of fortune that I almost missed the right flank where it appeared as if Lacellor had yet another force of less than a score horsemen. They, too, rode up toward the right half of the duke's heavy horse. Once again, two of their ranks broke forward, challenging the duke's knights with long lances.

All of the fortunes of this battle were ours, I realized.

The pikes were a mess and thus frozen in place. Some of our reserves were coming forward to bypass the breeches. There was no doubt who would win that fight when we had a flank on each of the blocks. We alone had the means of engaging them on more than one face. We had far more men at arms and were well spaced for the maneuver.

On both flanks, Lacellor appeared determined to engage heavier forces in mismatches by splitting his knights into two small groups that could easily be defeated or simply run out of the battle. My respect for Lacellor as a tactician fell. When they wrote a history of this, Lacellor would be mentioned as the world's worst battlefield commander for it, I imagined.

This was so clear to me that I became troubled by it.

Over to our right, the pack of priests, women, pages and old nobles were celebrating the victory even before many of the doomed enemy had died from the apparent advantages. No commands at all came from our nobles, for the course of each group's actions seemed obvious. Lacellor had simply fit his fingers into our glove as if he'd willed his rebellion finished.

Something wasn't right.

I had to find the missing part of the unfolding drama. Was Lacellor through with the war? Did he will the death of his men in some grand ending? From what I'd read, it was not unheard of.

Then, just before the enemy knights on the far right turned, I saw something truly unusual. Their horses appeared lighter than they'd been in the last battle. I squinted to see more from my great distance, observing that their breastplates had the color of shale. This was the case for all of the armor on every man other than the two sent forward with the ceremonial jousting pikes. The way the enemy horsemen moved seemed far too agile as well. No small horse could bear so much armor without falling under the weight of it. That could only mean one thing: The enemy armor was no more than clay castings or tinker's tin. That, of course, meant we'd not seen the enemy knights at all but were looking at messengers who were likely to outrun any pursuit.

The right flank of our cavalry took off after the enemy ruse. They were soon so far into the blue spruce that they had no hope of returning to the fight anytime soon.

"Return to the ranks, Abe!" commanded Captain Barker. Without knowing it, my horse had taken several steps to our front in my strain to see so far forward.

Before I turned, I noticed the enemy foot starting to flee the field. It was a rout, and then it wasn't, for two ranks of the enemy held their place with a wall of interlocked shields. They would die for the sake of time, though not without some delay to us. The last thirty of the enemy's ranks broke into lines of well organized companies and double-timed into the back fields with good order. All of the enemy's ranks did this, not just one or two of the blocks, and they did so, it appeared, at one blast of the rebel's horn.

Finally, the duke's flags went up, ordering the left and right reserves to advance around the far edges and chase, but I knew the maneuver would be far too great of a marching distance, both to the sides and forward. The enemy had organized their retreat too well, even leaving the small field catapults where they stood, knowing them lost to our swarm.

In the rear, Lacellor's archers broke into teams, some shooting while others withdrew, halted, and then allowed the former to retreat in turn. This forced our own men to work forward at a slower pace than the retreating foot of Sir Lacellor.

Soon, some of the pikers were too far away to even be seen by me. Hills and forests quickly hid them entirely. If we wanted any of the enemy footmen, we'd have to send quick horsemen to charge over the nimble archers. Those horsemen were gone off on their own futile chases. Then we'd have to reorganize and find another field, lest we be ambushed as we scattered. My admiration for Lacellor's tactics were revived when I saw those foolish enough to race after the retreating soldiers singly falling under the well aimed arrows. Enough of that promised to even their losses.

I remembered the lay of the land and realized there was a river two miles distant. Lacellor would have boats and leave none to us. I found that amusing and laughed.

Sir Barker cast me an angry stare.

"Don't you see? He is masterful!" I shouted to Captain Barker, who was getting red in the face while watching me prancing around on Ella. Others continued celebrating, oblivious to Barker and me.

"Back in the ranks, soldier!" he yelled with his hand on the hilt of his sword.

"None but two catapults, a handful of iron-plated knights

and a few hundred foot. Do you not see it? He's managed so well in the face of defeat! We'll lose nearly as many to his archers, if we persist." I yelled at Sir Barker, as if it was his fault. Of course, that was not the point. The point was, Lacellor had an unknown reason for his madness, and, in the eyes of every man I could see, all we saw was victory. Their eyes longed to join in the futile chase. Even our horses complained of their restraints, sensing the desire in their riders to run.

In the meantime, our main forces filed farther and farther to the front, already out of the control of the duke and his ally, the baron's brother, and into rougher land favoring the defense.

"I command you to return to your place, or I'll put you under arrest, Abe!"

Having heard Sir Barker, even Sergeant Hadarm came over from the other end of our ranks.

I ignored the fools and took my horse around them to our rear. There I looked into the wooded hills at our back and sides.

I whispered, "What must he do next? It cannot be enough just to trade a few peasants and four knights."

My arms tingled with tiny bumps. The hair on the back of my neck stood and waved like the centipede's legs. The smoke and noise of battle took a step back in my interest. This ruse from Lacellor had been for something, and one didn't need the blessings of the Goddess to feel it. Or did they?

Sergeant Hadarm and Captain Barker came up to either side of me. They were yelling and making nuisances of themselves. Threats bounced off my ears, unheeded.

We were so far back from the horror that I wondered why the birds didn't chirp in the trees to our rear. None of the leaves danced in the wind either. Yet, I sensed a low, throaty growl coming, as if the world was announcing an earthquake.

"They are coming." I didn't know if they heard me, though I'd shouted.

A murder of crows burst from the trees.

"Turn the men. They're coming from our rear!"

I felt Sergeant Hadarm's fingers clasp around my left wrist. His other grabbed my reins. I looked at him and laughed at his stupidity. Then I pulled my sword out and both of them backed away.

"They're coming, you fools. Damn you, turn the men! Don't you hear me it? There's no time!" I roared.

Captain Barker backed his horse away from me. His eyes were orbs of fear and anger aimed at the madman in front of him. Sergeant Hadarm, however, no doubt thinking me his own personal mistake, wouldn't budge from his station a horse away. I feared I'd have to kill him if he moved to his sword as he threatened.

I turned and rode before the men. "Men of Lettoir. Turn your mounts!"

I shifted Ella until we faced the woods. Golden Eyes stood there at the woodland's edge, alongside some of his pack. I knew what he was thinking. Oh, the folly of humans killing humans.

Over in the next group, the baron's brother gave our movements some of his attention.

The surprise, however, was behind me when I glanced over a shoulder. The men of Lettoir turned. They'd learned to heed my voice, probably because it had kept so many of them from being killed so far.

"You'll be put in irons for this insubordination. You're not but a peasant!" started Captain Barker.

But then his eyes fell from me and my men. They jerked toward the noisy woods. The first of Lacellor's knights came roaring into the clearing at our rear.

There were soon a score of knights riding like the coming wind. Then another twenty emerged behind those. Still a third rank of ten trailed the rest. They were unstoppable metal on huge beasts, long lances aimed at the ladies, pages, priests, old men and fat leaders in the middle of us all.

Lacellor was going for the head, and he had it in his hands. Thus I came to love him as a great leader, for we both knew the source of our misery.

Chapter Fifteen

I switched to my spear and yelled, "Pick the outriders and aim for their horses!" Then I took off, looking for stragglers.

It didn't matter to me if any followed. The situation seemed hopeless. The field was already lost to their knights, even though they numbered less than half our gnats.

Women and priests went down first, thrown by their own tiny and frantic horses in most cases. They hadn't been the enemy's goal, I assumed, but the trampling couldn't be avoided. Servants, squires and pages, in the way, fought for one stroke before they were soundly hacked and sent under the charging hooves. A handful were brushed aside without injury and thus left to scatter to safety. Lacellor's knights even ignored the light cavalry on the flanks. He trusted his armor as defense against us and aimed only for the better targets.

In minutes, all that remained were a few old knights and commanders. They organized into a mass of no more than a score. In it I saw both the duke and the baron's brother. They joined the fighting themselves, no doubt hoping to break through the clogged up charge and save both of them from the disaster.

I stabbed a horse, hamstrung a knight's knee and then killed a second horse before I noticed my own men busy killing and dying around me. Most had the good sense to pick a target, poke at it annoyingly and pull their horses away like I'd been showing them. Still, the knights were killing four of us to every one of their fallen horses. Most of the enemy who fell fought on. There were plenty of stranded horses left behind by the party of nobles, affording them remounts. It was as if none of the enemy truly perished.

Over on the other side, the White Shirts were pressing into the far side of Lacellor's charge with no success at all. The enemy trusted his armor as shields, leaving their swords free to kill the White Shirts as quickly as they came up and laid the first useless dent onto their plating.

Sir Wencor wasn't to be seen. I thought he might have been among the first into the churning steel, though I was too busy to be certain.

I picked out a knight who was trying to climb back onto a horse. I came around with a two handed swing of my teacher's sword and bashed the base of his helmet so hard I could hear his neck break inside. The snap mixed in with the clang, as if part of the same noise.

Another came at me with a huge axe. I let him swing it while I ducked all the way back on my far stirrups. When the axe swung past, I pulled myself back on my saddle and kicked the giant off his horse for having the stupidity of having gotten himself so far off balance. I stayed in that spot for a while so Ella could kick him around like a barrel. When I left, he was getting up again, forcing me to admire his staggering persistence, though I had no more time for him. Instead, I killed his horse that was just standing around. The axe-man screamed worse than did those dying around him, but, by then, I was off to find someone else.

Every one of the enemy knights was good and seemingly always winning. Only the men of Lettoir were still a decent fighting unit, though we were half our former size by the time I got through with the screaming axe-man. The older soldiers among us had the good sense to not press the irretrievable issue. Only Lacellor's doggedness at getting to the duke kept him from turning his force and swatting us away.

As for our effect, we managed to distract them just enough for the duke and baron's brother to break through. They slipped past ten of the White Shirts. All of Sho's men fought like the devout. I witnessed them gladly giving their lives in order to allow the duke's small party a little time. Considering the confusion, the duke might enjoy a ten or twenty minute head start, I guessed.

I finally saw Sir Wencor in their midst. There was a boy who'd feared every moment of battle, and yet he stood firm. I regretted harsh feelings we'd shared in the past. His thin line of light horses held for whole minutes, too. It seemed impossible. Perhaps it was their God that preserved them. Still, one by one, the White Shirts fell. Soon, the only man left was the boy Wencor. He must have died under the swarm of twenty enemy knights.

Sergeant Hadarm and Captain Barker showed good sense in getting out of my way as I rallied a few and raced after the duke and baron's brother.

To the rear were two full days of open road and vulnerable supply wagons between the duke and his castle. Not many were there to defend the castle if the gates were open, even against only a score of raiding knights. With a few torches, they'd sack the town and battlements, even if the duke should be impossibly lucky and reach the gates to close them. By the time the duke's knights came, great damage could likely be done.

I caught up to them after only two miles of hard riding. Every one of their horses had been bloodied. The duke's horse had fallen across the whole width of the road.

A teen squire was giving the duke his own horse. The duke seemed quick to gather the reins, as if they belonged to him, which I suppose everything and everybody did in his eyes. The squire swore to ward off the whole of Lacellor's heavy forces by himself, and on foot, though he could barely kneel from a cut above the knee. His wound bled severely, perhaps more than he could accept, as he continued to ignore it.

Over on another part of the roadway, Randolf, the baron's brother, waited impatiently for the older duke to steady the horse and pull himself up. The third time the duke failed to do so, I realized he couldn't get up there in all of his armor without the aid of all his servants.

Two old knights looked steady enough to fight. They gambled away time by idly watching the duke try to get up on his horse without help. The others, a handful, barely sat upwards on their horses, some certain to die before shelter from the looks of them. As I watched, one fell to the road. He didn't even twitch inside his coffin of steel plates.

I had seven with me, and none of them wore as much as a breastplate, save Captain Barker. Sergeant Hadarm was among them. Both the Captain and my sergeant hesitated, as if forcing me to make yet another decision.

"We can't do anything for these men," I said. "However, Dorne may be threatened. Race back through the battlefield. One of you must break through and bring back our knights."

"How can we do that? Who'll defend the duke?" asked Captain Barker.

I held up my sword. "I will hold the road. Now go!"

"You can't do this alone. I'll remain with you. The others will go," said Captain Barker.

Sergeant Hadarm wasn't as foolish. He nodded, then turned the other four and dashed them back down the road. I saw them divert into the woods even before they were fifty strides. We all knew the enemy knights would soon leave the field and find this road. In fact, it was impossible for me to believe that Sergeant Hadarm could bring the duke's knights in time.

I turned from it and rode in among the nine remaining

nobles. "You four can't fight. We'll waste our time defending you. Take these two who are able and retreat to the woods. Make your way back to the duke's castle and close the gates."

"Who are you to tell my men what to do?" asked Sir Randolf. "You are but a serf."

I laughed at him. "You'll remain and fight like the rest of us! Sir Lacellor may only be interested in you and the duke, so we'll satisfy him with your presence and be done with this!"

"Ah, now I remember you. Do you see this, Duke Crestlin? This is the soldier who came before us at court. He's the one who caused the disaster in the last battle. He thinks himself a leader, but he is nothing. I was right. We should have hung him for his insubordination when he last came before us."

The duke looked us over and nodded. He was too winded to speak. He took his breastplate off. Next, he added his helmet and arm braces to the pile. Then he kicked the squire over and used him as a step to get up on the horse. The squire didn't get up after that, but he slumped over. In seconds he was unconscious and nearly dead in his own blood.

I wasn't dissuaded. "The duke will fight. You will fight. Sir Barker stands, as do I. We four will hold the road while the others escape and warn the castle of the mess you two have made."

"Nay!" declared Sir Randolf. "These four who are beyond saving will stand, and the duke and I will make for the castle with the escort of these two able men. When we get there, we'll send word to arrest you for once again causing a disaster."

"You won't make it. Scouts will run you down and delay you for the heavier knights. Otherwise, once they have you and the duke, they won't care about the others. It saves lives to stand. Even the men in the field will be left in peace. Besides, if you try to run away like the last time, I'll kill you and the duke myself."

I drew up next to the duke where I could make good my threat. My sword was ready to stab him through the gut. The duke was an old man of little value to me. I knew that already he plotted with Sir Randolf to blame me for his mistakes, and this time hang me for sure. Still, he knew to keep his hand away from his sword.

"How dare you threaten the duke!" scolded Sir Randolf from where he'd hedged several horse lengths closer to the distant castle.

"He's the cause of all this, not me or the men of Lettoir. I'm thinking he even lied about wanting to find the queen and ending this war."

The duke yelled, "Oh that! Why does it matter? As long as the Debrecians are fooled by our looking long enough. Once Lacellor is defeated, we'll tame those women with ease."

"So that's why you only had a few of us looking, and kept us to the camp."

"I suppose I gave her as present to a peasant," said the duke. "I care not where she has gone. What's done is done, and I'll not waste time looking for her everywhere."

"So it's true. Everything in Farstand is a lie, and more to come."

"Enough!" yelled Sir Barker. When he moved his horse to come around, I put my sword up tighter to the duke's body, causing Barker to stop.

I told the duke, "You're all liars. The only man who ever spoke fairly to me is two seasons dead. Do you remember sending us forward to wait under the arrows in the last battle? Ah, I can see that you don't. You put us under the arrows and didn't care to notice. My friend died for nothing, just as this battle was for nothing."

Captain Barker saw the danger in me. Unlike the others, he knew me well enough to fear it. He shifted his horse a little more, but I kept the duke between us as I continued, "Why did I stay silent during my trial? What good did my silence bring us, given your second example of bad leadership?"

"Watch your tongue, peasant!" yelled Sir Randolf.

"No, now is the moment of truth, and it will all be said."

"Truth? What is this all about?" asked Randolf.

"You don't know his name, do you? I'll tell you then. His name was Ankind. Know this: He was a good man, worthy of a legend, for in the land your family rules, being a good man is a treasure. In his name you'll stand and die. Now send your men and give us at least one act of decency." I pushed the tip of my sword into the duke's skin, showing them I was serious.

"Leave!" shouted the duke. "All go, save Randolf! I am too winded and battered to run anyway."

The six knights watching were too sickly and tired to protest. They turned their horses and fled to warn their families. Armor clattered on the road as they tossed it off one piece at a time, ridding themselves of the weight. This left only us four and the dying squire.

"There is no chivalry in this," protested Sir Randolf. "Leave me to go and prepare the castle in case of siege. We have more men in the field than Sir Lacellor, and, when we gather for another battle, this will be reversed. Considering Lacellor's insult at striking to our rear, the king himself will raise twice this army and next year put an end to this forever. What does defending this road serve us? Leave it to this traitor."

I told him, "You have the right of it, Sir Randolf. All who remain here will die, excepting the intervention of the Goddess. In this you are mistaken: It's not the duke who is telling you to stay. It's me, speaking for the lost soul of the queen and all of the men you have both starved and persecuted."

"You insolent pig! I'll have you boiled in oil," warned Randolf.

"And I will help you," said Barker.

Dust became visible around the distant bend. It was too late for running now; we would soon be within their sights. I said, "Only the voice of the Goddess commands me."

Randolf yelled, "Do you hear him? Now what do you say to that, Barker! This is the one who speaks to God, you said. Did you ask him which one?"

"Is that true, Abe?" asked Captain Barker from where I kept his horse dancing on the other side of the duke's animal.

"I favor the Goddess. I declare myself free of you and your God. I quit you. I quit you all. Oh, great Goddess of earth and sky. Show my face to these fools. *Tpunwvw Own!*"

I felt myself changing. My breasts swelled and hips widened. Cheeks grew fat and warm. Touching my sword arm with the other caused me to realize my skin had regained its smoothness.

The duke's eyes widened. He whispered, "The accursed queen! No, that was years ago, and she would be old and wrinkled."

His eyes drifted inward as he recalled something that haunted him. "No, of course, we cut that old queen so she couldn't run, and I was first among those who raped and broke her until she grew feeble of mind. I gave her to a common soldier's bed. This cannot be that woman."

Then he took another look at me. "Ah yes, I am mistaken, for many years have passed. It was a trick of the light. That old queen has no-doubt died from a hard life under a hard man by now. As is befitting."

I rode from side to side before him. "Did you once know this queen? Did you truly befoul such a woman?"

"Maybe, maybe not. She was not worth much memory. I was only certain that she was overly proud, much like you. I've had more important things on my mind than the memory of a witch."

We'd moved farther apart. I glanced away, seeing the armored men of Lacellor rounding the bend, no more than a hundred gallops distant. The distraction gave the duke time to put his hand on the hilt of his sword. I could tell he was thinking he'd overestimated me; after all, I was just a woman.

It wasn't right, for I would be feared. My eyes spoke murder as clearly as they had with Bullor on that log nearly two years past. Just as then, when the crone took possession of my soul, the duke couldn't have mistaken the storm swelling within me.

He pulled more frantically at his sword, but I was no longer under any obligation to wait. Could the man truly be so arrogant that he thought I'd sit there and let him kill me? I kicked his hand. The sword cramped up against him so he couldn't finish freeing it. That's when I slipped my own blade into his neck. Blood fell across the mane of his stolen horse.

He dropped his sword and clutched to stem the leak. Old Duke Crestlin tried to speak a curse at me, but there wasn't enough flesh left intact between his lungs and mouth to do it.

I told him as he faded, "That was for befouling the queen and hiding her from us. Oh, dead duke, tell Sho it was just a cow who killed you, for I doubt he'll be speaking to me after this!"

While the duke slumped over his horse's mane, Captain Barker came up and crossed his sword with mine. I circled to his hilt then briskly slashed his arm. It wasn't a deep cut, for I'd told myself I wouldn't kill him. I bashed his sword away without real trouble. I'd thought Sir Barker would put up a greater fight, but maybe I'd surprised him by not pretending my skills were small.

He pulled back on his reins, causing his horse to step back. "You are most foul to have used God as an excuse for your evil. How long have I served beside you, unaware of your cursed womanhood? Now, you have murdered our duke, the brother of our king! There will never be a place left for the likes of you to hide, regardless of the outcome of this day!" He spat on the road near me.

Sir Randolf raised an empty hand, and, after his speech, so, too, did Sir Barker raise a hand. They were surrendering, not to me, but to the knights that had come up. By the time I turned to see the knights stopping ten horses in front of us, the mass of their cavalry filled the roadway.

The duke was dead, falling even then from his squire's horse. Only the three of us remained, and Sir Barker was unarmed. I found it strange to think that the men I was with had surrendered me as well; was I ever to be my own person?

Behind us, Sir Randolf seemed smaller with his arm raised in half surrender, half salutation. Perhaps he was praying to Sho in his mind. Maybe he was good at it even. After all, Sho had let him come to this world as one son next to a baron. Sho must have seen something promising in Randolf in a past life that led him into the error. For whatever reason, Randolf was the kind of man whom Sho admired more than others, for he had given him the job. The biggest surprise of the day was behind us though. Out of the woods to our rear came ten Debrecian warriors. They were loosely led by the great and honorable Beckli Kahnsa. I was most pleased to see her again, for I was ready to ask her many questions.

Others I knew as well. Behind Beckli were the cantankerous Catrina and the taller, though steadier, Gerta. Those two saw and knew me, but only with freshly curious eyes and no hint of a mocking smile.

There, in another group, rode a one legged warrior. She looked ten times the woman I'd helped out of the prison. She didn't seem to know my face. I was glad to see her well. Also, to her side rode the good scout I'd crossed paths with across the river, still the most watchful of the flanks. Neither of them knew me, though that pair glanced my way continually.

I took one long look at the young girl whose name I hadn't yet learned and bowed my head to her politely. She was the only one to whom I did so, and the others among the Debrecians were not slow to notice my observation. The teen girl bowed her head back at me, though much more reverently than I'd thought she might. It was the way she did this that caused many of the Debrecian women to murmur amongst each other.

"A challenge!" screamed Sir Randolf, breaking the moment's peace. He was still a formidable man and strong of voice, though he'd suddenly found that he was without many allies.

"I challenge your champions, this one and me against your two best! It is a noble's right to do this, assuming there is any honor among you." The madman pointed at me. Did he really think I'd stand beside him in his defense?

Before I could protest, the faceplate came off the closest knight. The finely featured Sir Daren Drake was behind it. "I accept. Your best will stand against our best. Let Sho's knight stand aside, for he is injured and out of the fight. He shall be free to go, as will all of your men still on the battlefield. These two alone will defend the honor of King Falstaff against the best of us and our hesitant Debrecian allies, completing the day of battle. Sword to sword. Is this sufficient for you, Sir Randolf?"

Sir Barker dropped down to pick up his sword. Regaining his horse, he pranced around, angrily looked into faces, and then rode past the Debrecians who parted for him. The man disappeared down the castle road at a gallop, probably knowing he'd get no better offer. I knew he'd pause around the distant bend and bear witness to the outcome.

"It is more than sufficient. Even if we ruled the moment, I would request it." Sir Randolf dropped from his horse and shooed it away.

"And you? Yes, you will join us," the knight told me, as if I mattered to one of noble birth such as him.

"Ah! I have no more dealings with these fools. Didn't you see me quit their army just now, and in grand fashion?"

Randolf answered for them all, however, when he insisted, "She is a murderess. She has killed as many as a dozen of your peasants, and often without honor, Sir Drake! Only a coward quits the field in the last moment, even the moment when a challenge has been offered. What say you to murderers and traitors, regardless of stripe? Come to think of it, if you prefer, kill her outright, and we'll fight alone."

"That's a lie," I protested. "The count is well over a hundred, and if it was mostly peasants, then it was knights who put them before me."

Sir Drake looked me over, and, seeing that I was also a peasant, even he couldn't help but dismiss my opinion. "She'll fight and die, as is befitting killers and cowards. The time for quitting ended at the first flying of the catapults, but still she is surrendered, so I won't slay her without a contest."

"Have I surrendered?" I'd not thought so. Still, I dropped from Ella. I then took my time taking the white tunic off. This left me in just my oldest dark grey. The tunic was not my best and in tatters. It was held together by only one button at my chest, but I preferred the lady's colors and felt like I could breathe again.

As I prepared, I told him, "I have no heart for this, for I have dismissed all loyalties, save to the good Lady Lettoir and the one in the sky. Still, if it will end the day and set things right between us all, I shall entertain you in this joust. A good practice round of swords always amuses me."

The man was almost in front of me. He sniffed at my comments, and so I took but one step and was nearly in his shadow. He fidgeted, as if surprised that I was so calm.

My, but Sir Daren Drake was a handsome beast of a man. It would be a pleasure watching him as we fought, I decided. It was the kind of pleasure I had felt only while looking at Sergeant Ankind long ago when I thought him so fanciful. That is except that it was worse than ever just looking at Daren. I'd fallen out of love with Sergeant Ankind, but I couldn't imagine ever forgetting this man's face.

"No," declared Sir Drake. "That is not the deal. I won't fight such a frail creature; it's below my dignity. I have a duty to fight Sir Randolf, as he is the nearest equal in rank and stature."

He didn't even have the decency to look at me while rejecting my challenge. I took my sword out and flashed it by his own, tapping him on his metal breastplate for the insult. My sword was up and recovered before he could protest the clatter.

From behind I heard a known voice. She said, "Ah now, calm yourself, Sir Drake. It's my duty to revenge the queen, not yours. We don't see rank as you do, but we do see our duty in similar light."

Sir Drake shook his head in disagreement, but he took his dented breastplate off anyway, readying for my murder.

Then I heard the sword of Beckli Kahnsa leave its sheath. She was behind me, and, thus, I couldn't watch her and keep my attention on my opponent as well. Still, she was the one I needed to know the most. I had much to ask her, but it seemed we'd have to wait until after the contest to have our conversation.

Around us, the soldiers came, clearing away the dead horse, duke and squire. I was made to stand with the cursing brother of my baron. We were back to back, me facing the handsome face of Daren Drake. Randolf seemed eager to kill the diplomat,

Beckli Kahnsa. For this we'd all stripped out of our armor, though I had none to shed, doing much nervous standing about.

Randolf's back was quickly gone from mine. In its place I heard Beckli and Randolf parry swords. I was very curious to see it, for I knew both the prophecy Beckli had uttered and the basic pattern of her promised technique.

Daren, however, wasn't of the same curious mind as me, coming at me and forcing me to fend off his vicious downward slice. Oh, it was a good one, coming down at an arching angle from which I couldn't duck away. I had to fight him meeting his muscle with my own, which wasn't my best approach at all.

My sword stuttered in her singing, warning me that my technique was lacking. I used my whole body against his bulging arms. Good leverage and all my strength pushed him way.

"Can't you wait until I'm done watching the other contest, Sir Drake?" This seemed to offend him, so back he came, faster than before.

I tumbled away, racing off to the edge of the circle of soldiers, putting enough distance between us that I could see Randolf coming at Beckli Kahnsa with a flourish of well schooled parries. She fended them all without response, and then when his confidence was up, he probed too far forward. Beckli stepped past him with amazing ease, brought her sword up from low behind her and sliced a neat nick just under and behind his knee.

"Ah, that was masterful. It brings but a trickle of blood. Did you see it, Sir Drake?"

He was on me even as I spoke, forcing me to parry his best couplings of strokes. One handed, he was full of finesse and still so strong of arm that I had to fend him without much neatness and two handedly. Doing such, I'd have been better armed with my staff, which was hazelnut and not easily cleaved. Still, my sword sang to me, so I figured I was doing something right, perhaps by wearing him out as he backed me up one step for every pair of strokes.

As we danced about, I noticed almost all of the eyes were on the other contest. I thought the work of Sir Drake was better than that, deserving of more attention, so I caught his next swing, braced him guard to guard, and then stepped past, kicking him to the back of his knee. He bent a little as I slipped by. That gave me enough space to watch the great Beckli Kahnsa slice another piece out of the back of one of Randolf's legs.

"Ha!" I grunted.

Of course, I could have done the same thing to my opponent on the last pass, I reasoned. I was learning the fine details of the technique by watching her, but then again, I had no desire to mar such a beautiful creature as Sir Daren Drake of Lacellor.

The foolish sword tapping between myself and Sir Drake didn't catch the attention of most of the knights, but it did catch the attention of one young Debrecian girl. I don't know why, but to me this was enough. I lost my smile and met the next stroke from Sir Drake with just enough sword to deflect. I eased back to slide his sword past and then returned to stab him a tad. His shoulder showed a little blood.

With that, I returned nobly to the center of the roadway. There we fought, sword to sword, employing all of the teachings from our masters except, of course, killing one another.

Then, out of the corner of my eyes, I saw Sir Randolf drop to his knees. Beckli Kahnsa had done no more than stab him once again across the back of his bloody thighs. All of the way across the back of both legs, Randolf bled in tiny streams. By the time the blood met at his feet, it was a virtual river.

Beckli turned from him and started to walk away,

undoubtedly knowing there was no more the man could do to defend his bleeding body from the inevitable hand of death.

My attention was drawn to her, giving Daren his opportunity. He thrust with the point of his sword. The best I could do was duck back and push his sword down with the hilt of my own blade. It was nearly enough.

The tug of his sword stripped the only button holding my old shirt together. It flew open, baring my bindings. My necklace jiggled into the sun from where it dangled unhampered by the layer of clothing.

Twenty knights and Debrecian warriors got an ample display of my bouncing breasts. I was so offended by the affront to my dignity that I stabbed him in his other shoulder, giving him a matching pair of bleeding spots.

He in turn took offense. While I was still off balance, he stabbed me in the ribs a fair inch deep. The fun was rushing out of the contest, for the jolting stab might well have killed me, and it bled like it might still.

He parried again, but for the first time, I was frightened by the skill of the powerful knight. Such was a good time to remember my many lessons. This I took to my work with a vengeance of quickness, both of body and mind.

It was suddenly as if he was the old duke, slow and unworthy of his weapon, for all I saw was the swordsman who'd cut me deeply and ended only inches below my heart.

Each stroke I put aside, standing mostly in one place with frozen feet of determination. He dared not come at me, for my sword sang so loudly all could hear it. I myself heard its words for the first time, singing now clearly, "I am the teaching sword!"

Each time I turned one of his couplings aside, I poked some more of him, his tunic growing red with tiny cuts about his body. I wanted him to know I had no intentions of killing him, but he would also remember my face from where I'd carved its likeness upon his skin.

The gold coin dangled from my necklace and at my stomach. It flipped up into the sunlight by the jerking motion of my many thrusts. Fashioned by my mother, it called to the wolves in a wee howl that was so faint I barely heard it.

One by one the wolves burst through the startled ring of soldiers. Soon they surrounded me. They bore their long, sharp teeth and held up their rear haunches while they snarled and made it known they were eager masters of violence. Golden Eyes himself backed away the great knight, Sir Daren Drake. Even I couldn't get through them to fight him. It was a waste of magic, for I was doing well enough on my own.

Around the circle, men took a step back, and horses complained.

I heard the clanging of a tossed sword. Looking over, the idiot, Sir Randolf of Olan, defender of Helfax Hall, fell dead. His tossed sword had made it only halfway to where the great Beckli Kahnsa stood looking at me from near her horse.

Entranced by the sight of me and my new friends, she'd not even noticed Randolf's last and futile toss.

"By the Goddess, who are you, my child?" she asked, seemingly having already forgotten her fallen foe.

I put my sword away so I could hold my tunic closed with one hand and my worst wound with the other.

Over by the distant bend, a cloud of dust was rising. The duke's heavy cavalry was a minute before falling upon us. They were led by my friends, Sergeant Hadarm and the remaining men of Lady Lettoir.

Lacellor's knights broke the circle. Sir Drake shouted his frustration and then turned to his own horse. They, led by the skilled Debrecian scouts, slipped into the woods. My wolves, apparently no longer sensing any danger to me, followed behind the fleeing feet of Golden Eyes.

Only Beckli Kahnsa remained unmoved by the danger. She lingered for my reply, even daring a step closer.

The spirit of my mother and the soul of the crone both filled my mouth. It seemed that a little of the cloud lifted. The crone herself moved my lips, for it wasn't my own mind that spoke. I said, "I am Abi, Shaman Warlord of the greatest Debrecian tribe!"

And then I knew that what I'd said was true.

The Debrecian glanced up to the sky. "Ah, so it is this that I'd not foreseen. Such are the many mysteries set before us by the Goddess."

Her eyes flew to the knights charging at us. They came as hard as they could ride. She, too, ran and leapt upon her saddle without help from a single stirrup. She turned her horse in a swift and spinning circle.

I saw pleading in her eyes, but there was no more time for even little gestures between us.

"We shall meet again," she yelled before turning away at last.

The great Debrecian leader disappeared into the trees while the bulk of the duke's knights followed, only to get clogged in the brush.

Search for the Queen
A Hidden Shaman Novel

Sneak Peek

Chapter One

I had tunics with only minor blood stains and boots the nobles had barely worn. These were the winnings of war. Though it was illegal for me to read, I'd started a collection of four books. The last two I'd taken from the duke's ravaged train as his army had been overrun. Our loss in that battle no longer mattered to me, for I'd quit the duke's army when I'd murdered him. It seemed the right thing to do, though it hadn't even slowed the war for me.

Beef was salted away with a whole round of cheese. Two half-full sacks of grain draped my horse.

Copper, silver and even golden coins were fastened about my person and hidden within my saddlebags. I tried my best to spend them out, but each place I went in Farstand I gathered more from the fallen than I could waste.

The town before me promised no exception.

The first place I went was the posting board.

Again I found my picture, looking nothing like me. The drawing was terrible. My jaw wasn't square, as drawn. My eyebrows didn't continually scowl. My lips were much fuller than depicted. They'd colored a red spot marking a demon in my eye. Perhaps my long disguise as a man had shaded their perception?

Even the colors were faulty. My true hair was light, with tints of red and slowly turning waves, not russet and straight. I had green eyes instead of brown. The biggest insult of all was the description of my breasts as flat and like that of a boy. I nearly wished it so. I'm tall; that they had right, as did they the description of my strong body.

It was a good thing the peasants couldn't read, for none would have ever recognized me from the script.

The existence of my horse always pointed me out. Few who weren't of noble blood had horses, much less saddles, and even less, saddlebags that overflowed with spoils. When it was a peasant woman on such a horse's back, even the village idiot figured it out.

I'd had to dye the elk saddle the same brown peasant color that I'd dyed all my clothing. The colors of the guards of Lettoir weren't well known, but I drew nearer to Lettoir's holdings and my clothing remained finer than those on any other peasant in Farstand.

I would not dye Ella; it's an insult to each of us to hide so completely that we forget who we are deep inside. I'd learned this from my last mistake of being someone other than myself for too long and too completely.

Neither the poor description, nor the dyeing of clothing helped. From the moment I went into any village, it was only a matter of their courage, not their discernment.

I reached down and tore the parchment off the posting board, in plain view of the curious who passed. I rode my horse on the main street, staring down every soul I met. Even the old women and small children were not spared my challenge, though sometimes I saw one look back and, of all things, smile.

When I went into the newly-planked tavern, I sat at a corner table and ordered the whole house chicken, not mutton or nibbles with beans.

Whispers passed from lips to ears. The one with the most eager ear waited until he thought I wasn't looking. Then he escaped through the doorway, in search of assistance.

One man barely looked up, almost seeing my face, clearly mistaking me for someone in need of instruction. His eyes were on his fellows when he said, "Houses of drink are meant for men."

I ignored him, saving it for the main battle. It was time to eat at a table, and I had little enough time to spare on the chore.

The chicken had been whittled down to bones by the time the two town guardsmen came in to arrest me. I pulled out my sword and killed them quickly without much tinkering. Next I killed the man who'd done the whispering and finally the man who'd told me the tavern was only for men. Everybody else fled the twirling splatters of blood. I note this quickly, for it cost me nothing in time, sweat or sympathy. My telling of it is as fleeting as the consciousness I paid it.

More than enough copper was found in the dead men's pockets to pay the tavern master for the chicken and to add two jugs of ale that I draped across my saddle horn. It seemed the whole town watched me slowly ride out. They'd been frozen by both the grandeur of my myth and the witness of my blade.

I couldn't spend all of the leavings from this war, and grew heavy from the collections. Too much success can leave a person empty. I found myself asking for the first time: What more is there to my life's new direction than treasures?

I didn't question that the shaman princess inside of me raged out of control and with no direction. Discerning war from peace is not the duty of a warlord. No, the wisdom needed to temper my violence was the duty of the unknown queen, who remained lost, in spite of my every effort to track her down. Not that I didn't feel her near every place I went, and thus nowhere at all, for she'd been rendered as invisible as my life had been before becoming an outlaw.

That night I made camp on a rise within a swamp where the dogs couldn't find my scent and the trackers were dissuaded by their beliefs in evil spirits rising out of water. I ate spiny fish and made flat bread over a raging campfire.

Sorting through my bags, I came upon my four books. I opened them one by one and read passages of poetry, battles or spells I dared not cast.

One book haunted me. I'd not touched it since before the battle that had killed the duke and baron's brother, for it was warded against anybody opening it. Many nights in the White Shirt camp I'd tried to break the spell holding it tight. I wondered who in that Debrecian cabin had carried it and about how easily I'd taken the treasure from the cabin wherein it had been placed in such plain sight. Did the former Debrecian owner miss it? Was she magical? Could she and no other open it?

Did she leave it specifically to taunt me?

Was she the queen?

Have I been riding in the direction meant for my life?

Not even the spells in the book of shaman magic had helped break the bonds protecting the mysterious Debrecian book from prying eyes. I laid awake nights, wondering about the powerful magic that defied the shaman spells. It fiercely fueled my curiosity, knowing the book's forbidden knowledge was so close and yet untouchable.

I picked it up for the first time since the final battle separating me from Farstand's iron fist, and as easily as can be, opened it to the very first page.

I couldn't believe I'd done it until it was open. The ward had vanished, though I could still sense its presence, ready to keep unworthy hands from the book's secret passages deep within.

At first there were no words, but as I watched, letters appeared as if an invisible hand inked the page that very moment. I was startled to find the script turn into a warning:

None may read these words, save the Queen.

Gary is the author of several short stories and the novel *Zombies in Our Hometown*. He is one of the founding members of the Ohio Writers and North Columbus Fantasy/SciFi writer's groups and is a longstanding member of the prestigious Columbus Writing Workshop. Gary has a BFA from the Columbus College of Art and Design, teaching certification from Otterbein College, an MBA from the Ohio State University.

VISIT THE LOCONEAL BLOG AT

www.loconeal.com

Breaking News
Forthcoming Releases
Links to Author Sites
Loconeal Events